# PRAISE FOR
# YOU SEE ME

"*You See Me* is an excellent look at the joy and agony, the triumphs and defeat, and the overall wonder that is teenage romance."

—**BRIAN KATCHER, AUTHOR OF *ALMOST PERFECT***

"Stars, drama, wisdom, and dreams merge in *You See Me*. Heart, beauty, and courage merge in this tale of what could be and what is. Author Dev Friedlander 'gets' high school and what goes into growing up in the contemporary world."

—**B. LYNN GOODWIN IS THE AUTHOR OF *NEVER TOO LATE: FROM WANNABE TO WIFE AT 62* AND *TALENT*, AS WELL AS THE OWNER AND EDITOR OF WRITER ADVICE, WWW.WRITERADVICE.COM.**

"Everyone can relate to some aspect of this story. It is an authentic portrayal of human emotion, vulnerability, and courage. A rich blend of suspense and romance."

—**DR. RIVKAH EIDEX, PSYD, PSYCHOLOGIST**

*You See Me*
by Dev Friedlander

Published by

 köehlerbooks ™

210 60th Street
Virginia Beach, VA 23451
800−435−4811
www.koehlerbooks.com

# YOU SEE ME

**Dev Friedlander**

VIRGINIA BEACH
CAPE CHARLES

*For Sherry, who gave me the gift of language.*

*And for Michael, who gave me the gift of love.*

# PROLOGUE

A WHITE LEXUS came to a halt in front of Ella, the window lowered.

"Get in the car, quickly," Jordan, her brother, demanded. He shoved his chestnut hair out of his eyes. "I don't want anyone seeing me driving this mommy-mobile."

"What took you so long?" Ella demanded, wiping beads of sweat from her forehead. "Your text promised me you would be here in five minutes."

"Everyone knows that's code for twenty minutes," Jordan replied. "Now get in."

Her brother looked about as happy to pick her up as Ella felt to leave the party early. A mad Jordan meant a mean Jordan. Ella knew better than to test his patience. She jumped into the front seat, reaching around for her seatbelt. She was thrown backward as the car accelerated .

"I'm not buckled yet," Ella yelled.

"Stop whining," Jordan replied, rolling his eyes. "I'm going like ten miles an hour. As a geek, you should be able to read a speedometer."

"I know how to read a speedometer, marble eyes," Ella retorted. She hated being called a geek, something she was called at least once a week along with the constant jeers about her red hair.

Ella finally managed to fasten her seatbelt, a task that would have taken her five seconds if the car were stationary. She sniffed the air and caught a familiar stench. "Jordan, you've been drinking!"

"Quit your griping, ginger root. I've only had a few beers."

Ella began to panic. "A few? You smell like you downed a whole keg."

"I could have if I'd stayed longer," Jordan said, rolling through the stop sign at the corner. "I had to leave Blake's party early because Mom made me come get you."

"It's not my fault," Ella said. "Mom is the one who ruined everything. I wish I could have stayed at Brittany's party longer." Ella touched her pale cheek, feeling the residue that remained from the kiss. She had waited three years for that kiss from Matt. Now her cheek was covered in perspiration, washing off all traces of his affection.

"Weren't you and Shelby going out tonight?" Ella asked.

"Shelby is in Savannah for the summer, remember?"

"No," said Ella. "I don't keep track of your love life."

The light up ahead turned from yellow to red.

"Jordan, the light is red," said Ella.

"Shut up," Jordan replied as he pressed with full force on the accelerator.

"Jordan, stop!" Ella shrieked.

"Ella, shut the hell up."

Then everything went into slow motion—the massive sound of metal hitting metal, glass shattering, and airbags exploding.

Ella was thrown to the side and forwards, hitting the airbag. The last thing she remembered before blacking out was a woman screaming for help from somewhere in the dark distance.

# CHAPTER 1

ELLA STARTED HER senior year of high school the same way she started every year at Dellpine Academy: completely and utterly disheartened. She had the normal first-day jitters like everyone else, but there was nothing normal about a seventeen-year-old girl with a limp. A limp that, after three years, showed little sign of improvement.

Ella opened her locker and pulled out her history textbook. She would never admit to anyone how studying about the English monarchy in history class led her to a three-hour search online for more information. She had discovered that the English monarchs did not have surnames until 1917, when all English monarchs would be called Windsor. Most high school students couldn't care less about these facts, but Ella could get lost in them for hours.

"Studying again?" Maria asked, peering over her shoulder, her raven hair brushing Ella's cheek. "Didn't you already take AP History?"

"That was AP US History. I'm taking World History now."

"Well, aren't you glad you haven't run out of AP exams like Barry? You would have nothing to look forward to."

"I do other things besides study."

"Like going to Madison's party on Sunday?" Maria asked excitedly. She was always trying to get Ella to socialize more.

"I wasn't invited," Ella replied as she put some books into her backpack.

"The whole class was invited."

"I don't think I will," Ella said.

"Stop being such a hermit, Ella."

"I'm not a hermit. I went out last week with Chelsey. We went shopping for riding boots."

"It's a wonder you can dress yourself without the help of your sister," Maria said, smiling.

"Not everyone has their own personal stylist," Ella said proudly.

Chelsey, Ella's older sister, was the closest thing Ella had to a Barbie. With blond hair and long legs, Chelsey broke guys' hearts simply by walking past them. She was studying to be a cosmetologist and took it very seriously. Their parents couldn't understand why their older daughter, who received straight A's in college, didn't pick a career closer to her field of study. But Chelsey decided to follow her true passion and loved using Ella as a guinea pig.

"Speaking of their own personal stylist," Maria said, bringing Ella's attention away from makeup and back to the present. "You will never guess who is joining our school this year."

It was not uncommon for a private school like Dellpine Academy to host celebrity students. Last year, Sarah Black, a girl with a promising country music career, had attended the tenth grade. She didn't last very long, shooting right to the top of the country charts and dropping out of school a few months later. Still, it was fun to claim that Sarah Black had gone to Dellpine Academy.

"So, can you guess?" Maria prodded.

"James Jude," Ella said, throwing out the only star name she could think of.

Maria nodded eagerly, jumping up and down. Ella put her hands to her mouth and shrieked with delight. James Jude was the latest teenage heartthrob. His father, Ian Jude, was a famous country singer whose songs played constantly on the country radio station. James had branched out into the pop music scene.

James found his boot in his mouth recently when he told a reporter that country music was a dying genre that "only rednecks enjoyed." Country fans led the battle cry against his remark, taking to social media, demanding "the little twit" gain some sense and go back to school. His own father showed disappointment over his son's words.

Attending his senior year in high school was clearly a publicity stunt, to lay low while the storm he created blew over. His latest album had bombed, and he was snubbed at the Grammys. Some of his greatest supporters urged him to give an education a try, saying James would be a role model for his younger fans. It seemed he had taken their advice and enrolled in school in his hometown, probably to prove he was comfortable with his Southern roots.

"When is he starting?" Ella asked, her voice shaking from anticipation. She'd had a star crush on him since he first started his music career at fourteen. She had all his albums, watched his music videos, and hummed his song all the time, but she kept her obsession to herself. Only Maria knew about the James poster hidden deep in her dresser's bottom drawer.

"I think he'll be starting sometime this week," replied Maria. It's just like James to miss the first week of school, Ella thought. She wondered what else the school would let him get away with.

Maria looked around. "Where is your cane?"

"I'm not going to be using it anymore," Ella said. "I found I can walk just as well without it."

"But the doctor said . . ."

Ella lowered her eyes, tightening her lips.

"I think you looked cool with the cane," Maria said.

"I looked like Mr. Peanut," Ella shot back.

"Only Brittany called you that." Maria threaded her arm through Ella's. "I just know James will fall madly in love with you. It will make Brittany so mad she will want to pull her hair extensions out. This is going to be your year, Ella. I can feel it."

Happy thoughts of holding James Jude's hand danced in Ella's head. It was completely unrealistic; his last girlfriend was a Delia clothing model. But daydreams were meant to be fanciful, and the idea of James holding Ella's hand was too wonderful for words.

The first day of school continued. Ella received a syllabus and the same speech in every class; the link between good grades and acceptance into college was reiterated over and over. Teachers warned against slacking off and senioritis, telling cautionary tales of the seniors who did not take their senior year seriously and ended up in community colleges because none of the more prestigious universities would have them.

Six syllabi later, Ella finally started the last period of the day, American Literature. Ella hurried from the science room in the west wing, determined to make it to the east wing on the other side of campus before the bell rang. The school had extended the time between classes so Ella could have enough time to reach each of her classes without being marked tardy. She felt ashamed when her mother told her the change in the bell schedule was because of her.

Ella got to class a full minute before the bell rang and eyed the vacant front row. Most students wanted to be as far from the teacher's watchful gaze as possible, filling up the back rows. Ella didn't mind the front and took the seat closest to the door.

"Good afternoon," Mrs. Salter said, a stack of papers in her hands. Ella had Mrs. Salter for British Literature last year and looked forward to being in her class again. Most students found Mrs. Salter's passion for literature insufferable, but Ella admired her. Mrs. Salter was true to herself, not caring about what was fashionable. She taught the details that many teachers preferred to skip over in favor of covering more ground. Last year, Mrs. Salter spent two full weeks teaching the history of Canterbury before reading a single tale. She was whimsical, speaking like a poet. Her words were like music, flowing and ardent.

"For those of you who love literature, this is going to be your favorite class," Mrs. Salter began after all the students took their seats.

"For those of you who are here simply to pass the AP exam, you will be disappointed. I am not a teacher who instructs towards an exam; I teach literature, pure and simple."

There were a few groans in the back of the classroom. Mrs. Salter ignored them as she handed out the class syllabus.

"I believe literature is a study in human psychology before the science of psychology ever existed. Literature explores the question 'why.' Why do we love? Why do we begin battles? Why is life worth living even when someone is in the nadirs of despair?"

A few of Ella's classmates gawked at Mrs. Salter, not understanding her enthusiasm—or even her English, for that matter. Ella looked over the coursework. She had already read several of the books and plays on the list. It seemed the first assignment was due next week.

Suddenly, girls screeched out in the hallway. A door was thrown open and a boy with hair gelled into spikes was practically shoved into the room.

Ella's heart skipped a beat. There he was in all his glory, James Jude.

James wore khaki cargo pants, with his light oxford uniform shirt rolled at the sleeves. The pants were not permitted according to dress code, but Ella was sure the school was making an exception.

Ella noticed he was on the slim side, yet he had enough muscle on him not to appear too bony. He looked, in one word, hot.

"Mr. Jude," Mrs. Salter said, "please have a seat." It was clear by her brisk tone that she was not impressed by James's grand entrance. James looked around the classroom. A girl named Samantha shoved a girl named Nicole out of the seat next to her, motioning for him to join her. Nicole returned the jab, sending Samantha tumbling onto the floor.

Mrs. Salter intervened before mayhem ensued. "There is a seat in the front, Mr. Jude."

James sat down next to Ella, his face indicating regret. He didn't seem pleased to be in the front row. He probably would have loved to sit next to Samantha, a cheerleader with shiny hair and a narrow waistline.

Mrs. Salter continued going through the syllabus. "As you will see, your first assignment is due next week. You will write a three-page essay about one of Shakespeare's plays. You may choose from the list on the syllabus. This is to be done with a partner."

Many girls in the classroom called out James's name, hoping to be the first to snatch him up. James turned with a wave that had clearly been practiced. Does he ever stop performing? Ella wondered.

"Partners have already been assigned," Mrs. Salter said sharply. "You will find your partner's name on the last page of the syllabus."

Ella's heart thumped as she turned to the last page. She ran her finger down to her name, her chest contracting when she saw James's name next to her own. She read it again to be sure. She couldn't breathe. Excitement grew inside her, choking her, taking over her senses.

"Who is Ella Heart?" James asked, looking around. He just said my name! She could have fainted from happiness right then and there.

"Me," Ella said timidly, holding up her hand.

James looked at her and took her in slowly. Ella was relieved to note he didn't look disappointed. He stuck out his hand, and she shook it. His hands were soft like her grandmother's had been—it was a little unsettling. Yet his eyes were green like a forest, which had Ella totally enamored. Ella's own green eyes felt watered down in comparison to James's emerald irises.

The class continued with Mrs. Salter giving more heartfelt words about literature. When the bell rang, two men in suits came in, and James was escorted out. Ella watched as James's cargo pants disappeared into the hall. Will those men come in every day? Will they let me speak to James outside of school? Speak to James—Ella sighed at the lovely thought.

"Ella, your book." Mrs. Salter pointed. Ella's attention returned to her desk. She had forgotten her pencil case as well. Her brain had gone off with James's security team.

Ella found Maria touching up her lipstick at her locker. Ella thought it funny that the first thing Maria did on the first day of school was place a mirror in her locker. The first thing Ella always did was tack up her class schedule.

"Maria!" Ella said. "You will never guess who was in my literature class."

"I think I can," Maria said, placing the lipstick tube back into her knapsack. "I have a class with James as well, Calculus."

"He is going to be my partner in AP American Lit," Ella hurried on. "This could be the best day of my life."

"It's the beginning," Maria said. "Next he will be composing songs for you."

"Don't be stupid." Ella's spirits sagged a little. "For Brittany, maybe."

"I read that he wants a girl with a big heart. If that's not you—"

"Stars will say anything if they think it will help their ticket sales." Ella didn't want to admit that she hoped Maria was right. She hoped James wanted more than what average American teenage boys normally wanted: a girl with more beauty than brains.

"Did you see his pants?" Ella asked. "They weren't in the dress code."

"Pants?" Maria said. "Did you see his hair? I bet he can't get too close to an electrical socket."

"Who can't get too close to a socket?" a boy in a red varsity jacket asked, a blue gym bag slung across his wide chest. It was their friend, Denzel Moland.

"We were just talking about James's hair," Maria said, her voice rising a notch.

"Man," Denzel huffed. "I think some auto repair shop is wondering where all their lube went."

They all laughed. Then Maria coughed. When she coughed again, Ella knew she was signaling her. She turned to see James, his knapsack slung over his left shoulder. He looked like he was modeling the back-to-school line at a department store.

"Hi," Ella squeaked.

"I wanted to give you my number," James said. "Maybe we can start working on that assignment this week?" James handed her a business card. "It's my agent, Evan Harris's number—he screens all my calls. I can't give out my cell phone number for security reasons."

"Thanks," Ella stammered, taking the card.

"Maybe we can meet Thursday after school? I don't think I have a recording session that day." James checked his phone. "Yeah, Thursday should be good. You should check with Evan just to be sure."

"Hey, James," Brittany chirped, dressed in her red-and-white cheerleading uniform. She was giving her best impression of a cat in heat. Her lips were parted, her pink-tipped finger winding a strand of silky hair into a curl. James made his way over to her, looking interested.

"He gave you his number. Sounds like a date to me," Maria said, nudging Ella. Ella watched Brittany play with his collar. He leaned into her, one hand against the wall, gazing at Brittany as if she were the most fascinating person in the world.

"Were you even listening to the conversation?" Denzel asked Maria in surprise. "He gave Ella a business card. It's not a date. And what is this crap about giving Ella his manager's number?"

"The manager screens his calls," Ella offered, though the words sounded hollow even to her.

"He could have given you his email or asked for your number," Denzel pointed out. "The guy is a douche if you ask me."

Ella also couldn't ignore the fireworks going off between Brittany and James. They seemed to only have eyes for each other.

"What do you know?" Maria jeered, bringing Ella's attention back to the conversation.

"Yeah, what do I know about the way guys think?" Denzel huffed.

Maria rolled her eyes. "Don't kill Ella's joy."

"I'm just being real," replied Denzel.

"And Ella can do better than James."

Ella wasn't so sure about that. Having James like her would be just about the best thing that ever happened to her. But she had to agree with Denzel. James didn't seem to take any interest in her now that the school queen had made her appearance. Ella had no illusions that it would be different when they worked on the school project together. Still, she did get to be his English partner and spend time with him. There were hundreds of fans that would pay anything to be in Ella's shoes.

# CHAPTER 2

AFTER SCHOOL, ELLA drove home. The weather was hot and sunny, perfect for a ride on her beloved horse, Dusty. She pulled into her driveway, parking her hand-me-down Volvo in the usual spot. This was the only house she had ever called home. It was her refuge from the cruel world she ventured into every day.

Ella found her mother in the garage, putting cans on the shelves. Mom wore a striped V-neck top with white slacks and sandals. Her red hair was cut short in a stacked bob, Chelsey's work. The look wasn't awful, but everyone agreed Mom looked better with longer hair and that Chelsey should stick to makeup.

"Hey, Mom," Ella said.

She turned and wrapped her arms around Ella, pulling her into a big mom hug. "How was your first day?"

"Same as the last three years," Ella replied.

"Let's leave the negativity," Mom prompted. "This will be a great year for you. My senior year was so fun I wish I could do it over again."

Ella groaned. "That's because you were Miss Popular."

"I made fresh cookies," Mom went on. "Why don't we share a couple and you'll tell me about your classes."

"Actually, I was thinking of going down to the stables. I've been sitting for so long that my legs have forgotten what they are good for."

"Maybe afterwards," Mom said wistfully.

"Okay."

Ella changed into her riding clothes and made the short walk to the stables, which were just a few dozen yards from the house. Willie was grooming Dusty when Ella came in. Willie Wilkens had been the farm manager for the past seven years and lived in the guesthouse with his wife, Amanda. A horse whisperer, Willie got the horses to behave without much effort. They were like his children. His own daughter, Robin, was grown, working on a nature reserve in Tellico Plains. Ella looked forward to Robin's yearly visits over Christmas. Their shared love of science and horses made for refreshing conversation. Most of her friends wanted to talk fashion and sports, which didn't interest her.

Ella patted Dusty on the nose, leaning her face close to his. Dusty was a taffy-colored Arabian with a gentle temperament and a fondness for rolling in the hay. He always listened to commands, never galloping faster than was asked of him.

Glenn, on the other hand, was an Appaloosa monster, his shiny gray coat dotted with white spots. He never did as he was told, only submitting his will to Chelsey. Even Willie struggled with Glenn, calling him a mule in horse's clothing.

Willie had used the horses to help Ella heal after the accident, restoring her confidence by showing her that she wasn't helpless. He taught Ella how to mount a horse without assistance—how to swing her right leg over the saddle without bending it. He never treated her any differently, never offering her help unless she asked, and he never compared her injury to other people he knew with similar problems. If Ella had a dime for every time someone suggested a fad treatment or miracle specialist, she would be featured in Forbes.

"Hey, Ella, how was your first day back at school?" Willie asked when he saw her, lifting one of Dusty's back hooves.

"Okay, I guess," Ella replied. She sat on a nearby stool. "Have you found an RV yet?"

"We have a few we're looking at," Willie replied as he picked dirt out of Dusty's horseshoe. "The RV will be our new home, so we have to choose carefully."

Willie and Amanda had been saving up for a "freewheeling retirement," as Amanda called it. They were going to travel the country in their RV, visiting all the national parks and sights. They would not have to worry about tending the garden or termites chewing up the house.

"Want to go for a ride?" Willie asked her.

"Yes, if that's alright," Ella replied.

Willie finished cleaning the other horseshoes before saddling up Dusty. Willie placed the saddle pad in the center of Dusty's back and then put on Dusty's saddle and secured the cinch. "Alright, he is ready for riding," Willie said, handing the reins to Ella. Willie knew Ella wouldn't go near Glenn, so he never offered him for riding.

Ella mounted Dusty and patted his neck, his mane soft and shiny from the brushing Willie had given him. Ella clucked her tongue. At the command, Dusty ambled forward, hay crunching beneath his hooves.

"Willie, may I ask you something?" Ella said.

"You know better than to ask such questions," Willie replied, removing Glenn's saddle, the tassels dancing on his duster jacket.

"Who will take over your job?"

"Haven't decided yet," Willie replied.

"Can't say I'm happy to see you guys go," said Ella. "No one can replace you. You can never replace family."

"Life isn't about standing still, Ella. It twists and turns. Soon you will be off to college and we will be touring the Smoky Mountains. Don't be sad about Amanda and me moving on. Focus on the path in front of you and the good times yet to come."

Ella knew Willie was right, but it didn't make the situation any easier.

"Happy riding," Willie wished her.

Ella put up her hand in thanks and trotted Dusty out along the worn lane, passing by the horse pen, the garden, letting go of modern life and all its tension. Dusty made long strides along the grassy path. His pace slowed when he reached the base of an incline.

"You can do it," Ella coaxed her horse. "The hill's not that steep." Dusty rarely faced an incline. Normally Ella stuck to more level terrain. The horse grunted and shuffled up the small slope of the meadow with his hooves clicking. A gust of wind blew a red-and-gold leaf into her mouth. Ella spat out the leaf, tasting the bitter sap on her tongue. She looked up to see a tree sprouting with fall foliage a few feet ahead of her, a black bird constructing a nest within its thick branches. Ella could almost forgive the leaf for the unpleasant taste after seeing the lovely home it had come from.

Ella surveyed the grass, which the dew had nurtured into a juniper green. A small stream leading to a pond shimmered with sunlight at the foot of the meadow. There was something so peaceful about pausing here with Dusty, stroking his velvet mane, the autumn wind nestling her cheek.

This was Ella's meadow, the one where she often took Maria. The serene seclusion magically pulled secrets from their hearts. Ella had told Maria how she wanted to go to medical school but was worried her leg would get in the way. Maria had told Ella she wanted to go to Syball, a prestigious performing arts school in New York; Broadway was the final destination. Maria was worried and embarrassed that she could not afford Syball's tuition, though. Maria confided only in Ella about her family's financial status, hiding that she lived in an apartment from everyone at school. Her uniform was secondhand— Samantha made sure to tell everyone that at lunch. And Maria used to miss school the day school fees were turned in. Sometimes, Maria said she wished she could trade places with Ella.

Ella craned her neck back to gaze at the slate rooftop of her family's three-story home. Having money meant she was not entitled to complain. "Be grateful," was a line Ella had heard over and over again. Be grateful she had two her legs. Be grateful that her parents had money for the surgery and therapies. "Be grateful, Ella, the accident could have been worse." Be grateful, grateful, grateful.

Ella proceeded after a few minutes of reflection. There were large rocks at the end of the pond where she could sit and think. Ella dismounted and sat, her riding boots touching the edge of the water.

Ella remounted Dusty and rode towards the house, galloping along the stream, the sun casting its pink rays upon the water. How free she felt as the wind brushed off her worries. She stopped at the edge of the meadow, gazing at the magnificent tree that had tried to feed her leaves. The blackbird had finished the nest and rested comfortably in a circle of pine. Ella rode Dusty to the stables and dismounted. She found Willie patting Glenn's forehead while Glenn happily munched on a carrot.

One day soon, Ella would wake up and find a new face tending the horses. No one could possibly replace Willie as a farmhand. Willie and Amanda were like an uncle and aunt to Ella. She would miss them a lot. She often sat in their living room in the evening eating pumpkin pie and listening to Willie tell funny stories about the horses—how Glenn was scared of mice despite his size and how Dusty danced to Alan Jackson songs when they played on the radio.

"Have a good ride?" Willie asked, taking Dusty's reins.

"Dusty didn't want to go up the hill," said Ella. She wiped her brow with the back of her hand.

"Dusty's never been adventurous," said Willie, patting Dusty's back. "But he's as dependable as hunger in the morning."

Ella dabbed at the beads of sweat on the back of her neck. The humidity had been particularly bad that summer—the price they paid for living in the South. Fall was the reward.

"Amanda made a pumpkin pie this afternoon." Willie gave Ella a big smile, showing aging teeth. "I'm sure she would love some help making sure the pie gets eaten."

"I'm on it," Ella said with a grin. No one had to ask her twice to eat hot pumpkin pie.

Ella washed up after being with the horses. She loved her Dusty to bits, but riding him always made her smell like the outdoors, and not in a good way. She changed into jeans and a T-shirt as the scent of BBQ chicken filled the air. Her dad must have started grilling while she was out riding. Ella came down the stairs, careful to use the railing. Experience and a sore bottom had taught her what happened if she tried to go down too quickly.

A feast awaited her at the kitchen table, a family tradition ever since Ella was in grade school. Kiwis and strawberries floated in a pitcher of fruit punch, and corn on the cob and wild rice lined the plates.

"Who's ready for dinner?" Dad asked, bringing in a tray filled with a rainbow of grilled vegetables. He was handsome, for a dad, with sandy gray hair and eyes the color of blueberries, her favorite fruit. Ella sat next to Mom, while Dad placed the tray on a trivet next to the BBQ chicken.

"So, tell me about school," Dad said as he ladled rice onto his plate.

"I got Mrs. Salter for AP Lit and Dr. Taylor this year for AP Chemistry," Ella said, taking some grilled vegetables—mushrooms were her favorite.

"I heard Dr. Taylor only teaches the top classes." Dad winked at Ella. She flushed and looked down at her plate.

"You know, she runs a cancer lab," Mom said, serving herself chicken. "The school is lucky she agreed to teach this year. I heard she'll be retiring soon to focus exclusively on her lab."

"I had heard that," Ella said. She poured punch into her glass. "I hope to get a chance to see it one day."

"Anything exciting happen besides getting your favorite teachers?" Dad asked before nibbling his corncob.

"James Jude joined the school," Ella said.

"Is that the boy who sings about guns?" Mom asked, her teeth clenched in disapproval.

Ella nearly choked on her rice, trying to swallow her laughter.

"I don't find the subject of guns to be amusing," Mom scolded Ella.

"It wasn't literal guns," Ella said. "He was talking about his biceps. That's why the lyric is, 'The only guns I'll ever need are the ones under my sleeves.'"

"Oh," Mom said, her mouth relaxing.

"He was forced to issue an apology," Ella went on, "saying he did not condone gun violence, but the song went to the top of the charts, proving that the rest of the world didn't care."

"You seem to know a lot about this James boy," Dad said.

Ella's cheeks burned as she cut her chicken. The thought of James being her partner set butterflies loose in her stomach.

The garage door slammed as Chelsey's well-formed figure came in holding a black box. Ella had once helped carry that makeup box to Chelsey's Volkswagen. It weighed as much as a potato sack.

"Chelsey, join us," Mom said, motioning to an empty chair at the table.

"I ate at work," Chelsey said. "I'm going to make some calls." With that, she rushed up the stairs. At twenty-four, Chelsey was embarrassed to still be living at home. She was saving up to move out, but it was hard to get by on her salary. Especially since she was still paying back loans for beauty school. Mom and Dad were unwilling to give even a dime.

"There will be leftovers if you change your mind," Mom called. Her green eyes grew sad as she watched Chelsey race out of sight.

"I think I need to get started on homework," Ella said, pushing her chair away from the table.

"Take your plate to the sink," Dad said.

Ella did as she was told. "Dinner was delicious."

"Glad you liked it," Mom replied.

Ella went up to her room and sat at her desk, the same light mahogany one she'd had since she was eight. She pulled out her AP

Calculus book and flipped to the homework. She enjoyed math—it was like one big puzzle to solve. Maria didn't get Ella's perspective, believing math was made for the sole purpose of torturing high school students.

Just as she was about to focus on her work, her phone buzzed. She looked down. It was a text from Matt, asking about her first day at school.

Ella sighed as she thought about Matt, her first boyfriend—the boy with copper hair that constantly fell in his eyes. They had bonded over spine-tingling horror novels during recess, daring the other to read the books that gave them nightmares. They'd talked about their parents and the boring school lunches. They talked about Barry, the school nerd, and Brittany, the class snob. They talked about sports, and tests and their fears about high school.

Matt gave Ella her first kiss, which felt wet and slightly sticky but had filled her heart with absolute glee nonetheless. During their freshman year of high school, Matt's parents got divorced and Matt moved to Connecticut, far away from Forest Hill, Tennessee. They remained friends, but Matt had moved on, or at least that was how it felt to Ella.

Ella replied to Matt's text, saying everything was good, and asked him about soccer. It was his favorite topic these days. He hoped to go to Stanford on a soccer scholarship.

She shook her head and refocused on the math problems. When she was finished, she got into pajamas and brushed her teeth, wondering if this year really was going to be her best year. The past few years had been excruciating as her leg eliminated her favorite activities one by one, the main one being dancing. If only she could dance. She would give anything to twirl around on stage with Maria, the music prodding her body along, giving her feet no choice but to move.

If only the accident hadn't happened, Ella thought regretfully.

If only she had a more responsible brother. If only . . .

# CHAPTER 3

POSTERS WENT UP all over school. The school was having a Sadie Hawkins dance—it was the girls' turn to scout out dates. Ella normally ignored the posters. Why should she bother asking anyone when she was just going to be rejected? But something was different this time. She wanted to go to the dance. It had been so long since she had been on the dance floor.

She pushed the thought out of her head. Her dancing days were over. Yet, the hope persisted.

Ella pictured herself in James's arms, his green eyes gazing into hers. The last period of her day had become her favorite. She got a whole hour to stare secretly at James, noticing his dimples when he laughed, his biceps when he lifted his books off the desk. His hair. Oh, Ella would give anything to run her fingers through his hair.

Her fingers suddenly felt sticky when she thought about the amount of gel he used, but she closed her eyes, concentrating on the wonderful image that was James Jude. Reality hit when she tripped over a backpack in the hallway. She landed splat on her face. It was a rude awakening, to say the least.

Ella lay on the floor, trying to figure out the best way to get back up.

"Need a hand?" a voice asked. It was James. Blood rushed to her head, and her cheeks reddened. She accepted the outstretched hand, knowing she would be unable to lift herself without his assistance.

"I see there is a school dance coming up," James said. He motioned to the posters. "You going?"

"I'd like to," Ella replied.

"Who are you asking? Is it someone I know?" His green eyes glittered with mischief.

"Perhaps." Ella held his gaze, playing coy.

"I'm sure anyone would be happy to go with you." James flashed a bright smile. Ella opened her mouth, then closed it again. Her word-forming ability completely escaped her.

"So, you are coming to my house on Thursday?" James asked.

"That is what your manager told me," Ella replied, getting lost in James's forest-colored eyes. He had not looked away from her the whole time.

"James," a boy called out, blond bangs covering the side of his face. It was Stefan—Mr. Popular, Mr. Lazy, Mr. Wouldn't-be-worth-much-if-Daddy-wasn't-a-member-of-the-school-board.

"See you Thursday," James said as he rushed off.

Ella's heartbeat intensified. Was James giving me a hint? Do I have the nerve to ask a celebrity out? One thing was certain, Ella was not invisible to James. Maybe Maria was right. Maybe James did want a girl with more heart than beauty. Ella could only hope.

Ella drove up to the Brookhaven Club, one of the most exclusive gated communities in Nashville. She stopped at the front gate and rolled down her window. The guard eyed her intensely, trying to assess if Ella was the type to cause trouble.

"I'm here to see James Jude," Ella said. The security guard asked to see her driver's license. Ella wondered how many girls came every day asking to see James. Not taking his eyes off her, the guard picked up the phone and dialed a number.

"Mrs. Gossett, a Gabriella Heart to see James."

Ella rarely heard her full name. Most people called her Ella, or Els. Then it dawned on her that he was talking to the famous Rachel Gossett, James's mother.

"Alright, I'll let her through." The security guard pushed the button, lifting the boom and allowing Ella entry into the private world of the Brookhaven Club community.

Ella waved her thanks as she passed. She drove past mega-mansions with immaculate front lawns decorated ornately with colorful flower beds in intricate patterns. Some of the driveways had more than four garages. She saw Rolls-Royces and Maseratis through tall, black gates. Most of the homes boasted half or even full-size Olympic swimming pools as well as movie theaters and bowling alleys in their basements. At least that was what Brittany Jones's house had; they also lived in Brookhaven. Ella hadn't been to Brittany's house since her middle school graduation party. She wondered if the gold ceiling in Brittany's foyer ever needed touch-ups or if the Andy Warhol painting was still hanging over the mantle in the grand living room. Perhaps they had replaced it with another expensive work of art.

Ella would have to keep wondering, since she had not been a welcome guest in the Jones home for a very long time. She decided she would ask Maria the next time she saw her. Maria had visited the Joneses several times just in the last month. Brittany needed Maria's help in producing new dance moves for the upcoming cheerleading competition.

Ella checked the address that Evan Harris, James's manager, had given her—137 Brookhaven Way. Talking with Evan Harris had felt like talking with a security guard at the airport—all business and no fun. Ella nervously pressed the buzzer on the gate.

"Hello?" a woman's voice crackled through the intercom.

"Ella Heart," Ella said loudly into the speaker.

After a few beeps, the gate swung open, welcoming her in. Ella entered the circular driveway, which had a giant fountain in the center. Water spouted from the mouths of ivory cherubs. Shockingly, the house's exterior looked like something out of a horror movie, with a gray brick face and large lanterns flickering on either side of the doorway; the door was dark oak with stained-glass windows and an old-fashioned knocker. Ella half expected a ghost to leap out of the bushes.

Ella's heart thumped along with the heavy knocker. Knock, knock, knock.

A woman answered the door. She had long, wavy hair the same golden-brown as James's, but her eyes were completely dark, no green in them at all. The woman looked to be about thirty-five, but Ella knew better. It was James's mother, Rachelle Gossett. Ella froze, feeling quite speechless. She was before country music royalty.

"I'm here to see James," Ella stammered. She felt like she was getting clearance to enter Fort Knox.

"James is just finishing recording a song in the studio downstairs," Mrs. Gossett said. "I'll take you to him."

Ella followed Mrs. Gossett past a gleaming white kitchen, a rustic-looking living room, and then down plush, carpeted steps. Ella thought James was not recording today; his manager had assured her Thursday would be a good day for studying. Ella guessed James had a song burning in his back pocket like an ice cream cone in a little boy's hand. A musician had to record, or the idea would melt away.

The basement was just as large as the Joneses', but it had been gutted completely. A person manned a large soundboard with another man in a gray suit standing next to him. Ella saw James through the glass window, in the vocal booth. He was singing into a microphone with large headphones covering his hair. James's voice lit up the soundboard in waves of green and red. The sound engineer adjusted the knobs on the board as James sang. Ella was hearing a song for the first time straight from the artist himself:

*I didn't ask to say goodbye,*
*you said you loved me, it's a lie*

*now I want to cry.*
*You told me you were gonna try*
*but my heart you went and fried.*
*Now I want to die.*
*Girl, don't you say goodbye.*

"Great, let's take a break," the man in the gray suit said. James took off his earphones and opened the door of the vocal booth. The sound engineer and the man in the gray suit huddled together, making notes about the song. Neither said a word to Ella.

"Hey, Ella," James said offhandedly when he saw her. She could not help but notice his looks; she soaked up everything about him so she could picture him later when she was alone. He wore a T-shirt under a blue-and-white-striped oxford shirt, and navy cargo pants. His bangs fell naturally to the side, and his mane lacked the usual gravity-defying gel. Ella decided she liked his hair better this way—natural.

"I like your song," Ella offered. The truth was, the lyrics were cheesy, and Ella had never heard the word fried in a song before. Yet the beat was catchy, and deep wasn't what most pop songs went for anyway. Gone were the days of Simon and Garfunkel's poetic hits.

"I'm starving. Do you mind if we work in the kitchen?" James asked.

"Sure," Ella replied, although the idea of traveling up the stairs made Ella feel tired.

James led Ella back up the basement steps and past the elegantly furnished living room to the sparkling kitchen. Everything in the kitchen was white. White granite counters and a white wooden table with wicker chairs complemented a huge, icy-white refrigerator and ornate, ivory-white cabinets. There were even white roses in a crystal vase.

"Want something to drink?" James offered as he scanned the fridge.

"Alright," Ella replied. James handed her a can of soda and continued his search for nourishment. "Leftover pizza," he said happily, taking out a slice.

Ella took out her literature folder from her school bag. "I thought we could review the play Romeo and Juliet. I've read it before and am familiar with the storyline."

"I think everyone is familiar with the storyline," replied James as he took a bite of pizza.

"Romeo and Juliet is one of the first stories about forbidden love," Ella went on. "Although some say Shakespeare based this play off someone else's work."

"Sounds good," James said as he shoved the crust into his mouth.

"Have you ever read the play before?" Ella asked. "Because I have the CliffsNotes if you haven't." She reached back into her bag to pull out the booklet.

"About the assignment," James cut in. "I'm kind of busy producing another album. I was hoping you would help me out with writing the paper. Maybe write it and email it to me and I'll see what needs to be added?" He rubbed his hands together, pizza crumbs falling on the floor. "I doubt I will need to add anything, since I hear you're the smartest girl in school."

James looked at her directly when he said this, turning his green eyes on her in full force. Ella felt sick. He was using her just like the rest of her classmates did. Why did I think he would be any different?

"There is something I wanted to ask you," James said. "I found out you volunteer at the local hospital a few times a month. Doesn't surprise me; I hear you have a big heart." James was sure turning on the charm.

"Yes, twice a month, in the children's oncology ward," Ella replied coldly, his charm sliding off her heart onto the floor.

"Yeah, with the children," James went on. Ella wondered if he even knew what oncology meant. "I was wondering if I could join you next time you go? Maybe play the children some of my new songs? I feel it's important to give back."

James is a walking cliché if there ever was one, Ella thought with disappointment. Yet she couldn't help but feel butterflies in her stomach at the thought of him accompanying her on her next visit to the hospital. She had seen pictures in magazines of him at charity drives and standing near children in hospital beds. He must be looking for the next PR opportunity.

"I think the kids would like that," said Ella.

"Cool," James replied. "You still have my manager's number, right? He'll tell me when you have arranged everything."

"Does your manager shower you as well?" Ella said tartly.

"What?" James sounded confused.

"I meant shower you with gifts?" Ella added quickly.

"Oh, he doesn't have to. My fans do that."

"Of course they do," Ella muttered, starting to regret she had ever been one of them.

"I have to get back to my album," James said. He was finished with his pizza, and Ella was no longer needed. She was being dismissed. "Making an album takes much more time than people realize," James continued. Ella didn't say anything. He was mistaken if he thought she was going to give him any sympathy.

"I'll start working on the paper," Ella said, packing up her literature folder. The study "date" had been a complete waste of time.

James seemed fidgety, anxious to get back to his studio. He waved goodbye as he hurried down the hall to the basement steps. Ella guessed walking her to the door was too much trouble for him. Ella walked to the foyer alone, passing photos of a younger-looking James. The man in the gray suit approached her.

"Miss Heart, can I have a word with you?"

Ella paused, looking at the man expectantly.

"I'm Evan Harris, James's manager. We spoke on the phone." He extended his hand in greeting. His hair was thick, and his eyes were a light brown. He would be handsome if he weren't wearing such a serious expression. "I don't know if James had a chance to run our idea by you," Mr. Harris went on. "We would like to accompany you on your next visit to the local hospital. Maybe you could give me the director's number, so I can speak with them about James giving a surprise concert for the patients?"

"I doubt the director would say no," Ella said. Ella wondered if Mr. Harris ever minded being James's lackey. Perhaps he was paid well enough to not let it bother him.

"Your leg," Mr. Harris said, pointing. "It was cancer, wasn't it? You walk so well with a prosthetic."

Ella gaped at him. He thinks my leg was amputated?

"I read a book once," Mr. Harris continued, "about a girl who had her leg amputated because of cancer. That is why you visit the cancer ward, to give back?" Mr. Harris sounded as if he had a crystal ball and was staring into her life. His magic ball needed cleaning, though, as none of the facts he had on Ella were correct.

"Nothing gets past you," Ella said, suppressing a giggle.

"It's a manager's job to keep a finger on the pulse," Mr. Harris replied. Might want to add more fingers to the pulse, Ella thought. He clearly had not picked up on her sarcasm.

"So, you will get me the director's number?" Mr. Harris asked.

"Yes," Ella said. She wanted nothing more than to leave and get on with her afternoon.

"We will be in touch then," Mr. Harris said, turning from Ella. Ella took the chance to escape to her car and avoid getting asked any more favors.

James was nothing like the compassionate heartthrob he was made out to be. Surely, not all singers were like this. Something had gone wrong along the way. Maybe his parents had a guilt complex about leaving their son to tour the world when he was younger—making up for lost time by giving their son all his heart desired. What James needs is a good dose of reality, Ella thought. He was unlikely to ever receive it.

# CHAPTER 4

ELLA TOLD THE hospital director about James's request to sing for the children. The director was thrilled, calling Evan Harris on the spot. But Ella could not feel excited. Her fondness for James slipped away, and seventh period no longer held the thrill it once contained. James didn't deserve any favors from her, especially when he had dumped the whole English assignment in her lap. But Ella's heart softened when she thought about the children and how ecstatic they would be to see James perform.

The following Friday, Ella turned in their assignment. James contributed nothing but a smiley emoji when Ella had emailed him the paper, asking for his feedback. After school, Ella went home with Maria to spend the night. They'd had countless sleepovers at Maria's house over the years, and Ella felt at home there, comfortable, like part of the family. She loved sitting on Maria's bed, looking at the posters pinned up on the wall—posters of Broadway classics such as Cats, Les Miserables and Ella's personal favorite, Into the Woods. Ella felt confident that one day Maria would be on someone's wall, a Broadway star.

"He has his own studio?" Maria asked in disbelief, lying next to Ella. Ella had spent the last hour complaining about her star crush—now her star resentment.

"James has his own everything. Manager, driver, bath filler," Ella replied.

"He has everything except sense," Maria added.

"No, not much of that."

"Did the director set up the surprise concert yet?"

"Yes," said Ella. "It's next Sunday."

"I get the sense he likes you more than you think he does," Maria said, hiking herself up on her elbow. "He could pick any hospital to perform at. Interestingly enough, he chose the one you volunteer in."

"He dumped the whole assignment into my lap."

"You said he was working on an album," Maria pointed out. "I bet he was just really busy and now he is really grateful."

Ella hadn't thought about it that way. James did seem grateful, offering her his pen during class when her mechanical pencil ran out of lead. Perhaps she had rushed to conclusions. It wouldn't be the first time.

"Maybe you should ask him to the Sadie Hawkins dance." Maria nudged her with a pillow. "He is probably waiting for you to make the first move."

"Weren't you listening?" Ella asked Maria. "The guy thinks I exist to write his school papers."

"Have you thrown away the poster hiding in your T-shirt drawer?"

"No," Ella admitted.

"You still have a thing for him."

Ella couldn't deny it. He was rude and lazy and still the most beautiful person she had ever seen.

"Ask anyone to the dance yet?" Ella said, tired of talking about her lack of a love life.

"No."

"What about Denzel?"

"It's complicated," Maria said.

"Actually, it's quite simple," said Ella. "You are both stuck in neutral and neither of you knows how to change gears. A Sadie Hawkins dance is the perfect time for you to make the first move."

"What if it doesn't work out? I don't want to lose him as a friend."

"Ah, but what if it does?"

"Alright, the deal is this." Maria was on her knees now, her nut-brown eyes bright with an idea. "I'll ask out Denzel to the dance if you ask James."

"That deal is not fair in the slightest."

"The problem is you're both in neutral," Maria mimicked Ella. "Get it in gear, girl."

Ella rolled her eyes. She should have known by now that Maria always gave back as good as she got.

"It's a deal then," Ella said. "We'll shift gears together and hope for the best."

Maria gave a triumphant smile.

Ella's eyes wandered to a wooden picture frame she had given Maria with the word besties carved at the top. The photo showed them in the hammock in Ella's backyard. Maria's hair was pulled back into a French braid, and Ella wore her hair in a half pony. Ella's knee was wrapped in a white cast. The picture had been taken a few weeks after the accident.

Ella remembered having to miss Brittany's skating party, something she had been looking forward to. But Maria surprised Ella by coming over instead of attending the party. They had spent the day hanging out, eating ice cream and pizza.

"Do the Joneses still have a gold-gilded ceiling in the foyer?" Ella asked Maria, thinking of Brittany.

"Yes," replied Maria. "They did touch-ups last year. Apparently, a pint of gold paint costs an absolute fortune."

"I wonder how many cans of paint is needed for one ceiling?"

"Better figure it out, because it will be on your next math test," Maria joked.

"What about the Andy Warhol picture above the fireplace?" said Ella.

"The picture has been exchanged for Brittany in a leopard-print dress," said Maria.

"What?" Ella exclaimed. "They exchanged an Andy Warhol painting for Brittany in a leopard dress?"

"Terrible choice," Maria sighed. "Then again, no one asked me." The girls looked at each other and laughed.

Mrs. Garcia pushed open the door. "Who's hungry? I made Mexican corn with chipolatas."

"Mom, I told you I am a vegetarian now," Maria whined.

"Really?" Ella raised a brow.

"I saw this YouTube video," Maria began. "There really is no humane way to slaughter an animal."

"Not again with the YouTube," Mrs. Garcia replied, placing a hand against her temple. "You know anyone can make a video and post it."

"But this really made me rethink my values," Maria insisted.

"What does your apron say?" Ella asked Mrs. Garcia to cut the tension.

"It says, 'The chef is always beautiful when dinner is on the table,'" Maria translated. Mrs. Garcia is beautiful without any food on the table or makeup on her face, Ella thought. Mrs. Garcia had a lovely olive complexion and bright brown eyes that held specks of gold. Her soft brown hair came to her shoulders in layers, making her look much younger than her forty-nine years. Ella marveled at Mrs. Garcia's face, radiant despite the sixty-hour workweeks the woman endured.

Ella went with Maria to the kitchen; the food was laid out on the table. Ella couldn't wait to dig in. Maria avoided the chipolatas, while Ella took two spoonfuls. She didn't see the harm in eating meat, and she wasn't about to miss out on one of Mrs. Garcia's dishes.

Monday started out like any other Monday. Ella went to first period, which was French, and second period, which was World History. On her way to the library to study through her free third period, Mrs. Pierce, the guidance counselor, stopped her. "Ella, can I have a word with you please?"

Mrs. Pierce motioned for Ella to take a seat. Ella pulled out the chair and sat down, aware that it took her longer to sit than most people. She felt Mrs. Pierce's gaze and saw the sympathy on her pretty face. Ella didn't like being watched when she struggled with activities most people did with ease. And she certainly didn't need sympathy.

"Going through your file," Mrs. Pierce began, after Ella was finally seated, "I have uncovered the fact that as of now, you are short one credit, which means you will not be graduating along with your class in the spring."

"How can that be?" Ella said, panicking. "I've taken more than the required number of classes."

"Yes, but you are lacking an elective," Mrs. Pierce said. "You need two elective classes to graduate. I see the last elective you took was Music in ninth grade."

Ella shuddered at the memory of that horrible class. Mr. O'Shea, the music teacher, had given Ella the harmonica to play. "It will be fun," he had assured her. "You will learn fast."

Two-thirds of the way through the class, sticking out her blue, plump lip, Ella had begged Mr. O'Shea to let her bang the cymbals. Mr. O'Shea refused, insinuating that she was musically challenged and therefore unqualified to play any other instrument. "Those who can't play, teach," Ella muttered under her breath, apparently not quietly enough. She was handed the cymbals and a pink detention slip. Four years later, she still avoided Mr. O'Shea in the halls.

"Ella, are you alright?" Mrs. Pierce asked. "You keep pointing to your lip and muttering."

"I won't be graduating," Ella wailed. What will I tell my parents?

"Relax, Ella, all hope is not lost," Mrs. Pierce said brightly. "Let me have a look at what is still available." She ran a French-tipped fingernail down the computer screen. "There are still spots available in Dance, Art and Woodshop this semester." Mrs. Pierce's maple-colored hair came loose from the clip holding it back. Ella decided she like Mrs. Pierce's hair better down and wondered if she should say something, then thought better of it. Instead, she considered the electives to choose from.

Dance is not an option, Ella thought sadly. She enjoyed Art History, but her own drawings were chicken scratch with no imagination. The answer would have to be . . .

"Woodshop," Ella said.

"You know that class consists mostly of boys?" Mrs. Pierce said, clicking her hair back into place, instantly aging ten years.

"Is that a problem?" Ella asked.

"No, not a problem. I'm just pointing it out." Mrs. Pierce took a deep breath. "You have missed the deadline for switching classes. If you take Woodshop, you will have to stick with the class until the end of the school year."

Ella wondered if Mrs. Pierce tried to talk all girls out of Woodshop or just Ella. "I'll stick it out," Ella said.

"I must stress, Ella, the class is a graded class like any other class in school, which means it must be taken seriously."

"I will take the class seriously," Ella insisted, showing Mrs. Pierce she would not back down.

"Alright, I'll sign you up for Woodshop," Mrs. Pierce replied, typing Ella's name into the computer. "Mr. Geller is the teacher." She scribbled something on a piece of paper and handed it to Ella. "The class has already started. Off you go."

As Ella left Mrs. Pierce's office, her stomach started to bind. She wondered what she had just signed herself up for. On the one hand, she now had a mission to prove that girls could succeed in Woodshop. And Ella had no doubt many women could. On the other hand, Ella had never fixed anything in her life. This class was going to be a problem, plain and simple. Instead of heading to the library to study, she had been thrust into Woodshop to fulfill some silly, bureaucratic, state-mandated requirement to allow her to graduate.

Ella made her way back up the east wing and towards the lawn, to where Woodshop was located. The walk took longer than she expected, and her right leg gave her more trouble than usual. Panting, Ella pushed open the door of the workshop timidly. The room looked like a glorified garage, with wood beams crisscrossing the cork panel ceiling, the smell of pine and sawdust overwhelming her senses.

Mr. Geller, a tall man with a tool belt, stood at the head of the class with pieces of wood laid out neatly on the table in front of him.

"Can I help you?" Mr. Geller asked. Ella noted the mild tone.

"I will be joining your class," Ella said, handing him the note from Mrs. Pierce.

He took the note with his callused fingers and looked it over. He nodded and handed Ella a nylon sack. "This is your tool bag," Mr. Geller explained. "You will need to bring it to every class." He then gave Ella a stack of wood. "Now, have a seat next to Max." Mr. Geller indicated a boy with dark hair and stubby fingers. Ella knew Max. They were in World History together.

Ella clung to the bag and wood, making her way to her seat. She managed to stay upright, but her pile of wood landed with a loud thump next to Max, and he jumped.

"Hi, Max," Ella whispered, slipping as fast as she could into her seat.

"Hi," he murmured back. He didn't seem to be happy sharing a table as he glanced around at the other boys who had tables all to themselves.

Ella was much happier about the seating arrangement. Max was a nice guy, known for being quiet and helpful. Brittany often referred to Max as adorable and pinched his cheeks. Ella wondered if that was why Max had joined the wrestling team—perhaps he was trying to shed his adorable image and pinchable cheeks.

"Start by taking the base of the birdfeeder and set it lengthwise," Mr. Geller said without even the slightest introduction, demonstrating with a square piece of wood.

Ella looked frantically for the pieces that matched Mr. Geller's. All the pieces looked alike to her. Finally, she found a piece of wood that appeared slightly wider than the other four pieces scattered in front of her. She assumed it was the base Mr. Geller was referring to.

"Now take the back-wall piece and line it up with the corresponding poles on the base of the bird feeder," Mr. Geller went on.

Ella saw Max line up the wall along the base. She copied him, lining up the pieces of wood exactly as Max had his wood pieces. The directions were more complicated than she had expected.

"Take four screws," Mr. Geller instructed, "and screw the wall to the base of the birdfeeder. Repeat the process until all walls are connected to the base. We will deal with the roof separately."

"What tool is he using?" Ella asked desperately, looking at the tools before her. Max noticed her frustration.

"This one." He shoved a screwdriver in her direction. "Honestly, aren't you supposed to be the smartest girl in the school or something?"

Ella wanted to respond by pinching his cheeks but decided she needed Max as a friend if she was going to survive this class. She took the Phillips-head and tried screwing in the screw from the base to the wall. It didn't want to go in. Ella pressed harder.

Mr. Geller rushed to her aid. "Never force a screw in; you will strip it." He pulled the screw out, showing Ella the damage she had done to the top. Ella saw some of the boys smirking at her, and she knew then and there that Woodshop was going to be her least favorite class.

It was the longest hour Ella had experienced in her life. Her birdfeeder looked like it was put together by a kindergartener. The glue she used for the roof wouldn't stick, meaning Mr. Geller had to help her remove the roof and try again. Mr. Geller stayed by Ella's side the whole time, his sympathetic eyes starting to look irritated. Yet he kept his tone even, showing he had lots of patience. Ella left dejected, having scored no points for women's rights. She had just furthered the stereotype that some women were hopeless with tools.

# CHAPTER 5

AFTER A TOUGH week at school, Ella was glad when Friday finally came. But the weekend wasn't as restful as Ella hoped. Evan Harris badgered her if the hospital director delayed even ten minutes in returning his calls. This is not the presidential inauguration, Ella wanted to shout at Evan. Who cared if the streamers were purple instead of white or if James entered from the back? Ella was glad when Sunday finally arrived. All the plans for James's surprise concert were finished. And if anyone mentioned the word James or concert ever again, she would scream.

Ella arrived at the hospital during the Sunday visiting hours. She wore a white sweater and blue jeans, her hair down and straight, her makeup in neutral tones. "The effortless look," Chelsey called it—when one wanted to look stylish without appearing to have tried. Ella told her sister she wanted to look presentable for the children, but she left out the part about impressing James.

Ella settled into a game of chess with a boy named Arthur Kalaf, one of the patients in the common area of the hospital. Arthur had a type of brain tumor called juvenile pilocytic astrocytoma. They had performed surgery a few days before; bandages were wrapped around his head, black hair sticking out at the ends.

The kids in the common room were in varying degrees of health. Some were getting stronger, and some weaker. Ella could never judge them just by appearances. One girl had looked like she had one foot in death's door, only to be sent home in full remission a month later. Another boy looked fit as a football star, hardly any bruising or hair loss, but he died a few weeks after meeting Ella due to complications. Ella never took for granted that she was a visitor at the hospital instead of a patient. She hoped she would always be on this side of the curtain.

"You cheated," Arthur said with an angry pout, bringing Ella's attention back to the game.

"I didn't cheat," Ella protested.

"You let me win."

It was true. She felt sorry for Arthur and could not help but feel like he needed a boost.

"I can win without you cheating," Arthur said furiously, his thin arms crossed.

"We will see about that next time," Ella replied as she placed the lid on the chess box. She stood and stretched, looking around for who to visit with next.

"Ella, I see your balance has improved," commented Nurse Hellen, one of those nurses that everyone knew. Her smile was always wide and welcoming. "Are you still going to physio?"

"Stopped two years ago," Ella replied. "You really think I've improved?"

"Definitely," Hellen said, flashing Ella a wide grin. Then she whispered in Ella's ear, "Big James is here."

"So exciting," Ella replied. She hoped Hellen didn't notice her blush. She reminded herself that James had come to be with the children.

"It's alright." Hellen patted her back. "My daughter has a crush on him too." Hellen put a finger to her lips, giving Ella a furtive smile as she walked off to the nurse's station.

Ella went over to a young girl sitting in an armchair. Nia Burton was one of Ella's favorites, always cheerful despite fighting a losing battle against an aggressive bone cancer, osteosarcoma. Nia had trouble walking as the cancer continued to attack her legs. Ella identified with Nia and held a great admiration for her. She was far more courageous than Ella ever could be. Nia also tried to bring joy to others even though she was in a dark place herself.

Ella found Nia listening to music, her headphones resting on her hairless scalp as she bounced to the beat.

"What are you listening to?" Ella asked Nia.

Nia took off her headphones. "James Jude."

"Really? How much would you like to meet James?" Ella asked. She bit her lip to suppress a smile.

"More than anything," Nia responded, dreamy-eyed.

Right on cue, a high-pitched noise pierced the air. Everyone instinctively covered their ears, but soon the kids heard a young voice singing a familiar song.

"Hey girl, / yes, I'm talking to you. / Hey girl, you seem too good to be true."

James entered the room, holding a microphone. The young patients went ballistic. James looked like a rock star with a backwards baseball cap and a layered T-shirt. He was wearing baggy pants, but it fit with the look. Nia screeched, in utter shock. Even the boys watched James as if he were a superhero.

James gave each boy a manly high five and he serenaded the girls, gifting them each with a long-stemmed rose. He made every child feel like the only one in the room. He tossed T-shirts and caps into the intimate crowd. The children had never looked so happy; James made them feel like a million bucks.

When the performance was over, James helped Ella serve the children pizza and drinks in the back room. He spent time with each child. He asked them about their hobbies and favorite TV shows. The cameraman followed him from patient to patient, snapping photos James promised to send to each patient. When he got to Nia, she was shaking with eagerness to talk with her idol.

"Hi, pretty lady," James said, taking the seat next to her.

Nia could barely contain herself. "You're the greatest. I have all your albums."

"Do you now?" James pulled out a disc in a plastic CD cover and handed it to her. "My new song, 'Wanna Cry.' You have it before the radio stations."

Nia threw her frail arms around his neck. "This is the greatest day of my life," Nia said, still holding James. She seemed like she was on cloud nine.

"Meeting you was the best thing that has ever happened to me," James answered. Ella knew he didn't mean it, but it was nice of him to say.

"May I take a picture with you?" James asked. Nia nodded.

"Okay," said the cameraman, "frown." Nia's face broke out into the widest grin Ella had ever seen.

"Ella, join us," James instructed. Ella leaned over Nia's shoulder, and another picture was snapped.

"Can I have a copy of that?" Nia asked.

"Sure, we will send some pictures to the hospital," James replied.

"James, do you have a girlfriend?" Nia asked.

James grinned. "Not yet."

Nia blushed. It was clear from her expression that James had made her feel she had a shot. This was a new side of James, a side Ella wanted to see more of.

James and his crew were packing all their equipment into his fancy RV. It had been a wonderful few hours. Ella felt her star crush returning. James had seemed kind and generous, without so much as a trace of the arrogance she had come to associate him with. Maybe she did have the nerve to ask him out.

As the crew loaded the last of the speakers, Ella called out to James. He turned to her.

"What you did for those kids today, you gave them more happiness than some of them will have in a lifetime," Ella said, hoping she didn't sound too gushy. "Some of them may not be here tomorrow," Ella continued. "You gave them incredible memories."

"That's why I do it. Knowing I can bring these children some pleasure in a difficult time is important to me." James looked like he meant it.

"I saw you with that girl, Nia," Ella went on. "I think you made her year."

"She looks up to you," James said.

Ella flushed from the compliment. "We just understand each other, I guess." Ella swallowed. Her window of opportunity was shutting rapidly. "James, would you like to go to the fall dance with me?" Ella blurted out.

James lifted his baseball cap and ran a hand through his hair. He had bleached it blond, making his skin appear sallow. He looked uncomfortable. "I would love to, Ella, but Brittany already asked me."

Ella just stood there, not knowing how to respond.

James broke the silence. "I'll see you in school," he said. Ella nodded, her heart sinking.

With that, he climbed into his RV and shut the doors behind him. It had been a nice day, but it felt spoiled now. Ella should have known Brittany would get to James first. She didn't feel any braver for trying; she just felt miserable. Miserable for believing the situation would end any other way.

Ella came home that evening feeling worn out. She flopped down in front of the TV and flipped through the channels, not having the strength for anything but vegging out.

"Hey, Ella," Mom said, joining her on the couch. She was wearing her favorite funnel-neck sweater from Talbots. "How did it go today at the hospital? Were the kids surprised to see James?"

"Yes," Ella replied. Hearing his name made her wince a little.

"It was nice of James to volunteer his time," Mom went on. "Why don't you invite James over for a movie one night?" Her mother was under the mistaken impression that they were friends.

"He is busy with school and becoming a world-famous singer," Ella told her mother. She didn't see herself asking James for anything, ever again.

"Ella, don't sell yourself short. James would be lucky to have you as a friend."

Ella didn't respond. She turned her attention back to the TV. She wondered how Maria was faring with her situation. Maria had asked Denzel over to study math together, a subject that Maria hated with all her might. Denzel was an expert at math, always getting the top scores, setting the curve. Tonight, Maria was going to ask him out. Ella was sure Maria would have more success than she had.

She felt a twinge. She hated being jealous of Maria. Maria was her best friend and never bragged or made Ella feel inferior. But Ella couldn't help wondering what it was like having boys get shy and lose their words around her. If Maria had asked James, Ella was sure James would have said yes. Will any boy ever want me? Or should I just get a cat and be done with it?

A commercial for cat litter came on, causing Ella to drop the remote.

"Oh, did I tell you we are having the Lowells for dinner tomorrow night?" Mom said. The Lowells were their next-door neighbors.

"Do we have to?" Ella whined. "Shane and I have nothing to say to each other." Shane was the Lowells' only child. There was a debate between Mom and Dad whether Shane was spoiled or simply a moody teenager. Either way, Shane's attitude made him painful to be around.

"They're our friends," Mom pointed out. "Remember how Paul helped your dad install benches near the house so you would be able to take rests on the way to the stables after the accident?"

Ella did remember, mostly because her mother never let her forget.

"Will they bring Otis?" Ella asked. Otis was a Mackenzie River husky, and by far Ella's favorite member of the Lowell family.

"I don't really like big dogs in the house," said Mom. "Ros is always complaining about the shedding and the mud Otis tracks onto her carpet."

"Can I invite Maria?" Ella begged.

"I'm sure you and Shane can think of something to talk about." Mom patted Ella's shoulder. "Maybe tell him about the college application process. I'm sure he would appreciate it. He will be a senior next year."

Ella groaned, thinking she needed to go to sleep. Sleep made everything, better. Right?

# CHAPTER 6

THE NEXT MORNING at school, Ella trudged to her locker, feeling miserable. She didn't know how to face James. She knew he had not rejected her outright, that someone had simply gotten to him first, but Ella couldn't help wondering if James would have said no to her even if he was free to go with her. That was her fear—that James didn't want her, that nobody wanted her.

Maria bounded up to Ella in excitement.

"Guess what?" Maria asked, nodding.

"All your dreams came true," Ella said in a dismal tone.

"Yes, but why do you sound so depressed?"

"James is taking Brittany," Ella muttered.

"Well, it was a long shot asking James Jude," Maria sighed. "Aren't you glad you tried?"

"As glad as you were to try calculus?"

"Don't remind me," Maria said, scrunching up her nose. "Hey, why don't you ask Bar—"

"Don't say Barry," Ella warned.

"Why not?"

"Haven't you noticed he hangs out with Stanley a lot?" said Ella, opening her locker.

"Stanley is artsy and Barry is a smarty pants. They are like a copy of us—so what?" Maria shrugged.

"Take a better look next time," Ella said. "You will see exactly why I can't date Barry."

"You think?" Maria cocked her head.

"I do," said Ella.

"My dad said I could drive the Mercedes to the dance," Denzel said, coming up behind them, his brown eyes shining. Maria grinned back. Denzel and Maria looked like they were going to live happily ever after.

"Ella, may I speak with you for a moment?" It was Dr. Taylor, her chemistry teacher. Ella left Maria and Denzel gazing affectionately at one another. They were so charming together it was almost sickening. Ella tried to shake off the bitterness in her heart. Maria was her best friend; she should be happy for her. Ella followed Dr. Taylor to the science room, wondering what her teacher wanted to speak with her about.

"Have a seat," Dr. Taylor said, motioning for Ella to sit at one of the desks.

"Is it about the test we just took?" Ella asked.

"You got a ninety-five, beating Barry by two points." Dr. Taylor was aware of the ongoing competition between them. Ella tried to hide her smile. She felt a little smug but didn't want to show it.

Dr. Taylor pushed back her chair, her short, dark hair bobbing around her chin. She had kept the same hairstyle since she first started teaching at Dellpine Academy three years ago. "Ella, what would you say about helping me in my laboratory once a week?" Dr. Taylor asked.

"You want me to work in your lab?" Ella asked in surprise.

"Your lab work is always excellent. I thought this would be a good experience for you. You would be performing basic tasks such as cleaning vials and recording results from the microscope slides you will be inspecting. Oh, and Barry will be joining you."

Ella gritted her teeth. If she heard Barry's name one more time . . .

"I will need you every Saturday between eight in the morning until about noon. Of course, allowances can be made if you need a weekend off now and then. The lab will also be closed for all holiday weekends."

Ella didn't have to think too deeply. Working in Dr. Taylor's laboratory would be a wonderful learning opportunity, not to mention it would look nice on her college application. Dr. Taylor worked at the CDC in Atlanta until she was hired as the director of the program in cancer research at a nearby university. She was one of the first black women to hold such a prestigious position. How the school convinced her to teach even one science class at Pines, Ella would never know, but she was grateful for the chance to be her student.

"Yes, I would like to," said Ella.

"I was hoping you would say that," Dr. Taylor said. "Now, can you please find Barry for me? I thought I saw him in the computer lab."

Ella grimaced but agreed to go find him.

Barry was just where Dr. Taylor thought he would be. He was taking an intelligence test online. His sandy, untrimmed hair lay shabbily around his geeky face.

"Trying to beat your score?" Ella asked him.

"What do you want, squash head?" Barry replied, his eyes focused on the screen. Barry always had nicknames for her, usually something orange themed like "carrot top," "pumpkin bomb" or "sour tangerine."

"Dr. Taylor wants to see you," Ella replied, not taking the bait.

"It's about the test we took," Barry said confidently. He pushed his oversized glasses closer to his face. "She probably wants to congratulate me."

"Not quite, Mr. Humble. I beat your test score by two points."

Barry scowled.

"You will like what Dr. Taylor has to say though," Ella continued. "The only downside is that we will be working together."

Barry pushed his chair back. "The upside better be freaking fantastic. Why do people always group us together? It's like putting together a stallion and a donkey to pull a load."

"I couldn't agree more," Ella replied. Barry glared at her, his beady eyes contracting as he sauntered out of the computer lab.

The end of the school day could not come soon enough for Ella, although she was not looking forward to seeing James in American Lit. When James entered the classroom, he gave her a half smile and inched his desk away from her. After that, he acted like she didn't exist.

"We will be diagramming sentences," Mrs. Salter announced at the beginning of class. "Sadly, most of you do not understand the basic structure of a sentence." There were groans as Mrs. Salter turned her back to the class, picking up a dry-erase marker from the whiteboard. Her scarf rustled as she wrote on the board. Ella's throat tightened. *How is Mrs. Salter wearing a scarf over a turtleneck?* she wondered, tugging at her shirt collar.

Mrs. Salter drew a horizontal line with a small vertical line down the middle.

"First, we must identify the subject of the sentence," Mrs. Salter continued, pointing to an example. "'The dog chased the cat,'" Mrs. Salter read to the class. "Can anyone tell me the subject of this sentence?"

"Oppression," Samantha called.

The class laughed. James and Samantha bumped fists.

"Perhaps we should use some examples from your last homework assignment, Miss Bell," Mrs. Salter said, crossing her arms.

"It's the dog. The dog is the subject," Samantha said quickly.

"Very good, Miss Bell," Mrs. Salter replied. She wrote dog on the left half of the horizontal line.

Mrs. Salter had the class diagram more than twenty sentences. Ella's right hand came close to retiring. What was worse, her bladder was about to explode. Just when Ella thought she could not diagram another sentence or hold up her pelvic floor muscles any longer, the bell rang, signaling sweet relief.

After a stopover in the ladies' room, Ella made her way to the parking lot.

"Hey, Brittany, I found your twin sister." Stefan's voice carried across the lot. Ella saw him hold up his cell phone.

"Let's see," Brittany said, reaching for the phone. The whole gang was gathered in her red convertible, the top down. James and Brittany were in the front, Samantha and Nicole in the back, and Stefan sat near the trunk. Ella hid behind a Range Rover, not wanting James to see her.

"I guess I see the resemblance, but I wish I had the model's nose—mine is square," Brittany sighed, tossing Stefan back his phone.

"Your nose is just fine," James said.

"Ahh, Jimmers," Brittany said, laying her head on his shoulder. James stiffened. Ella guessed he didn't like the nickname. As her knee complained from being forced into a crouch, she wondered how long she would have to stay in hiding. Unfortunately, no one looked like they were going anywhere anytime soon.

"Did you really eat a whole chocolate bar?" Samantha asked Nicole, holding up a wrapper in the back seat. "It has like four hundred calories."

"So what?" Nicole answered. "I'm not calorie counting."

"Only that freshman Maple Muffin Top needs to calorie count," said Brittany.

"That's mean," Nicole said, tossing her blond hair over her shoulder. "Besides, everyone still has some baby fat until they're, like, sixteen."

"I never had baby fat," Samantha said. She popped gum into her mouth and held out the package. Brittany and James each took a piece.

"I heard Ella Heart asked you to the dance," Stefan said to James, his legs dangling into the back seat.

"She did," James replied. "And I . . . considered it."

The whole gang burst into laughter. Ella could hear Brittany's snort and Stefan wheeze, "Can't breathe, can't breathe."

"She tripped over my water bottle this morning," said Samantha.

"Let's face it, the girl would suck at dancing."

Ella's heart quivered, tears welling in her eyes as the sound of laughter echoed in her ears. She couldn't stand hiding behind the Range Rover anymore and emerged, red cheeks and all. She passed Brittany's car, pushing hair into her face. She didn't want them to see the trail of tears falling from her eyes.

"Do you think she heard?" Samantha whispered to Brittany.

"Looks like it," Brittany whispered back.

"Come on, Ella. You know we were just joking," James said, reaching for her shoulder.

Ella swerved and James's hand slid off her. He pulled his hand back, lowering his head.

Ella found her car keys and got into her car. She pulled out of the parking lot, leaving behind wide eyes and gaping mouths. But Ella knew their embarrassment would wear off much faster than she would forget their painful comments.

# CHAPTER 7

ON THE DRIVE home from school, tears poured down Ella's face. How could she have been so foolish to believe James would want her? No guy would ever want her. She just had to accept the reality of her situation.

Her cell phone rang, interrupting her sorrow. She pulled to the side of the road carefully and answered, trying to make her voice stop trembling. "Hello."

"Hi, Els. Wait, Ella, are you crying?"

"No, Chelsey," Ella answered reflexively.

"You are crying," said Chelsey. "What happened?"

"I don't want to talk about it," Ella answered.

"I called because we ran out of cotton balls at the salon," Chelsey went on. "Can you pick up some at the drugstore on your way home?"

Chelsey worked in an upscale beauty boutique only a ten-minute drive from the house.

"Sure." Ella's voice was still quivering.

"I see I have a cancellation," Chelsey continued. "I'll come to the house. We'll talk then."

Chelsey was the best big sister Ella could ever ask for. Slightly pushy, but with a heart as big as Jupiter. She protected Ella and wanted her to see the bright side of life. Chelsey made sure Ella always looked nice, doing her hair and makeup for special occasions. She called Ella her muse. Ella felt her heart start to relax knowing Chelsey would be there to comfort her soon.

Ella pulled into the drugstore parking lot and glanced at herself in the rearview mirror. Chelsey always told Ella that her complexion was like peaches. Now it looked more like oranges: sallow and splotchy. Her green eyes were swollen from crying. She dabbed at her eyes, pinched her cheeks and got out of the car.

While waiting in line at the drugstore, Ella stared at the magazines by the checkout. There were the usual tabloid headlines—divorces, marriages, scandals. Then one story line caught her eye. "James Jude, the high school heartthrob. Meet his teachers, friends, and the girl who changed his life—Ella Heart."

The girl who changed his life? Ella thought in disbelief as she grabbed the magazine and flipped the pages till she found the cover story.

"Are you going to buy that?" the lady behind the checkout asked.

Ella put the magazine down to be scanned along with the cotton balls. When she left the store, she quickly read the story in the parking lot. There were pictures of James posing with the principal and the gym coach and pictures of him in the lunchroom. She recognized Brittany's ponytail and Stefan's side bangs. He was sitting at the cool kids' table, shooting the breeze with his friends. No one else was in the picture besides them. The picture had been staged.

Then Ella saw the picture she took with Nia and James in the hospital. The caption read, "With his best friend, Ella, and Nia, one of the patients they visit together every Sunday."

Every Sunday? Ella thought incredulously. She could tell this article would be about as truthful as children telling the babysitter their bedtime.

"I met Ella in American Lit," James was quoted as saying. "She had the most beautiful smile. I could tell right away we had a connection." He went on to say, "We also bonded over our love of helping others. Ella makes me want to be a better person." Ella's mouth fell open when she read about how she had lost her right leg due to cancer spreading to the bone. "It just couldn't be saved," James said. Ella burst into laughter. "Ella is such a strong person. She never complains."

Ella touched her right leg just to be sure it was still there. It seemed James's manager had never followed up, taking Ella's sarcasm all too literally.

When asked if the fact that Ella only had one leg bothered him, he replied, "No, I don't see Ella as disabled. I just see this incredible girl—we do everything together. Nothing stops her." The reporter asked if James had a crush on Ella. James acted coy by replying, "We are friends . . . for now."

What a liar! Ella thought, recalling the conversation she overheard in the parking lot. James was disgusted by her. This whole article was a glorious fabrication. Entertaining in parts, but still a lie. Apparently singing and making up crap were James's main talents.

It suddenly hit her that she had been had. James had used her for a publicity stunt—keeping up the narrative of James having a big heart by dating a disabled girl. His fans would eat it up. Anger shot through her. She got in the car and drove home in a rage.

Ella screeched into the driveway, almost hitting the blue-and-white truck parked there. Her heart sank further—the new farm manager's car. Willie and Amanda had left early that morning. The tears and hugs had all been shed and given the night before.

Today, more than any other day, she would have loved to talk with Willie and get some sage advice. Ella couldn't bear the thought that he was gone. She was sure she was going to dislike the new farm manager, if only for the simple fact they just weren't Willie.

Ella walked into the house, where the smell of freshly baked cookies hit her nose. This was definitely a day that needed cookies. Ella poured some milk and took a cookie from the tray—it had M&Ms and chunks of caramel baked into it. She sat on a barstool near the kitchen counter and shoved the cookie into her mouth.

Slowly, her anger subsided. The cookie was a tonic for her bad mood. But her bad mood returned when she saw the ingredients on the counter. She had forgotten the Lowells were coming for dinner. Ella's head drooped. She was not in the mood to make polite conversation with Shane, the muskrat.

"That bad, huh?" Chelsey asked. Ella lifted her head. She was sure her face was covered in chocolate, but she didn't care. In contrast, Chelsey looked chic, wearing a ruffled shirt with tight jeans and kitten heels. Ella marveled at how Chelsey could be glamorous at every hour of the day. Chelsey would never have anything smeared on her face.

Ella licked her fingers before nudging the magazine article into Chelsey's hands. Chelsey took the magazine and read. Her pretty face turned to outrage. "Leg amputated because the cancer spread? His best friend?" Chelsey's fist came down on the magazine. "What a lying, badly bleached bastard. He is going to pay for this. I have a contact at People. He is going to regret this interview." Chelsey looked on top of the kitchen counter. "Where is my purse?"

"No purse," Ella said, glancing underneath the counter.

Chelsey bumped the palm of her hand against her forehead. "Left it in the car." Her heels clicked as she went to get it. Ella continued reading the magazine, drowning out her sorrows in sugar and celebrity news. One celebrity had bought their dog a mansion.

A few minutes later, Chelsey returned, excitement burning in her blue eyes. Ella knew this look. It was the same one Chelsey wore the time her favorite super-expensive hair product became available at half-price in the local supermarket. She took Ella by the hand and led her upstairs. "Come, we have to get you dressed."

"Why?" Ella asked, a chill running through her. "Did you arrange an interview?" She wasn't sure she wanted to do a "tell-all" with some reporter and see her words trending on Twitter. Shaming people wasn't Ella's style.

Chelsey yanked Ella up the stairs and into her bedroom. She rummaged through Ella's closet, pushing hangers aside, scrutinizing

Ella's wardrobe. Chelsey pulled out jeans and a pair of shiny black riding boots. "Now we need a top." Chelsey wrenched open drawers until she came to Ella's sweaters. "Yes, this is just the one." Chelsey tossed Ella the gray sweater. "Why aren't you changing?" Chelsey asked, her hands on her hips.

"Are you going to tell me why I should?" Ella replied.

"Change!" Chelsey instructed. Reluctantly, Ella obliged. It was easier than fighting her sister. As soon as Ella was in the gray sweater and jeans, Chelsey started on Ella's hair and makeup.

"High pony, low pony?" Chelsey asked herself. "We'll go with a low pony." Ella was used to Chelsey talking to herself while she worked. It seemed to soothe her.

"Chelsey," Ella tried again.

"Shush," Chelsey said as she went over Ella's hair with a straightener. When Chelsey was satisfied with Ella's pony, she proceeded to makeup. Chelsey kept a bag of makeup in Ella's bathroom nicknamed "Ella's survival bag," which Ella did amazingly well without during most of the week. In the bag were dozens of eye shadows, blushes, bronzers, lipsticks, glosses, concealers and mascaras. All tailored to Ella's complexion.

Chelsey looked at her different palette choices of eye shadow. "I think we will go with metallic gray with a hint of periwinkle blue." Chelsey dabbed the thin-tipped eye shadow brush into the shimmery powder. "Now close your eyes." The brush gently stroked Ella's eyelids; it was almost like a massage for the eyes. Chelsey went on to line Ella's lips with several layers of lipstick and gloss.

"Beautiful," Chelsey said, gazing at Ella's face, admiring her handiwork. "I almost forgot blush." Chelsey pulled out a compact case and dabbed Ella's cheeks with the blush brush. "There, all set."

"Set for what?" Ella tried again.

"To go to the stables," Chelsey replied as if this was the natural answer.

"Because the horses don't recognize me without makeup," Ella quipped.

Chelsey placed her hands firmly on Ella's shoulders. "You will thank me for this—trust me. Now, go down to the stables, and when you return I want to hear every last detail." Chelsey gave her a wink. "Good luck."

"Okay, Charlie Townsend," Ella replied, giving Chelsey a salute. She felt like one of Charlie's Angels on a secret mission.

Ella walked to the stable. Am I ready to meet this new farm manager? Willie hadn't said much about the new hire. Ella thought again about Chelsey's bizarre behavior. What on earth could Chelsey be thinking, making her get all dressed up to ride horses? Silly, Ella thought. Silly, silly Chelsey. And then she saw him.

He was in blue jeans and a white T-shirt bearing the Titans' logo, raking a pile of hay. Ella froze, studying him from a distance. His brown hair was cut short in a tapered style. His jaw was strong and smooth, his biceps perfectly defined as he swept the barn hay into a pile. Is he real? With sudden horror, Ella slipped on a pile of leaves as the guy turned.

"Hi," Ella said, gripping the fence.

"Hey," the young man said. He gave a big smile, showing bright, straight teeth. Sticking out his hand, he came towards the fence. "I'm Brandon Cunningham, the new farm manager."

# CHAPTER 8

ELLA'S THROAT TIGHTENED, and she struggled to return the handshake. "I'm Ella," she choked out. The gorgeous human standing before her made it difficult to speak—or stand, for that matter. His handshake was firm, with hands that were obviously used for manual labor. They were not delicate like James's had been.

Brandon let go of her hand and moved to shovel up horse manure, emptying the pile into a pail. Willie had used the same method. He called it the "pooping pail" and collected the manure throughout the day, then threw the pail into the forest far from the house.

"I should have warned you about the leaves," Brandon said as he shoveled. "They can become slippery after the rain."

"Yeah," Ella replied, flushing down to her red roots. Blame her imbalance on the leaves? She could go with that.

"So, you're taking over Willie Wilkens' job?" Ella said, shoving herself off the fence.

"Yes," Brandon replied. He picked up a fresh bundle of straw.

"Will you be living in the guesthouse?" Ella asked, trying not to sound too hopeful.

"Nope, I live in Greenbrier with my family," said Brandon.

"I guess this is a good job to have when you're in college," Ella said. "The hours being flexible."

"Even better when you're a senior in high school," Brandon replied.

"I'm also a senior," Ella said.

"Where do you go to school?" Brandon asked as he shook new hay into a stall.

"Dellpine Academy."

"Where Sarah Black went?" There was a note of surprise in his voice, his eyes growing wide. Ella noticed large specks of green dotting his brown irises. "I bet you're used to seeing celebrities in the hallways," Brandon went on. "No one famous at my school except the one boy whose mug shot made it into the news. What it is to be rich," Brandon muttered.

"So, because I go to Pines you think I'm rich?" Ella was taken aback that Brandon had already passed judgment on her.

"Your father is retired, and you have horses—I'd say you're rich."

"So, because my parents have money, you think you know me?" said Ella. "That I'm this spoiled snob who has no worries?"

"I didn't say that," Brandon replied.

"Yes, you did," Ella insisted.

"Actually, I just said you were rich," Brandon pointed out. "You added those other adjectives."

Ella realized he was right, although not about using adjectives in the plural sense. Really, she had only used one adjective, spoiled, as the word snob was a noun. Best not to harp on it though, or he would label her as a geek.

"How about we each give the other a clean slate?" Brandon put out his hand to Ella and she took it, showing she was open to the do-over.

Dusty snorted. "Hey, Jackson," Brandon said, as he affectionately stroked the horse's tan forehead.

"His name is Dusty," Ella corrected him.

"I believe all horses should have presidential names," Brandon replied. "This here is Jackson and that horse over there with the spots is Nixon."

Ella laughed, looking over at Glenn.

"Which one did you want to ride?" Brandon asked her.

"Jackson," Ella said, playing along. Brandon led the toffee-colored horse into the middle of the stable. He took one of the saddle pads and placed it on Dusty's back.

"How often do you ride?" Brandon asked as he centered the saddle.

"A few times a week," replied Ella.

"A horse needs exercise every day," Brandon said as he tugged on the cinch, making sure the saddle was secure. He handed Ella the reins. "He's all yours."

As Ella took the reins, she looked over her shoulder. Brandon was filling up Glenn's food bucket.

"Would you like to join me?" Ella asked. She spoke before thinking. All she could do now was wait for his response.

Brandon looked around the stables. "I've got a lot of work to do still. Maybe a different time."

"I'll help you," Ella offered, stunning herself yet again.

"You know how to clean stalls?" Brandon raised a brow.

"Ugh," Ella said, tilting her head back in frustration. "I thought we were past the judgment phase? Besides, the horses could use some exercise. They normally just graze in the field."

"Fair enough," Brandon said as he grabbed another saddle off the wall. He opened Glenn's door and tried tugging the horse out of the stable. Glenn dug his heels in and gave a big huff.

"Oh, come on, Nixon," Brandon said, as he tugged harder on the reins.

"He might come if you call him by his name," Ella suggested. "It's Glenn."

"Nah, he won't come unless you give him a truckload of carrots," Brandon replied. At the word "carrots," Glenn looked around excitedly. Brandon grudgingly pulled a carrot stub out of his jean pocket. Glenn reached around with his long neck and snatched the carrot stub right out of Brandon's hands. While Glenn chewed, Brandon threw a saddle over him. Before the horse realized what was happening, Brandon was on his back, holding the reins.

"Who's the boss now?" Brandon said happily as he dug his boots into Glenn's side. Glenn gave a defeated huff and started walking. Ella was in complete amazement. She had never seen Glenn submit to anyone besides Chelsey and Willie.

Ella marveled at how steady Brandon was on a horse. Horse riding took lots of core strength—perhaps that was why he rode so well. Ella had taken lessons when she was younger, but she was never as adept as her sister. Seeing Chelsey ride was like watching one of the greats. Chelsey rode as if she were one with her horse. The relationship she shared with Glenn was strong; he would do anything she asked, never backing down from a jump.

Ella led Brandon down a grassy path and up a small hill to her meadow. It was covered in purple and red wildflowers; the trees still had their coppery leaves. Never did the meadow look so pretty and welcoming.

Ella came to a stop near the pond by the rocks. Swinging her leg over, Ella dismounted the horse and Brandon followed her lead.

"I come up here whenever I want time to myself," Ella said as she sat on one of the rocks. Brandon sat next to her on the grass. He craned his neck to make sure the horses were still there.

"Don't worry. I bring the horses here all the time. They've never run off." Well, it was true about Dusty. Ella hoped Glenn would stay put.

Brandon relaxed, stretching out his long legs. "Are we still on your property?" he asked.

"Yes," replied Ella.

Brandon looked around the meadow. He seemed pleased with what he saw.

Ella asked Brandon about his family. She learned he was one of three, with an older brother who was married and a younger sister still in middle school. They talked about Dellpine Academy—Brandon wanted to know if they had a bowling team and if famous people taught at the school. Ella told him that they didn't have a bowling team, but the head coach had played pro football and her chemistry teacher was doing advanced cancer research. The afternoon slipped by, and soon the sun began to set, lighting up the sky with beams of pink and orange.

"I think I need to get back," Brandon said, standing up. "I still have to finish cleaning the stalls and washing the horses."

When they returned to the stables, Ella kept her promise and helped Brandon. She rubbed down Dusty with a mild shampoo, while Brandon cleaned the stalls. Ella was careful to keep away from Dusty's hind legs. A kick from a horse could result in a serious injury.

When all the new hay was dispersed and the horses were stabled, it was time for Brandon to leave. She walked him to his car, the blue-and-white truck she had almost smashed into a few hours before.

"Do you go to school with that Jude fella, the singer?" Brandon asked.

"It's not as cool as it seems," replied Ella.

"His hair looks like he puts syrup in it, but my sister is crazy about him," said Brandon. "Holley has been begging to go to his Thanksgiving concert. And after what she has been through, she deserves some happiness."

Ella looked at Brandon, trying to make sense of what he was saying.

"Holley had leukemia," Brandon said quietly. "She has been in remission for a few months. It would be nice if I could give her something to look forward to."

"Poor thing," Ella said, wondering if she had ever met Holley. No Cunninghams came to mind.

"I tried to win tickets from the radio," Brandon went on. "But it's like playing the lottery. No one ever really wins. Maybe you could see if he has any nosebleed seats left?" Brandon looked at Ella hopefully.

Ella took a deep breath. She would rather eat worms than talk to James.

"I'll see," she said.

"Thanks," Brandon said, climbing into the front seat of the truck. The engine roared to a start, like a jumbo jet taking off. She watched Brandon back up the truck, one hand on the steering wheel, the other lying over the passenger seat. Ella was never able to back up that way, having to use her mirrors. Soon all that was left was the smell of gas fumes, reminding Ella that she had not just imagined his presence.

Ella leaned against the outside wall, feeling the stucco on her back, not ready to come off the cloud her head was on.

Ella heard heels clicking against the pavement. "Put a fork in her, she's done," Chelsey said when she saw Ella standing in a dream-like state.

"He is . . ." Ella had trouble forming sentences.

"Gorgeous, handsome, hot as a wildfire," Chelsey said, her pretty face smug with victory. "Now, about getting revenge on James. I had some ideas."

"Who's James?" Ella asked. Right now, he was like an ant to her, completely insignificant.

"That's the spirit," Chelsey replied.

Ella kissed Chelsey on the cheek. "Thank you."

"It's what big sisters are for," replied Chelsey, wrapping her hands around Ella's waist. "That and to tell you, you smell like a horse."

"Brandon was able to ride Glenn," Ella said. It was the only comeback she could think of.

"Glenny would never cheat on me," said Chelsey.

"When was the last time you rode Glenn?" Ella asked.

"Yesterday." Chelsey gave Ella a so-there look.

Ella noticed Chelsey had changed out of her blouse and skinny jeans. She was now wearing a white evening dress with a black blazer and pumps.

"Where are you off to?" Ella asked.

"I have a date," Chelsey replied.

"Can I come with you?"

"That would be a . . . no."

"But the Lowells are coming for dinner."

"It won't be that bad," Chelsey assured her. "Just ask Shane about what he's watching these days."

"I don't care what Shane is watching these days."

"Bring up what you're learning in World History. He might find it fascinating or be so bored he'll ignore you. Either way, you win."

Chelsey has a good point, Ella thought, watching Chelsey get into her pink Volkswagen. Ella took a breath. Time to face the Lowells.

# CHAPTER 9

DINNER WITH THE Lowells was what Ella thought it would be. Her parents had a lively discussion with Paul and Ros while Shane and Ella stared at their food.

"This salmon is delicious," Ros gushed, taking another bite. "How do you make it so tender, Pattie?"

"I cook the salmon on a low temperature," Mom replied. "Dry fish is almost as bad as raw."

"These are the best spuds I've ever tasted," Paul said. He stuck a piece of potato into his mouth.

"My wife is an excellent cook," Dad said, raising his wineglass. "Which is why I never take her out for dinner. The best food is at home."

All the grown-ups laughed and Mom shook her head at Dad.

"How is school going?" Ella asked Shane, unable to bear the silence any longer.

Shane shrugged, putting a hand through his red hair. His nose was small and square and his eyes reminded Ella of a swamp. Some people said they looked alike. Ella hoped their hair color was the only similarity between them.

"I hate fish," Shane grumbled, moving a pink piece around with his fork. He pushed his plate to the side and took out his cell phone.

"Shane, what did I say about having phones at the table?" Ros scolded with a bony finger.

Shane sighed and put his cell phone in his pocket. He took a dinner roll and smeared it with butter, plopping it into his mouth.

Ella wondered if it would be rude if she went upstairs and never came down.

"So, is it nice having horses?" Shane asked, bits of the roll stuck in the gap of his front teeth.

"Yeah, I love them," Ella said. She sipped some water.

"Do you have cameras in the stables?" Shane asked, reaching for another roll.

"No," Ella replied.

"What kind of security do you have?"

Security? Shane wants to talk about security?

"I don't know, I'll ask . . . Dad," Ella called, trying to pawn the red weed that was her conversation partner onto someone else. Dad mouthed, "Not now," before turning his attention back to Paul.

"You seriously don't know?" Shane asked, lifting a scraggly brow.

"We have a home alarm system," Ella offered.

"I thought you guys would have more security. I mean, anyone can walk up and steal the horses."

"And if this was the seventeen hundreds, I might be more concerned. Not many people steal horses these days. They are a lot of work."

"I saw you have a new stable boy."

"The proper term is farm manager, and his name is Brandon Cunningham." An involuntary smile crept onto Ella's face.

"Why do you keep grinning like that?" Shane asked.

"Grinning like what?" Ella countered, trying to relax her mouth.

"Forget it." Shane shrugged. Looking around the room, he asked, "Where is Chelsey?"

"On a date," Ella replied, happy to see his mouth droop at the corners.

"Does she ever talk about me?" Shane's muddy eyes grew big, his lips parting.

"Sometimes," Ella replied.

Shane leaned forward. "What does she say?"

"Who wants dessert?" Mom said, holding a frosted cake.

Saved by the cake, Ella thought as Mom handed her a piece. She took a bite, the chocolate frosting melting on her tongue.

After dinner, Ella went to her room to study. She had a World History exam coming up and a lot of material to memorize; there were so many wars and battles. Couldn't there be peace for a few years in the Dark Ages? The conquerors had not considered the amount of material they would be forcing future generations to remember.

Ella thought about Shane's strange question. Is he planning on stealing the horses? Strange didn't even begin to describe that boy.

Thinking about horses made Ella think about Brandon. She smiled as his hazel eyes filled her mind. Ella thought of the request he had made of her, wondering if things would end the same way with Brandon as they had with James. The parking lot incident came to Ella's mind.

Brandon is not James, a voice whispered deep inside her.

Ella smiled, deciding she was going to be brave and see what happened. Then it struck her: James had given her the perfect opportunity to get back at him. She would get those tickets for Brandon's sister—only, they would not be in the bleachers. They would be front and center. After all, James would do anything for Ella—at least that's what he had said.

The next day in school, before first period, Ella went on a search for James. She found him easily by following the sound of Brittany's voice into the school cafeteria. Brittany was whining at James to buy her a soda. Samantha and Stefan were there too. They were like a school of fish, sticking together even in the dullest of situations.

"James," Ella called. James turned to her. The bleached parts of his hair clashed with his darker roots. He gave her a slight nod in the way of a greeting.

Ella found no use in beating around the bush. "I was wondering, James, if I could have two concert tickets to your Thanksgiving show?"

James looked slightly miffed at her request. "Maybe try the radio stations?" he offered. "Last I heard they are still giving away tickets." James spoke to Ella as if she had asked him to give her directions to the bathroom. He did not expect a response, turning back to his gang.

"Please," Ella said. She kept her voice neutral. "I really need them—it's for a good cause."

"Listen," James said, his voice annoyed. "I'd love to help, but I'm afraid there are no tickets left. I'm just too popular." He laughed, but no one else did.

"What Mr. Modest is trying to say," Samantha said, her shiny black ponytail bobbing to the side, "is that you were just too slow."

"When is Ella ever quick?" Stefan murmured. Laughter rippled amongst the group. Ella felt her courage melting, but she drummed up her strength. She would get those tickets and bring these hyenas to their knees.

"I don't think you heard me," Ella said. "You will get me two tickets, in the front row, with backstage passes."

"Ella, come on," James said, his frustration clear.

"Ella, just stop." Brittany held up her hand, bracelets jiggling.

Ella ignored Brittany and faced James. "You will get me those tickets, or I will go to the press and tell them we have taken our relationship to the next level."

James's mouth tightened. "Now wait a second, Ella."

Ella took out the magazine from her backpack and began reading aloud. "I don't see Ella as disabled. I just see this incredible girl—we do everything together. Nothing stops her. We are friends . . . for now."

"Oh, she got you." Stefan smirked, brushing his straw-colored bangs out of his eyes.

Brittany's jaw clenched in anger. "You didn't tell them I was your girlfriend?"

"I thought we agreed on keeping that under wraps," James said. "For your protection," he added quickly.

"You are so full of it, Jimmers," Brittany said, rolling her eyes.

"I told you not to call me that," James hissed.

"Why, because that's what your mommy calls you, Jimmers?"

The pack howled as James scowled at Brittany.

"Two tickets," Ella said, enunciating every word. "Front and center, with VIP passes, by Friday. Or me and my real leg will be sitting down for the interview of the century."

With that she walked away, slowly so as not to stumble. She didn't want to lose her swagger by falling on her face. Right now, Ella felt taller than a statue; revenge was truly sweet.

A few days went by, and James didn't so much as glance in Ella's direction. Ella wondered if James thought she was bluffing. Well, she wasn't, and he had two days to get her those tickets, or she would make good on her promise to expose him.

Ella sat with Maria at lunch, picking at her sandwich. It was Friday. James had better deliver.

"I sent in my Syball application," Maria said. "My relatives think I'm crazy. Am I crazy for thinking I can get into a school like Syball?"

Ella sipped her water. She didn't answer Maria, her mind focused on James. Ella would expose the Jimmers if it came to it, but she really didn't want to. What she really wanted were those tickets.

"Hello," Maria said, waving both hands at Ella.

Ella shook her head and brought herself back into focus. "All the great ones were crazy," Ella replied, demonstrating she was listening to Maria after all. She bit into her peanut butter and chocolate sandwich. She had been eating the same sandwich for lunch since she was six. Might be time to change things up a bit, Ella thought as she eyed Maria's cheese burrito.

"So, you think I'm crazy?" Maria asked.

"Crazy talented," Ella replied. Maria smiled. "You want to know the truth?" Ella asked, putting down her sandwich.

"Yes," Maria said. She gripped her burrito.

"I think you're one of the most talented people I know," said Ella. "You steal the show every time you perform. And if you don't steal the hearts of every one of the board members of the Syball entrance committee, I'll eat my chemistry book."

"You mean it, Ella?" Maria looked bashful.

"I do," Ella said, "but please don't make me."

They both laughed.

Just then, a white envelope was slammed down on the table in front of Ella, startling her.

"Two tickets, two VIP passes," James spat bitterly, like he was handing Ella his soul. "The seats are in the third row, by the aisle. The front row was full." James looked like he wanted to kick something. "The tickets were supposed to be for Samantha and Brittany."

"Shame," Ella replied, without a trace of guilt.

"You know, you could have asked me nicely instead of being a bitch about it," James said. His bangs were gelled together, forming a cone on top of his head.

"I tried being nice and you treated me like a minion," Ella replied.

James was quiet, and Ella wondered if he was trying to figure out what a minion was.

"Well, see you at the concert," James said crossly. He was clearly pissed.

"Actually, you won't," replied Ella. "These tickets are not for me; they are for a girl who battled cancer. She adores you, probably because she hasn't met you yet."

James scowled at Ella as he slinked away.

"Wow," Maria said. "I've never seen brave Ella before. Where have you been hiding her?"

"It's amazing what can happen when you're in love," Ella said.

"With James?" Maria asked in disgust.

Ella frowned. "Not him."

"So, who is this love of yours?" Maria said as she leaned closer, her eyes sparkling with intrigue. Besides James, Ella had not talked about a crush in a long time.

"His name is Brandon Cunningham, and he makes James look like a mouse in comparison."

"How good looking are we talking about?" Maria asked.

Ella blushed. "Let's just say I almost fell over the first time I saw him."

"He's that good looking?" Maria shrieked.

"Yup," Ella said, feeling her cheeks flare.

Maria nearly flipped her chair over. "How did you meet?"

"He's the new farm manager."

"Is he in college?"

"He is a senior, like us."

This made Maria even more excited. "Ask him to the dance!"

"What is with you and this dance?" Ella moaned, but she secretly had the same thought the night before.

"I really want to meet the love of your life," Maria insisted. "When did he ask you out?"

"He didn't. We just met."

"Oh." Maria sounded disappointed. "Well, there goes your engagement party. I was already planning the guest list."

"I was worried you might be," said Ella.

"So, who are the tickets for?" Maria asked, eyeing the envelope.

"Her name's Holley. She's Brandon's younger sister. If anyone deserves those tickets, it's her."

"You're trying to get on his good side, aren't you?" Maria wagged a finger at her. "You have enough to offer without resorting to bribes."

Ella wasn't so sure, but it was nice of Maria to say so in any case.

The bell rang.

"We will talk more," Maria said as she packed up her lunch.

There was a pop quiz in Calculus. Luckily, Ella had done well on the homework and the problems were familiar. Ella continued with her day, dreading American Lit. It had gone from highlight to heartache. Ella wished James didn't sit next to her. He radiated contempt now. And she could have sworn he stuck his foot out as she passed him the other day.

Ella entered American Lit and waited for class to begin. She let out a sigh when she saw James was absent. He must have gone home early. Maybe she had scared him off. She sat taller, the tickets safe in her wallet.

After school, Maria stopped by Ella's locker.

"Our deal is still on. You have to ask Brandon to the dance," Maria said, picking up the conversation back where they had left it at lunch.

"No, it's not," Ella said. "I already asked James and he said no. The deal is null and void."

"You are forgetting the clause that says you have to do what I say."

"What clause?" Ella asked indignantly, as she put her books in her locker.

"It's the best friend clause. It states when my best friend becomes too scared to follow her heart, I must step in and make her."

"Fine." Ella shut her locker in defeat. "I'll ask Brandon to the dance."

"And we will go shopping together," Maria squealed. Then, looking serious, she added, "No offense, Ella, but I can't let you go shopping alone."

Ella laughed. Her sister would have said the same thing.

"I have one condition," Ella said.

Maria looked at Ella expectantly.

"We go to your house for dinner on Friday. I'm craving your mother's cornbread and salsa."

"Deal." Maria smiled, linking her arm with Ella's. They walked together to the parking lot.

# CHAPTER 10

ELLA WENT DOWN to the stables, her heart beating faster when she saw Brandon. Her tongue instinctively glued itself to the roof of her mouth. She took a deep breath. She had the tickets with her and had every right to be at her own stables. She willed her tongue to move.

"Hey, Ella," Brandon said when he saw her. He was wearing a red T-shirt with blue jeans. Ella wondered if he owned any other type of pants.

"Hi," Ella said back. "How is Nixon behaving today?" The tickets were burning a hole in her hand; she wondered the best way to give them over.

"Only snorted at me once," said Brandon, patting Glenn's leg. He was cleaning out Glenn's hoof with a hoof pick; there seemed to be a rock jammed inside.

"You're really good with horses," said Ella as Brandon pried the rock loose from Glenn's horseshoe.

"I should hope so," replied Brandon. "I've been around them my whole life. My grandfather owns a ranch."

"Do you want to be a horse trainer?" Ella asked. She leaned against the door of Dusty's stall and patted his forehead.

"Nope," replied Brandon, scooping out grass from Glenn's horseshoe. "I want to be a soldier."

"Isn't being in the military dangerous, especially with a war going on?" Ella asked. An image of Brandon marching into a dusty village formed in her mind, his tan helmet shadowing his war-painted face and an M16 in the low and ready position.

"Everything in life has an element of danger," Brandon said, placing the hoof pick down and wiping his forehead with the back of his hand, his temples glistening. The day was unusually warm for autumn. "How about you? Lawyer, horse breeder, fortune cookie writer?"

"I want to be a doctor," Ella said, almost reflexively.

"Isn't that dangerous, being around all those sick people?" Brandon mocked her. "What's in your hand?" Brandon asked.

"It's a court summons," Ella said, handing him the envelope. "Glenn is suing you for emotional distress."

"I'll bet he is." Brandon laughed. He pulled out the two tickets and his mouth fell open in astonishment. "How did you get these?" He peered into the envelope once more. "VIP passes? Holley is going to scream till she turns blue."

Ella was hoping for that reaction.

"How did you get James to give you the tickets?" Brandon asked as he ran his thumb over the VIP passes. He seemed in shock.

"I threatened to take away his hair gel," Ella replied. They both burst out into laughter.

Brandon looked down at the tickets again. Then he placed the tickets inside the envelope along with the passes and put the envelope into Ella's hand.

"You're giving them back?" Ella asked, starting to panic.

"I think you should be the one to give them to Holley," replied Brandon.

"How? When?" Ella became flustered, her plan evaporating.

"Maybe at our family BBQ this Sunday?"

"Come to your house for a BBQ?" Ella stammered. Her mouth hanging open, Ella just stood there until a fly went for the opening.

She shut her mouth as quick as a switch and shooed the fly away. "I'd like that," she said, trying to sound more grateful than ecstatic.

She felt like jumping for joy but knew that would make her look strange. Instead she challenged Brandon to a race. "I'll race you to the meadow," Ella said, opening Dusty's stall door. He had his saddle on. Was Brandon expecting me to ride him?

"No starting till we both get on the horse," Brandon said as he got out Glenn's saddle. He seemed to take his time getting Glenn ready to ride. "Come on, boy," Ella commanded, digging in her heels. Dusty headed for the meadow. Brandon was not even on his horse yet.

Ella knew she had cheated, but there was no turning back now. She galloped as fast as she could to the meadow. She kept her back straight, throwing her weight into her heels just like Chelsey had taught her. She arrived at the meadow first, Brandon not far behind.

"You didn't even let me get on the horse," Brandon panted. "I demand a redo."

"That's what losers demand," Ella said, her eyes bright from the exercise.

"Never start a fight you can't finish," said Brandon. "You'll see. Next time I'm gonna win—that is, if you'll let me get on the horse before scampering off."

As the sun went down, there was no time to stay at the meadow and chat. Brandon had to be off for the evening. They turned and rode side by side back to the barn in an awkward yet comfortable silence.

At the barn, Brandon slid off the horse in one easy motion. He made a clicking noise with his tongue, leading Glenn to his stall. Brandon took Glenn's saddle off without much fuss and rewarded him with a carrot stick and a pat on his gray forehead.

"Hey, Brandon?" Ella said. Am I really about to ask him out?

"Yeah?"

The words were on her tongue, aching to be said. But fear got the best of her and she swallowed them.

"Does your family like cake?" Ella asked instead.

"We are humans," Brandon replied, looking puzzled.

"Good, I'll bring one on Sunday."

"Thanks, I'll let my mom know."

"Okay, goodnight."

"Goodnight."

Brandon got into his beat-up truck and drove off.

Ella let out a deep breath, relieved, but also disappointed that she hadn't gone through with asking him out.

Ella entered the kitchen and the smell of meatballs hit her nose.

"Hey, Ella," Mom said, handing her a cutting board and some red peppers.

Ella began dicing the vegetables after giving her hands a good scrub down.

"He sure is handsome," Mom said as she chopped cucumbers. "But what I like most about Brandon is how respectful he is towards your father and me. He always says, 'No ma'am' and 'Yes sir.' I'm not used to it. Makes me feel like I'm an old woman."

"Glenn likes him," Ella said.

"He's not the only one," Mom replied, giving Ella a knowing smile.

"We're just friends," Ella said. She slid the cut peppers into the salad bowl.

"Just friends?" Her mother eyed her. "Oh, and speaking of friends, guess who might be coming to town for a visit?"

"Aunt Leslie and Uncle Ned?"

"Matt Granger."

"What?" Ella nearly toppled over the barstool in shock.

"He's coming to check out Vanderbilt University," Mom explained. "Matt's father is encouraging him, hoping they can form a better relationship."

"Does Matt want to go there?" Ella asked.

"His mother, Florence, thinks he wants to go to Stanford, but Matt is willing to check out the university. Wouldn't it be nice to have Matt close by?"

"Matt and I aren't really friends anymore," Ella replied, her stomach squeezing. She had buried that part of her past long ago, yet she couldn't help wondering what if.

"Maybe you can ignite the old spark." Mom winked at Ella.

Ella wasn't sure she wanted to continue this conversation. "Grades are coming out soon," she said. "I'm a little concerned about French class and Woodshop."

"Well, getting a B isn't the end of the world," Mom said as she poured her homemade vinaigrette dressing into the salad. The family complained when Mom served store-bought dressing. Salads were to be eaten with her dressing or not at all.

"I think you might be valedictorian again like you were in middle school," Mom went on. "At least that's what the guidance counselor told us at parent-teacher conferences."

"I'll be happy if I get into Johns Hopkins," Ella answered. She nibbled on a piece of red pepper straight from the salad bowl. It was slightly sweet and crunchy, just the way a pepper should be.

"Stop that," Mom scolded Ella, pushing her hand away from the bowl. "Spoons are for serving; fingers are for rings." It was a saying Mom used frequently.

Later that night, Ella sat at her desk in her room, going over French words. Ella could see the stables from her window, and her mind drifted to Brandon and how he wore blue jeans like they were required for the job. A warm sensation pulsed through her when she thought about him in a T-shirt. She knew her feelings were natural; her teen magazines were filled with hot, shirtless guys. But this one was real, almost within her reach.

These strong feelings were all new to her; the last time she even remotely felt this way about a boy, she was only thirteen. She thought about seeing Matt again. She had sent him an email about book titles she thought he might find interesting, and Matt responded with exactly one word: thanks.

Ella thought about working in Dr. Taylor's lab on Saturday. She scowled when she remembered Barry would be joining her. A notecard slipped from her hand to the floor. She picked up the card; the words très bien were written on the front.

Ella shut her eyes, trying to recall the meaning. She knew Mr. Durand used the words often.

"Very good," Ella said, and then flipped the card over. Very good, she laughed to herself, pleased to get the word correct.

She felt butterflies at the thought of being valedictorian. But Barry was a walking search engine, so Ella wouldn't count on it.

Turning on her microscope, Ella's hands quivered as she slid in the plastic slide. It was Ella's first time in Dr. Taylor's lab. Everything gleamed. The equipment was state of the art, expensive, fragile. Ella had almost dropped one slide and was using all her concentration to keep this one secure between her thumb and index finger. The slide held tiny pieces of human tissue taken from the participants in the research study. Ella's job was simply to record what she saw. Dr. Taylor was, of course, overseeing the lab and always double-checking Barry and Ella's records.

Ella enlarged the focus on the microscope. She was looking at tissue taken from someone who had a sarcoma diagnosis. The tumors looked like black dots in a sea of purple passion fruit seeds. By the number of black dots, it seemed the tumor was quite large. Ella recorded what she saw.

"How are you progressing?" Dr. Taylor asked. Ella showed Dr. Taylor the records she had been keeping. Dr. Taylor looked in the microscope and then at the ledger. "You're doing well. You have noted the diameter exactly."

"Is the patient going to die?" Ella asked quietly.

"The prognosis doesn't look hopeful," Dr. Taylor said solemnly. "That is why they agreed to participate in my study, not having many other options. Now, if you wouldn't mind helping Barry with the washing up."

Donning rubber gloves, Ella joined Barry at the sink. Their task was to sterilize the vials, a job Ella thought simple at first but quickly found challenging with its many steps. Harsh chemicals such as chromic acid were used to make sure no residue was left on the glass. When using the pressure canner, she had to be punctilious or risk losing a hand. Ella soon realized she was not cut out for working in a lab day in and out like Dr. Taylor. Four hours each Saturday was plenty.

"How many slides did you record?" Barry asked. He took a flask out of the pressure canner, making sure the steam from the canner pointed away from his face.

"Not everything is a contest, Barry," Ella replied as she swished a pipette around in one of the vials. A wave of weariness overwhelmed her. She felt like she had recorded a piece of death.

"So, how many slides?" Barry nagged.

"I don't remember," Ella said testily. Barry was straining her nerves.

"Sounds like you lost to me."

"These are people, Barry. It's not a joking matter."

"Jeez, who spit in your Lucky Charms this morning?" said Barry, pushing his glasses closer to his squinty eyes.

"It was Cornflakes," replied Ella. "So that's zero for you in the breakfast category."

"Now who's cracking jokes?"

Ella rolled her eyes. The thought of seeing Brandon tomorrow was the only thing keeping her from wringing Barry's frail little neck.

# CHAPTER 11

"HOW DOES THAT look?" Mom asked, stepping back from the chocolate creation they had spent the last three hours forming. The layered cake took four mixing bowls and six different wooden spoons. There was not a clean spatula left in the house. The result was an edible, incredible masterpiece.

Ella turned the cake around. The homemade chocolate icing was decorated with sprinkles. The inside was sponge cake layered with butterscotch icing. Mom got out her cell phone and snapped a picture.

"Almost too pretty to eat," she said, taking another photo.

"Almost," Ella replied. She resisted the urge to add more sprinkles. Ella liked every inch accounted for, while her mother was more of a minimalist.

She got her cell phone from the charger and plugged in the address Brandon had texted her—over a forty-minute drive. I'd better get going.

Mom helped Ella move the cake to a portable cake dish. A few of the decorations fell off in the process but were easily restored.

"I really appreciate this," Ella said. She kissed her mom on the cheek.

"I hope they like it," Mom replied, putting an arm around Ella's shoulder. "Oh, and I have something else you can give the

Cunninghams." Mom reached into the cupboard and pulled out a box of tiny soaps shaped like pinecones.

"Who gave you that?" Ella asked, her nose wrinkling at the strong scent of cinnamon.

"A friend," Mom said. "Aren't they cute?"

"So cute you are regifting them?"

"They are pretty tacky. I think the cake is enough."

"More than enough."

"Have a good time," Mom said. She brushed some hair away from Ella's cheek. "And don't forget to help clear the table. It's a sign of good manners."

"I won't," Ella said, shifting the cake dish so she could open the garage door.

Soon Ella was on the 440 heading north to Greenbrier, blasting Bruno Mars on the radio. She knew she was leaving city life behind when a pasture of cows overtook the rows of shopping centers and parking lots. Gone were the clipped lawns and designer flower beds of suburban living. Instead the grass grew free and the flowers wild.

Ella had only been this way once before, when she visited Glenn's breeder with Willie and Chelsey. Despite the breeder's protest that Glenn was stubborn and aggressive, Chelsey fell in love with him. Ella remembered Willie driving the horse float home, Glenn bucking and kicking behind the whole time.

Ella felt she could drive for hours enjoying the view. This was country living.

She turned down a small street lined with ranch-style houses. Ella knew she had the correct address when she saw a blue-and-white truck parked in the driveway. Ella pulled up in front of the house and turned off the car. She took one more look in the rearview mirror. Chelsey had helped her with her makeup earlier that morning. It was subtle, not overdone, the amber eye shadow bringing out the green in Ella's eyes. Her hair was in a half-pony with a few curls thrown in for "flair," as Chelsey said. Ella smoothed down her olive-colored skirt and took a deep breath. She carefully lifted the cake out of the car and walked to the front door.

Ella knocked.

Creak, creak. The porch swing swung back and forth. No sound of approaching steps. Ella looked around. The truck is here; someone must be home. She noticed an intact spiderweb strung across the top left corner of the doorway. It seemed the front door wasn't used very often.

Ella walked around to the carport, the cake dish fast becoming a dumbbell. She had a choice between climbing two stairs to a screen door or up a short ramp. Ella chose the stairs, eyeing the ramp. Is the home a former office?

Ella knocked on the screen door. After a few moments of eerie quiet, a young woman wearing a flared, powder-blue dress and tan cowboy boots answered the door.

"You must be Ella," the young woman said. "I'm Cindy, Chris's wife. Come on in."

Ella admired Cindy's ombré hair and slender figure. If Cindy was the standard for Cunningham women, then Ella didn't stand a chance.

"This is for you," Ella said, handing Cindy the cake dish.

Cindy opened the lid and peered at the contents. "I think I'm going to hide this cake and not tell anyone."

She led Ella inside. Ella gazed at the damask wallpaper and wooden fixtures lining the hallway. She was led into the den, where a boy with thick, blond hair was playing with blocks and cowboy figurines on a taupe-colored carpet.

"I thought Brandon was in the den. I guess he's outside," Cindy remarked. Squatting down, she turned her attention to the little boy. "Graham, I'd like you to say hi to Ella."

Graham looked up at Ella. His eyes were brown with specks of blue. "Why do you walk like Great-Grandpa Louis?" Graham asked.

"Graham!" Cindy reproached him, her face coloring with embarrassment.

"It's alright," Ella said. She sat down slowly in a chair next to Cindy. "I have a hurt leg. What are you making?" Ella asked Graham, to steer the conversation away from her leg.

"A city," Graham said proudly. "Here is the store Grandpa works in." He motioned to a pile of plastic tools on the ground. "And there is Ronald's Grocery," Graham said, pointing to a circle of blocks with a jar of mayo and a can of onion soup at the center.

"Did you take that mayo from the table?" Cindy asked.

"Yes, Mama," Graham said. He sucked on his fingers, looking guilty.

"I'll take it back," Cindy said, ruffling her son's hair and stacking the mayo on top of the cake dish. She stood with ease, her hands full. How Ella wished she could get up like that.

"Want me to help you?" Ella asked Graham. Graham nodded. Ella slid gently to the floor and helped him form the blocks into colorful roads, gates, and buildings, putting her limited Woodshop knowledge to use. Soon Graham's city looked like a city.

"What you got there, buddy?" a man asked. Ella turned to see an attractive man with fair hair roll to a stop behind Graham. He had Brandon's strong frame, but his eyes were bluish brown instead of hazel. He must be Chris, Ella thought. Ella was a bit taken aback by the wheelchair; Brandon had never mentioned his brother's disability.

"We made a city," Graham said happily.

"I see Grandpa's tool shop," Chris said as he hoisted Graham up and onto the chair.

"She made it with me," Graham said, pointing at Ella.

"I'm Ella," Ella said. She reached up to offer her hand.

"I'm Chris, Brandon's older, better-looking brother."

"You wish," said Brandon, joining them. He wore a red flannel shirt with a white tee underneath and his usual pants of choice, blue jeans. Ella's heart melted. How does he manage to be so good looking in such casual clothing?

"Hey, Ella," Brandon said. "I see you jumped right into Graham's little world there."

"Well, I couldn't resist a good game of make-believe," Ella replied.

"I think someone took the Halloween candy," Brandon said, eyeing Graham.

"No," Graham said defensively. But his hands went right to his corduroy pockets. Brandon swiftly lifted him and turned him upside down. Graham squealed as Brandon shook him gently, and he shrieked with laughter as candy corn flew out of his pockets like a slot machine.

"I knew it," Brandon said, turning his nephew right way around. "I should put you in the city jail. Where's it located?" Graham pointed to a spot on the ground with toy soldiers, and Brandon lightly placed him there.

"Ella, there is someone I want you to meet." Brandon motioned for Ella to follow him. Ella tried to stand, but her right leg locked. She went into the cat position to push herself up. Nothing happened. Brandon made a motion towards Ella, but Chris put out his hand, blocking him.

"Let her try," he whispered.

Ella felt her cheeks redden and was grateful to Chris for stopping Brandon. She should have anticipated this problem before she sat on the ground. Flustered, she looked around hastily to see if anything could help. She saw the couch a few feet away. She pushed against it with all her might and, with great force, willed herself into a standing position.

Graham clapped as if Ella had just put on a show. "I bet Great-Grandpa Louis can't do that," he said innocently. "You should teach him how to use the couch next time he falls."

"Good idea, Mr. Man," Chris said, placing Graham back onto his lap. "Let's go see if Grandpa Gary needs any more help with the grill in the backyard."

Completely mortified, Ella followed Brandon down to the basement, holding tightly to the railing as they went down. The basement was outfitted with the same aging carpet as the upstairs. The only furniture was an ancient-looking sofa and armchair. An old TV rested on a wooden crate, videos stacked on top of it.

There were two bedrooms, one on either side of the sofa. Ella saw Holley in block letters tied up with pink ribbon on the door to the left. Ella assumed the other door was Brandon's. Brandon opened Holley's door. Holley was on her bed reading a magazine, a James Jude poster on the wall behind her, his music blaring in the background: "You told me you were gonna try / but my heart you went and fried, / now I want to die."

Holley sang along to James's latest single, her head bobbing up and down. She looked like a more effeminate version of her brothers, with soft brown hair and bright brown eyes. Ella noticed bruising on Holley's arms, a common side effect of the chemotherapy treatments.

"Holley, there is someone here to see you," Brandon said.

Holley put down the magazine and looked at Ella.

"Hi, I'm Ella," Ella said with a small wave. Holley just stared at her, looking confused.

"Brandon, bring up some folding chairs," someone called from upstairs.

"I gotta go back upstairs to help my dad," Brandon said. "See you soon." Brandon went to the door and was gone, leaving Ella alone with Holley. It was a brief introduction to say the least.

"So," Ella said, sitting on the edge of Holley's bed. She was never comfortable with silence. "I hear you like James Jude."

"Like?" Holley cried. "We are getting married; he just doesn't know it yet." Ella saw what Brandon meant about Holley adoring James. Her preteen crush was innocent and pure. Ella decided not to waste any time.

"Perhaps you can ask him at the concert," Ella said, handing Holley the white envelope.

"James Jude concert tickets with backstage passes!" shrieked Holley when she pulled out the tickets. She rolled off her bed and jumped up and down. "I'm going to meet James Jude! I'm going to meet James Jude!"

Then, to Ella's surprise, Holley threw her hands around her neck and hugged her tightly. "You are the best!"

Ella patted Holley's back awkwardly.

"I have to show Momma." Holley grabbed Ella's hand and yanked her up the stairs, practically throwing Ella into the kitchen. "Momma, Cindy, look."

A slender woman with sandy blond hair stopped chopping vegetables and turned around. Cindy paused in stirring a boiling pot of water with tea bags brewing inside.

Holley waved the tickets. "I'm going to see James Jude in concert!"

"Did you win them from the radio station?" Cindy asked excitedly.

"She gave them to me," Holley said, motioning towards Ella.

Brandon's mother extended her hand to Ella. "Hi, I'm Paulina."

"Ella Heart," Ella replied, shaking Paulina's hand, which was cold from peeling vegetables.

Paulina struck Ella as a fading beauty. Not because of her face, which had few lines and wrinkles. It was the way Paulina seemed to shrink from her surroundings, as if weariness consumed her. Paulina indicated her daughter-in-law. "This is Cindy."

"We met," Cindy replied. "She built a city with Graham. I think Graham wants Ella to come over every weekend." Cindy winked at Ella. Ella flushed, thinking there was nothing she would like more. She had been so nervous about meeting Brandon's family, but their warmth put her at ease. She breathed a little easier now. No one had given her the cold shoulder, and no one had mentioned her leg except Graham. Ella could hardly blame a four-year-old for stating the obvious.

"So, you are the one who brought the chocolate cake?" Paulina said. "Puts my blueberry pie to shame."

"I love blueberry pie," Ella said, wondering if she had gone a little overboard with the cake.

"Hello, has everyone forgotten about my James Jude tickets?" Holley said, flapping the tickets in her mother's face.

"We are very happy for you," Paulina said. She stroked her daughter's hair. "It will be my first pop concert."

"I was hoping Cindy would go with me," Holley said. She glanced down, shifting the tickets in her hand. Paulina quickly turned back to the sink. Taking a knife, she began chopping lettuce.

Cindy gave Paulina a sympathetic glance. "Maybe your mom should take you."

"But I want to go with you," Holley begged, shaking Cindy's arm.

"We can talk about this later," Paulina said stiffly. "I'm sure Ella is hungry. We should eat."

Ella, who normally ate as if there were a famine on the horizon, found she was not hungry after this odd exchange. Holley grabbed Ella's hand again and hurled her onto the back deck, where a table was set with a blue-checkered tablecloth and all the trimmings for a tasty BBQ. There were chicken wings and hamburgers, pork chops and coleslaw, fresh corn and Ella's favorite, red-skinned potato salad.

Ella looked up at the sunless sky; rain threatened at any moment, and the cold chapped her lips and hands. Still, she would sit in rapids if it meant being next to Brandon.

The family gathered around the table where Ella was introduced to Gary, Brandon's father. Gary looked remarkably like his son. His light-brown hair was thick, only his sideburns fading into gray. His eyes were bright and hazel, his arms toned and strong. Ella thought that if this was what Brandon would look like in thirty years, he would be as handsome as ever.

Before anyone touched a single serving spoon, they all put their hands together and bowed their heads. Gary led the family in grace, and only when he was finished did they begin to eat.

"Ella," Paulina said, "tell me about your horses. You have an Arabian and Appaloosa, I understand?"

"Yes, we do," Ella answered.

"Most people say Arabians can be finicky and mischievous, but I find them to be sweet," Paulina continued. "I had one named Buttercup. She used to play hide-and-seek with me. I know it sounds odd, but she did."

"Dusty is the sweetest horse I have ever ridden," Ella said, confirming Paulina's assessment.

"Poor Dusty has to put up with Glenn, though," Brandon said. "Just like Chris and me. One wild horse, one tame as a kitten."

"I can tell Ella stories about you that would make her hair stand on end," Chris shot back. "How about the one where you shot Cindy with the BB gun?"

"Or the time you beheaded all my dolls because they had a war with each other?" Holley glared at Brandon.

"Or the toast you gave at my wedding," Chris added with a glance at Cindy.

"I think we should play Ella the video," Cindy said, stifling a laugh.

Brandon gagged on his burger and coughed wildly.

"Now, now," Gary said, "Let's not air all our dirty laundry out at once." Gary turned towards Ella. "Brandon tells me you are going to study medicine."

"I hope to," Ella said as she ladled a helping of potato salad onto her plate.

"Are you going to chop 'em or drug 'em?" Chris asked, recklessly squirting ketchup onto Graham's burger.

"Chris," Cindy hissed as she tucked a napkin in the front of Graham's shirt.

"I don't know," Ella replied. "Maybe both?"

"We are very grateful for Holley's doctors," Paulina said, looking wistfully at her daughter. "Her doctors are wonderful. We are able to call them night or day."

"I can't believe I'm going to see James Jude," Holley said, a far-off look in her eyes.

"Brandon is going to West Point," Gary said proudly.

"I haven't gotten in yet," Brandon said. He didn't look as certain as his father.

"You will, son," Gary said confidently.

Cindy poured herself the freshly brewed tea that Ella had seen her working on in the kitchen. "Iced tea?" she offered Ella.

"Yes, please," Ella said, handing Cindy her cup. The flavor was strong and sweet, like liquid candy.

"Paulina, did you tell everyone your good news?" Cindy asked, taking some coleslaw.

"It's nothing." Paulina waved her hand.

"It is so not nothing," Cindy chided.

"What is it, Paulie?" Gary asked his wife.

"I got into veterinary school, that's all," Paulina said modestly.

"Mom, that's great!" Brandon cried.

"It's about time," Chris said. "You have been working with animals long enough."

"Stop all this fuss," Paulina said, looking embarrassed. "It's not like I got into something special like medical school."

"Some say it's harder," said Ella. All eyes fell on her.

"I think this calls for a celebration," Gary said proudly. "Let's get the scotch."

"I don't know if I will even go," Paulina said. "The tuition is awfully high."

"We will manage," Gary said, placing a hand over hers.

"After lunch, can we build another city?" Graham asked Ella enthusiastically. His face was smeared with ketchup. Some had landed in his hair. Ella thought he was the cutest thing she had ever seen.

"Now, Graham," Chris reproached. "Ella didn't come here to play with you." Then with a cheeky grin, he added, "She came to play with Brandon."

Ella felt her cheeks redden and hoped no one would notice.

"None of that, Chris," Gary admonished his son.

"Like Ranny comes to play with Brandon?" Graham asked.

Ella noticed that Brandon paled a little.

"It's not fair," Graham complained, crossing his arms, his tiny lips in a pout. "Brandon has so many people to play with. I want to have friends too."

Chris was about to answer Graham when Cindy glared at him. Ella got the sense that Cindy had two children to contend with. Chris swallowed his smile and took a bite out of his pork chop.

"Will Ranny be coming later?" Ella asked.

"Not today," Brandon said. He seemed uncomfortable.

"Well, he is missing a good BBQ," Ella replied as she bit into her burger.

Chris's cheeky grin returned before he replied, "Ranny is a girl, short for Raeanne."

"Oh," Ella said. She felt as though she had been kicked in the stomach.

"Do you know how to shoot, Ella?" Chris asked, changing the subject as Brandon threw him an icy stare.

"No," Ella said. *Is this something I should know?* she wondered.

"Well, you gotta learn. Everyone should know how to defend themselves," Chris replied.

"Chris is a firearms instructor," Gary explained to Ella.

Ella saw Paulina and Cindy slip inside and return with Ella's cake and a blueberry pie. Paulina lifted the lid off the cake dish.

"Ooooo," the table went.

"You made that?" Brandon asked, turning to Ella.

"My mom helped me," Ella said.

"Ella, you didn't need to make me such a big cake," Gary said, pulling the cake towards him.

"Cut it out," Paulina said. She pulled the cake back to her. "Everyone will get a piece."

After lunch, Ella helped bring plates and bowls inside. When the table was cleared, Chris motioned for Ella to follow him to the backyard. Ella felt scared; she wasn't sure she wanted to learn how to shoot, but she didn't want to look like a wimp. Ella straightened her shoulders and took a breath. She could do this. She would do this. She would be brave.

# CHAPTER 12

CHRIS NAVIGATED THE uneven ground in the backyard like a pro, stopping a few yards from a round target hanging from a steel stand. "Your target is the red in the middle of the bull's-eye. This is what you're aiming for, every time. I know it sounds obvious, but you have to know what the target is if you are ever going to hit it. See the X on the ground?" Chris motioned to an X about twenty yards away from the round target. "That is where you will be shooting from. Never cross the line, you hear?"

Ella nodded, wind blowing against her face and through her hair. She was not sure that learning how to hold a gun while shivering was the best idea. She looked up at the darkening sky, wondering when the downpour would begin. The clouds looked low and loaded with hair-damaging droplets. She would look like a permed lion if water touched her mane. Ella shut her eyes and mentally willed the rain to hold off.

Brandon handed Chris a rifle.

"This is an air rifle," Chris said, showing Ella the gun. "Great for beginners, which you are. Now, hold the rifle with your dominant hand and press the butt of the gun tightly into your shoulder." Chris demonstrated, holding the rifle as naturally as Ella held a glass of water.

He handed Ella the gun. "Now you try."

Ella felt like she was holding a bomb ready to explode. Where to begin? She tried to place the end of the gun against her shoulder like Chris had shown her. Something didn't seem right. She looked around. "Where's Graham?" Ella asked.

"He's inside, nice and safe. We never let him in the yard during a lesson," Chris replied, leaving her no wiggle room.

"Press the gun tighter into your side," Brandon instructed.

"What?" Ella asked.

"Like this." Brandon pushed the stock of the gun into Ella's shoulder. She felt his breath on her neck as he let go of her elbow. It was a simple touch, but it might as well have been an electrical shock.

"Brandon, did you release the safety?" Chris asked.

"Yes," Brandon answered.

Release the safety. Is that a good thing? Ella didn't understand gun speak. She never thought she would have to.

"Okay, Ella, when ready, aim and pull the trigger," Chris commanded.

Ella froze. Shoot? How? She was worried the gun would send her backwards, or perhaps she would shoot sideways and the bullet would ricochet off a tree and knock Chris in the head. The many ways the bullets could travel filled her mind.

"Shoot," Chris said again, more forcefully this time.

Instinctively Ella pulled the trigger. The force of the blast knocked her off balance, but somehow she managed to stay standing. Chris stared in amazement as the bullet shot between two bushes, coming nowhere near the bull's-eye.

"Well, I've seen worse," Chris said. "Try again. This time hold the rifle tightly into your shoulder. That way you won't jerk back as much. And squeeze the trigger, don't pull it."

"Squeeze, pull, what's the difference?" Ella asked, confused. Chris might as well have given her instructions in Italian.

"Think of the trigger like a lemon, and squeeze it," Chris replied. "You'll get it in time."

Time? How much time? Ella thought. She didn't see herself getting monthly passes at the shooting range. Jordan had expressed interest once, but nothing ever came of it.

Ella aimed again, the gun tucked tightly into her shoulder. She squeezed the trigger with all her might.

"The girl's got aim!" Chris said, his voice full of surprise when the bullet hit only a few centimeters from the center. "Who would have thought after seeing the first shot?"

Ella shot again, hitting the periphery. It was nowhere near the bull's-eye, but at least she hit the target.

"You're on your way," Chris said. "Now, hand over the rifle."

Ella shifted the gun, the barrel pointing at Chris.

"Wow," Chris cried. "Never hand over a gun that way; you could kill someone. Here is your second lesson of the day—gun safety. Point the barrel of the gun to the ground and make sure your hand is nowhere near the trigger, placing your hand instead on the grip. Usually I'd ask you if the weapon is cleared of ammunition, but you don't know how to check that yet. I'll teach you next time. For now, just point at the ground, for goodness sake!"

"Like this?" Ella asked, tilting the front of the rifle down, her hand away from the trigger. She worried the gun would explode into her palm.

"Very good," Chris said, holding his hands out for the rifle, which Ella was grateful to give back. He took the air rifle and shot a bullet straight through the bull's-eye. Chris didn't even gloat. Ella guessed success got old, eventually.

Chris handed the air rifle to Brandon like he had taught her, with the barrel down. Brandon held the rifle in the correct position with the same ease his brother had. The air rifle let out another bang. He came closer to the mark than Ella had, but still not a direct shot like Chris.

"You have to practice more," Chris chided. "You don't want to be the poor sap in your unit who can't shoot."

Brandon hunched his shoulders. "I know, I know."

Bang. A bolt of lightning shot through the sky, and Ella felt rain on her head and shoulders.

"Chris, Brandon, Ella—come on inside," Paulina called from the porch.

"I think that's it for today," Chris said, wheeling himself towards the house. Even he couldn't fight the rain.

"You did good today," Brandon said, patting Ella on the back.

"My aim is awful, and I have no idea how to manage a rifle," Ella pointed out.

"Those things come with practice," Brandon replied. He led Ella past the kitchen to the living room. The living room reminded Ella of her grandparents' home, with a Chesterfield sofa and a wooden shadow coffee table. Gary sat by a piano, a guitar propped against the wall nearby. Ella sensed a concert was about to happen.

"Have some hot chocolate," Paulina said, handing Ella a mug.

"Thanks," Ella replied. The warm cup felt like heaven in her hands.

There was a big bowl of tortilla chips and salsa on the coffee table. It seemed this was the Cunninghams' version of teatime. Cindy handed Chris a harmonica, and Brandon took the acoustic guitar by the wall. Just when Ella thought Brandon couldn't get any hotter, he went and draped himself in a shiny guitar.

Gary played a few notes on the piano. Ella recognized the Billy Joel tune right away. Chris and Brandon joined in, and the jam session began. Cindy stared at Chris like he was a rock star, and Paulina's eyes filled with pride as she watched her family play. It was the first time Ella had seen Paulina sit for an extended period of time.

The sweet melody filled the room. Ella became absorbed in the music and rested her head against the couch. Cindy sat next to her, Graham's little foot pressing into Ella's skirt. She gave his foot a playful tug, making him smile.

"Play 'Hey Girl,'" Holley begged—a James Jude song, of course.

"No freakin' way," Chris said.

"What about 'Blackbird'? It's one of my favorites," Paulina said.

"Remember when I took you to that Paul McCartney concert for our fifteenth wedding anniversary?" Gary said to Paulina.

"I remember," Paulina replied. They seemed to be sharing a moment, making googly eyes at each other. Her parents often did the same thing, making Ella and her siblings cringe. But it wasn't so bad watching somebody else's parents flirt; she found it sweet.

Graham yawned, prompting Ella to look out the window. The rain had slowed to a drizzle, and it seemed night had fallen. She looked at the wall clock. Is it seven o'clock already? Ella had to get going. She had only been invited for lunch—not lunch, dinner, and a midnight snack.

"I think I'll head home now," Ella said, standing, her right leg shaking a bit from being sedentary. She wavered but managed to stay upright. The image of her struggling to get off the floor brought a new wave of embarrassment. She hoped Brandon would forget the incident, but she knew she never would.

"I'll walk you out," Brandon offered.

"I can manage." Ella waved her hand. "Besides, it's still raining."

"And I can manage a little rain," Brandon said back.

Their eyes met, making Ella feel shaky again. She turned to Chris. "It was nice to meet you."

"Same here," Chris replied. "We'll work more on your aim next time you come. Say goodbye, Graham." Chris nudged his son.

Graham lifted his head. "Will you make another city with me?"

"We'll build an even bigger one next time," Ella replied.

Graham grinned and waved his fat little hand goodbye, his eyelids fighting to stay open.

After saying goodbye to the rest of the family, Brandon walked Ella to her car. The windshield was foggy. The rain had stopped completely, which Ella was grateful for—she hated driving in the rain.

"It was nice meeting your family," Ella said. She meant it. They had been so welcoming.

"Yeah, it's a real fun house around here," Brandon replied. "Not much peace and quiet."

Ella could believe that.

Brandon squinted at something across the street. Ella followed his gaze to a white flag with a circle. Inside the circle was a black sun with jagged edges that formed what looked like misshapen Zs. Ella went numb. The symbol was called the Schwarze Sonne, and it was from the Nazi era. She had learned about it in history class.

Brandon went over to the flag and ripped it into pieces, throwing the remains on the ground.

"You shouldn't have done that," Ella told Brandon when he returned to his driveway. "You should have reported it instead. They might come after you."

"We have reported it," Brandon replied, "but unless my neighbors become violent, there's not much we can do. We just try and cause enough trouble to make living here uncomfortable, hoping they will move. We can't stand people like them. They give us small-town Southern folks all a bad name."

"Maybe my dad can help," Ella offered. "He's friends with the governor."

"I think he mentioned that," Brandon replied.

Ella wondered why her dad would tell Brandon about his friendship with the governor. She pushed the thought out of mind, a more pressing question burning inside her.

"Can I ask you a random question?" Ella asked. Finding out who this Ranny was had been Ella's biggest concern until she learned about Brandon's neighbor.

"Sure," Brandon replied.

"Who's Ranny?"

"She's a friend that lives down the street," Brandon replied evenly.

"You see her often?"

"We go to school together."

Ella felt like she had swallowed an ice cube. She wrapped her sweater around herself, but the cold feeling wouldn't go away.

"Why do you ask?" Brandon gave her a curious look.

"Well"—Ella swallowed—"there is this dance on Saturday. One of the top DJs in Nashville will be managing the music. The theme isn't anything cheesy like a ship sinking."

"I'll go," Brandon said.

Ella was not sure she had heard him correctly, so she continued, "The food is supposed to be incredible. The company that owns Bessy Burgers is catering the event. They are also making soy burgers for people like my friend Maria who think eating meat is cruel."

"Ella," Brandon said a little more forcefully. "I'll go with you."

Ella could have jumped for joy but knew that would send Brandon running into the house. She decided to play it cool and give as natural a response as possible.

"Great—the dance starts at eight, so . . ."

"I'll pick you up at 7:30," Brandon finished.

"Okay, so 7:30 on Saturday," Ella repeated, still in disbelief.

"Eight on Tuesday," Brandon said.

"No, 7:30 on . . ." Then she saw Brandon's grin; he was messing with her.

"See you Saturday," Ella said as she got in her car.

"What day again?" Brandon asked, his hazel eyes twinkling with mischief.

"Goodnight," Ella said. She closed the car door.

The highway was empty, but Ella kept a steady, low speed. A few cars passed her, but she kept her cool, not wanting to hit a slick patch and slide off the road.

Ella could not believe Brandon had said yes. She was going to a dance, with an actual date. Maria was going to flip when she told her. Ella was glad that Maria had invented and then enforced the friendship clause. It led to her first date in almost four years.

Ella didn't go to the parking lot after school on Monday; instead she proceeded to the school auditorium. Maria had flipped when Ella shared the news about Brandon, and she instructed Ella to meet her after school so they could practice dancing. The word "dance" made Ella shaky.

She climbed onto the stage. The melody of "L.O.V.E." by Nat King Cole filled the hall. Maria swayed to the music, moving with every beat. Ella clapped and Maria halted.

"Why did you stop?" Ella asked.

"Because this is about you, not me," said Maria. "Now get up here." Maria motioned for Ella to join her.

"You sure we aren't going to get in trouble for this?" Ella asked, looking around for prying eyes.

"Mrs. Pierce is giving us one hour," Maria replied. "Enough talk. Let's get moving."

Ella stood with her feet apart, her right leg extended, toes pointed. When the music began, she tried a jazz walk, crossing her legs as she moved around the stage. Her knee gave in a bit, but she managed to stay straight. She tried a ball change. Stepping with her left leg out, she brought her right leg behind her, but her knee wouldn't bend. Ella tumbled to the ground.

"Try again," Maria instructed her, not giving Ella time to wallow in the fall she had taken. Ella started from the top, first in a jazz walk, shifting over to a ball change. Again, she found herself facedown, her hands sore from the impact. Ella covered her face with her hands, tears sliding down her cheeks. Maria put her arm around her.

"It's no use. I'll never be able to dance," Ella said, her body aching with disappointment. "Brandon will take one look at the other girls, dancing with ease, and forget all about me."

"No, he won't," Maria said firmly. "Besides, maybe he doesn't like dancing. Maybe he will be perfectly happy to sit with you and talk about King Richard III."

"I'm just kidding myself," said Ella. "I have nothing to offer Brandon, no reason for him to want me."

"There are many reasons to want you," Maria insisted.

"Name two," Ella challenged. "And smart can't be one of them."

"Alright," Maria said. "You are kind and bake yummy cookies when you feel up to it."

"I sound as appealing as a grandmother."

"And funny," Maria added, "but I'm not entirely sure you always mean to be. Come on, Ella." Maria helped her to her feet. "Dance with me?"

Ella sulked. "I think we established I can't."

"It's different when you dance with a pro," Maria said, holding out her hand. Ella tripped a couple times, but it didn't bother her. Falling in front of Maria was like falling in front of family.

When the song finished, they collapsed on the stage, spent from dancing. "Anything else you would like to practice while we're here?" Maria huffed, catching her breath. "Should we gaze into each other's eyes? I refuse to nibble on your ear."

"Eww," Ella said, scrunching up her nose. "And you know I always win the staring competition."

"Ready, set, go," Maria said, opening her eyes as wide as possible. Within a few seconds, she blinked them shut. "Damn it," she said.

"What are you girls doing?" a voice boomed across the auditorium. It was the principal. His arms were folded, his mouth taut, reminding Ella of an angry beanpole.

"Mrs. Pierce said we could be here," Maria said.

Mr. Howell's fat lips twitched. His mouth was the only part of him with any stoutness. He sighed and pulled out his cell phone, muttering something inaudible. Ella squeezed Maria's hand. She had never been on the wrong side of the rules.

"It seems you are telling the truth," Mr. Howell said. "But from now on, you must get permission from me before using the stage. Is that clear?"

"Yes, Mr. Howell," Maria and Ella said at the same time.

Ella and Maria gathered their things as Mr. Howell waited at the back door. He locked it after they exited, making sure they didn't have any thoughts about sneaking back in. The girls walked to the parking lot.

"You can breathe now, Ella," Maria instructed as she unlocked her car, a 2005 Saturn. Maria had worked three summers at a local daycare to afford it.

"I was so worried he was going to suspend us," Ella said.

"They would never suspend the school's golden girl," Maria replied. "Do you still feel scared about the dance?"

"A little," Ella admitted.

"We'll go shopping tomorrow. Maybe a killer dress will give you some confidence."

Ella wasn't sure anything but a new leg would do the trick, but the idea of going dress shopping did give her a thrill.

# CHAPTER 13

THE NIGHT OF the dance arrived, and Chelsey was doing her best to make Ella look beautiful.

"Hold still, Ella," Chelsey commanded. "Or the curling iron will give you a big fat welt on your shoulder." Ella tried to stay still but couldn't help it; she was so nervous. The black party dress that Maria had helped her pick out, the one that seemed so perfect in the store, now just didn't feel right.

The bottom half had lots of tulle, making it stick out like a cupcake. The dress was sleeveless with thick straps, the modest neckline reaching just below her collarbone. Yet it seemed to reveal so much of her. Ella's arms seemed pale and willowy, and the scars on her right knee were clearly visible. Well, there's nothing I can do now. She reasoned that the lighting in the dance would be dim, and everyone would be too focused on other things to notice.

At least her shoes looked nice. Chelsey had advised Ella to get thick soles instead of thin heels to help with her balance. The thought of dancing scared Ella enough as it was; she didn't need to add wobbling in her shoes. She wondered if Brandon would even offer to dance with her or if he would just assume she couldn't.

Chelsey pulled Ella's hair into a loose bun, leaving auburn curls dangling down the back of her neck. She placed special clips in Ella's hair so it wouldn't yank loose.

"There, all done," Chelsey said, stepping back and admiring her work. "You look as pretty as a fairy." Then she looked over Ella's face. "Something is missing. Lipstick." Chelsey reached into Ella's survival makeup bag and pulled out a silver tube. She dotted Ella's lips. "Rub them together like this." Chelsey demonstrated, moving her perfect pink lips over each other.

Ella did as she was told, not managing to be as graceful as Chelsey. "This lipstick is smear resistant," Chelsey went on. "That way your date's mouth won't be tinted pink." She winked.

"I think you have higher hopes about this dance than I do," Ella replied. Although she would never admit it, Ella had thought of little else. Each night, the scene was the same. She imagined herself nearly kissing Brandon, like in a fairytale. Brandon would be galloping next to her, their hair flowing in the wind. He would reach for her, but, disappointingly, she woke up right before his lips touched hers, every single time.

The doorbell rang. Ella heard her mother call, "I'll get it."

"I can't do this," Ella said, fear taking hold of her senses.

"None of that negative talk," Chelsey scolded. "I didn't make you all pretty so you could stay in."

"Hi, Brandon, don't you look handsome!" Mom said, loud enough for the sound to travel upstairs.

Ella put her face in her hands, reeling from embarrassment. "Mom didn't just say that."

"Mothers are supposed to embarrass their children," Chelsey said. "Now stop panicking. Everything is still going as planned."

Chelsey placed a thin, sparkly necklace around Ella's neck.

"Is it real?" Ella asked. The sparkles from the small diamonds were so lovely.

"No, my dear; I don't love you that much," Chelsey replied, giving Ella the matching earrings.

Ella put in the "diamond" earrings. Then she looked at herself in the mirror. Her arms were still pale, and her scar was still visible. Yet staring back at her was a pretty girl, keeping her date fashionably late.

Chelsey gave her a little nudge. "Go on. The more time you spend worrying about how you look, the less time you will have to dazzle Brandon."

Taking one more moment to gather her nerves, Ella pushed her insecurities aside and went down the stairs. Brandon stood alongside her mother in the living room, holding his suit jacket over his left arm; he was wearing a white button-down shirt, a navy-blue-and-teal-striped tie around his neck. His sleeves were rolled halfway up his forearms. He wore khaki pants instead of his usual jeans, and black loafers instead of his usual boots. While he certainly would not be the best-dressed guy in the room, he looked as handsome as ever.

"You look nice," Brandon said, handing Ella a single pink carnation.

"Thanks." Ella blushed, taking the flower.

"Now I want a picture of you lovely kids," her mother said, holding up a red digital camera. It was her new favorite toy, and she loved accosting her family with it at every family event and special occasion.

Ella stood awkwardly next to Brandon. "Come on," Mom coaxed. "Stand closer together."

Ella inched closer to Brandon, touching his shoulder. Brandon did not put his arm around her as was customary in most school dance photos. Perhaps he was just as nervous as she was. Ella's mother snapped a few pictures. She reviewed the frames, nodding with satisfaction.

"Don't stay out too late," Mom said as she handed Ella the white coat she had chosen for the occasion.

"We won't," Ella called, walking with Brandon to the front door.

The autumn chill made her wonder how long Brandon's truck took to warm up. He opened the passenger door for her. The seats smelled like hay. It wasn't an unpleasant smell, just unusual.

"Is the truck yours?" Ella asked.

"It was my brother's before he was wounded in the army," Brandon said as he started the engine. When the engine was at its loudest, Brandon pulled out of the driveway and headed for the main road.

"Do you know which way to go?" Ella asked him.

"No, but I'm sure you'll tell me." Brandon turned on the radio. A Garth Brooks song came on.

"Any more trouble from your neighbors?" Ella asked, the black sun flag whipping around in her mind.

"They don't mess with us," Brandon replied. "Chris's aim is legendary. But their son did beat my friend up pretty bad when he was walking his dog."

"I'm sorry," said Ella. "Was it because of your friend's race?" The words tasted bitter in her mouth. She was angry and sad that crimes like this still happened.

"That and his heritage," Brandon answered. "Seth's mother is from Kenya, his father is from Brooklyn. Makes him a great friend, but a target for losers. We had the last laugh though; Chris, Seth and I gave the bully a thrashing he couldn't come back from. Chris having wheels only gave him more leverage."

"Wish I could have seen it," said Ella, thinking the neighbors' son got what he deserved.

Brandon turned up the music and sang at the top of his lungs. Then he turned towards Ella. "Come on, sing."

Ella, whose singing voice sounded like a badly tuned piano on a good day, tried singing along, albeit in a quiet manner.

"Come on, louder," Brandon encouraged. Ella sang a bit louder, still worried the sound of her voice would make him cringe. "That's it," Brandon said, giving her a big smile.

Ella stopped caring what she sounded like and sang with complete abandon. Before she knew it, they were pulling into the school parking lot, which looked like the lot of an expensive car dealership. "Is that a Porsche?" Brandon asked, craning his neck to get a better look.

"Yes," Ella replied. She knew it was Stefan's car, but she did not mention that.

"The most expensive car they drive in my school is a Pontiac. What do you drive?"

"A Volvo," Ella replied, "but it used to be my mom's." While her parents drove expensive cars, they would never buy them for their children.

A Mercedes drove up behind them, parking in the next spot over.

"Well, we won't have any problems finding the truck," Brandon said cheerfully. Ella pulled on the door handle to let herself out but quickly pulled her hand away when Brandon shot her a look. Sure enough, he hopped out of the truck and walked around to her side, opening the door and extending his hand.

"Ella!" a happy voice shouted. Maria ran over, dressed in a red mermaid dress under a black duffel coat. Ella saw sparkling beads along the neckline. Maria's raven hair was in a side twist, hanging over her shoulder, crystal drop earrings dangling from her ears. Her lips were painted bright red. Maria looked simply stunning.

"You look amazing," Ella said to Maria.

"Me? Look at you!" Maria exclaimed. "Your hair looks so glamorous."

"The work of Chelsey." Ella touched her hair. The pins were digging into her scalp.

"I had no illusions, Ella, trust me." Maria gave Ella a playful nudge.

"Where is Denzel?" Ella asked.

"Denz?" Maria said, looking around.

"Something is wrong with the car," Denzel said, his mouth twisted in worry. "A light came on while we were driving. My father is going to kill me."

"You have a flat," Brandon said.

"Damn, you're right," Denzel said, peering down at his back left tire.

"He is fine," Maria whispered in Ella's ear.

"Denzel looks mighty dapper himself," Ella whispered back, eyeing his maroon suit and dark shawl lapel.

Denzel looked up at Brandon. "Do I know you?"

"Brandon Cunningham," Brandon said, extending his hand.

Denzel shook it.

"Can we go inside?" Maria shivered. "I'm about to lose some fingers."

"But the car?" Denzel motioned to the Mercedes.

"Do you have a spare tire?" Brandon suggested.

"Yeah, but I need a car jack," Denzel replied.

"I've got a jack in the truck. I can get it for you if you like."

"Could you?" Denzel said, not taking his eyes off the deflated tire.

"Sure," Brandon said. He walked to his truck and returned with the jack a few seconds later.

"Thanks, man," Denzel said as Brandon placed the jack near the tire.

"Should we leave the car mechanics?" Maria suggested. "I think they might be a while."

"Let's go inside," Ella agreed, wrapping her coat tighter around her.

"Hey, grease monkeys," Maria called to Denzel and Brandon, "we're going inside."

Denzel put up a hand to signal that he had heard her.

"Shall we?" Maria said, offering Ella her arm. Ella took Maria's arm like couples did in classic movies. Together, they went inside.

The gymnasium had been turned into a neon rock club with brightly colored arches and strobe lights. Any student wearing white was suddenly luminous.

Without even discussing what to check out first, Ella and Maria strode over to the guy manning the milkshakes. "What can I get you lovely ladies this evening?" the waiter asked.

"What are our choices?" Maria inquired.

"Soda, juice and three different flavors of milkshake: strawberry, chocolate and pistachio," the man replied.

"Strawberry," Maria said.

"Make mine a mix," said Ella. "Chocolate and pistachio."

Maria looked at her in bewilderment. "This coming from the girl who has the same peanut butter sandwich for over eleven years? I see Brandon is bringing out your wild side. Soon you'll be getting tattoos and skipping school."

Ella laughed. Maria knew nothing in the world would cause her to voluntarily miss school.

"Here you go." The man handed them their shakes. The milkshakes had hot chocolate sauce drizzled on top of whipped cream mountains, and each featured a glow-in-the-dark curly straw.

"Cheers," Maria said, clinking her strawberry milkshake against Ella's pistachio-chocolate blend.

"Mmmm," they both said at the same time.

"Where should we sit?" Ella asked.

"By the food," Maria answered, eyeing the burger bar. "Hey, they have my soy burgers!" Maria pointed to a sign next to a tray of thin, shriveled burger patties.

"Knock yourself out, Maria. I'm sticking to the original," Ella replied. The real burgers looked thick and juicy, and she couldn't wait to chow down.

Ella piled her plate high with mini burgers and onion rings, while Maria took two soy patties and some salad. They sat down in a corner near the table but away from the crowd.

"How is your burger?" Maria asked.

Ella took a bite, gravy spilling down her hand. "Delicious. How is yours?"

Maria cut the patty neatly and had a taste. "Not bad." But she had trouble swallowing.

"It's awful, isn't it?" said Ella.

"Bite me," Maria said back.

"I think I'll stick to biting my burger, thanks," Ella said, finishing off the small bun.

"Here comes the brat pack," Maria muttered. She pointed her chin towards the entrance.

Ella turned to see Brittany and Samantha entering the hall in exceptionally revealing gowns. Brittany wore a long sheath dress in ruby red, her brown hair in perfect waves. Samantha was in a silver dress with an embellished bodice, her dark hair pulled back in an elegant bun. Ella noticed Nicole conspicuously absent from the group.

James wore a white tux, his hair shaped like a wave. Stefan seemed to be the only guy in the room wearing a classic suit jacket. But he didn't seem comfortable and constantly pulled at his collar.

Denzel and Brandon came into the gymnasium, hands covered in grease, chatting like they had known each other for years. Maria waved them over. Ella noticed Brittany rotate her head in their direction and lock eyes on Brandon. She stared at him, and her lips parted with the same expression Holley wore when talking about James Jude. A cat-like smile slid onto Brittany's face as she led the pack towards Ella's table.

"Uh oh, Brittany is coming this way," Maria said.

"No," Ella cried, wishing there was some way to stop her.

"It's your doing." Maria pointed an accusing finger at Ella. "You're the one who brought James Dean."

"Brittany already has a James," Ella said in desperation.

"Yeah, but yours is better looking."

Ella hoped that they would all stay far away from her, and she sighed with relief when James pointed to a table near the door.

"Who's better looking?" Denzel asked, taking a seat next to Maria as Brandon joined Ella. Both had milkshakes.

"Denzel, your hands are filthy," Maria said when she saw the grease on his fingernails.

"I thought your hair might need some more shine," said Denzel, his hands hovering over Maria's hair in a threatening manner.

"GROSS!" Maria shrieked, jerking away from him.

Denzel laughed. "'My hands are as clean as can be. We washed them at least ten times in the bathroom."

"You promise?"

"Smell," Denzel offered.

Maria took a tentative whiff and pinched her nose. "Your hands smell like a mixture of grease and disinfectant."

"Do you want to smell mine?" Brandon asked, sticking up his hands for Ella's inspection.

"No thanks," Ella replied. "I get enough of the smell of disinfectant at the hospitals."

"Whose call was it to put us by the food?" Denzel asked.

"Mine," Maria said proudly.

"That's my girl," Denzel said, giving Maria a squeeze.

"Ella, what a surprise," said a voice from across the table. Ella froze as she watched Samantha pull a chair out and sit down.

"I didn't think you owned a dress, Ella," Brittany said, sitting next to Brandon.

Ella swallowed. Her perfect night was about to be ruined.

# CHAPTER 14

"BRITTANY, LET'S SIT somewhere else," James hissed, but she waved him off.

"Who's this?" Brittany asked, turning to Brandon, her hair brushing his shoulder.

"Ella's date," Maria replied. "So you might want to back up a few inches."

"Aha," Brittany cooed, ignoring Maria's comment. "That is so sweet, isn't that, Samantha?"

"Adorable," Samantha agreed, resting her head on Stefan's shoulder. From a bird's-eye view, Samantha and Brittany's little act may have seemed genuine, even sweet. Ella knew better. They were having fun at her expense.

Brittany continued her fawning. "James, isn't that precious?"

"Bet he's rented," James muttered.

The table went silent. Samantha gasped while Stefan stifled a laugh. Brittany covered her face with her hands, giggling. Hot tears slipped down Ella's cheek as she fought the urge to run.

"Did anyone tell you that you are a jerk, James?" Maria asked.

"Did I say that out loud?" James gave a sheepish shrug, causing more laughter.

Just then, James's song "Wanna Cry" began playing.

Ella caught Maria's eyes. Maria mouthed, "Are you okay?"

Ella looked down, brushing away the tears. She had to stop crying or it would just confirm that she was the pathetic girl they painted her as.

"You sing this song, don't you?" Brandon asked James.

"Yup," James replied, placing an arm around Brittany's shoulders.

"I was wondering something," Brandon said. He leaned forward. "Is it wolves fly or whales get high? I can never tell when my little sister makes me listen to the song."

"Whales getting high," Stefan laughed. James gave him a warning look. Stefan coughed, trying to get ahold of himself.

The chorus for "Wanna Cry" came around again.

Without warning, Brandon sang out in a mocking voice, "Whales are getting high." He turned to Denzel.

"Just like donuts deep fried," Denzel joined in, making up another line.

"Now I want to die," Maria sang, reaching an impressive high note.

"Girl, this song sucks, but I sure would love it if wolves could . . . fly." Brandon held the note as long as he could, staring straight at James.

Cheering came from neighboring tables as Brandon took a bow.

James's nostrils expanded in anger; he looked ready to kill. He lunged at Brandon. Brandon swerved out of the way, causing James to land face-first on the table. Humiliated, James lifted his cheek off a plate. It was red from the impact.

"I think it's time for a dance." Denzel offered Maria his hand. Stefan and Samantha followed suit. James held his injured cheek, sending bullets at Brandon with his eyes.

"Would you like to dance?" Brandon extended his hand to Ella. Ella's heart filled as he led her to the dance floor, leaving a furious James in the dust. Brandon placed a hand around her waist and brought her closer to him. Ella felt faint under the strobe lights and loud music. She tried to steady herself, not wishing to fall and ruin the moment.

"James looks like he wants to murder you," Ella said, glancing at their table. James was still glaring at Brandon while Brittany talked to him, trying to calm him down.

"Let him try," Brandon said. "James is a guy who is used to other people fighting his battles. He'll run screaming once the punches start."

How different we are, Ella thought; she felt scared of everything. She placed her head on his shoulder, and his arms tightened around her waist. She didn't believe in heroes, and she knew she shouldn't need a boy to save her. But it sure felt nice to know Brandon had her back.

"Ella, why do you let them bully you?" Brandon asked softly. "Why don't you stand up for yourself?"

Ella didn't answer. What could she say? Most of the insults they swung at her contained some truth. Ella had learned it was better just to stay quiet.

"It's because you don't see yourself the way you should," Brandon went on. "You're better than them, Ella. Especially 'Flying Wolves' and that girl with the red claws—those two deserve each other."

Ella looked up, green eyes meeting hazel. Brandon slowly leaned into her, and their noses touched. Ella froze, not sure which way to go—to release the moment or give into it. Stefan chose for them.

"Psst," he whispered to Brandon, "got any juice?"

Brandon stepped back from Ella, his eyes darting side to side before he pulled out a small flask from his pants pocket.

"Now the party's starting," Stefan said. He took the flask from Brandon and placed it inside his suit jacket.

"Bet you fifty bucks you can't spike the principal's drink," Brandon said.

"Of course I can," Stefan replied, pushing his shoulders back and puffing out his chest, making his cummerbund look like it would burst off him.

"Prove it?" Brandon dared.

Stefan snuck off the dance floor towards the principal's table.

"That was almost too easy." Brandon grinned, watching Stefan hide behind a chair.

Ella looked at Brandon. Why is he carrying alcohol? Is the flask full? When exactly was he planning on drinking the alcohol? Ella went numb as memories of the accident took over. The sound of screeching brakes, the smell of Jordan's foul breath.

"I need to go," Ella said. Her magical evening was falling apart. She made her way off the dance floor towards the exit.

Brandon caught her arm. "Where are you going?"

"Out," Ella replied.

"Why?"

"I need air," Ella said, shoving off his hand.

"It's the flask, isn't it?" said Brandon.

"Yes," Ella replied.

"How about you take a sip instead of getting your nose bent out of joint?" Brandon suggested. "Show everyone you know how to have a good time."

Ella felt her blood rising. The cage of her inner lion sprang open.

"Because shooting at a poster and driving around in a truck is sooo entertaining," Ella mocked. "I guess I need a hick like you to show me what I've been missing, right?"

He stepped back from Ella abruptly.

"Brandon, what the hell—you gave me water?" Stefan threw the flask at Brandon's chest.

"Not the fastest train on the track, now are you?" Brandon said, putting the flask back in his pocket.

Water. That was all it was—plain old innocuous water. Ella's knees shook. She was about to fall over. She stumbled forward. Brandon caught her.

"Let's go," he said, and Ella nodded.

They made their way out of the gymnasium. Ella looked around for Maria, wanting to say goodbye to her, but she was nowhere to be seen. Ella and Brandon walked to the school parking lot, the silence stiff, like a bench between them. They got into the truck and Brandon put the radio on. They rode for a while, saying nothing.

"I'm sorry," Ella said, finding she could not take the silence anymore.

Brandon didn't say anything, his jaw clenched tight.

"I didn't mean it," Ella insisted. "I sometimes say things without thinking."

Brandon didn't answer her; instead he turned up the volume on the radio.

"I didn't know it was water," Ella defended herself over the music.

Brandon hit the power button. "I bet you wish it was moonshine in the flask, because then you could justify calling me a hick."

Ella didn't say anything, her heart breaking under the burden of a relationship destroyed just as it was coming to life.

"My uncle gave me the flask," Brandon said quietly. "It was my grandfather's. Keeps water cold and is easy to carry around."

"How does Jameson taste in the flask?" Ella asked, hoping to make him smile.

He turned away from her, letting her bad joke sputter and die. Ella leaned her head against the seat as guilt spread to every corner in her body.

"You know, you're no different than those snobby classmates of yours," said Brandon. His eyes were cold and angry. "You think if someone doesn't come from money, then they must be out on the street dealing drugs or slugging beers. You're a snob, Ella, and the shame of it all is I thought you saw me for who I am. It turns out you didn't see me at all."

"My brother drove drunk and ran a red light," Ella said softly, her face to the window. She couldn't bear to look at Brandon. "That's why I can't bend my leg enough to walk without limping. Seeing the flask . . . it scared me."

"You lost all faith in me in ten seconds. I think I deserve better than that."

"You do," Ella agreed.

They pulled to a stop in front of Ella's back door, near the stables.

"Goodnight," Ella whispered, opening the door of the truck. Brandon didn't respond. There will be no goodnight kiss, Ella thought miserably.

Ella watched as Brandon put his hand over the passenger seat and drove down the driveway, no wave, no goodnight. Ella stood with her back against the stucco of the house. The evening had begun with such promise. The food was delicious, she had danced without falling, and James had been publicly shamed.

Why did Brandon have to carry that flask? Ella thought bitterly. Why did I have to overreact when seeing it? She never knew alcohol could affect her like this. She had seen her parents drink wine many times since the accident and it had never induced panic. Ella realized her anger had more to do with her pride than her fear of alcohol when she lashed out at Brandon for implying she was a mossback who couldn't handle a bit of fun.

She took in a deep breath of crisp evening air and walked into the house. She wanted nothing more now than to take a warm shower and cozy up in bed with a book and forget this whole thing ever happened. As if she ever could!

Ella walked through the garage door, throwing her coat onto a barstool by the counter. She paused. The family lawyer, Richard Bailey, was speaking with her father. Something was wrong.

Has someone died? She didn't have any grandparents left; her grandmother Vivian had passed away last November.

"Hey, Ella, how was the dance?" her father asked. He looked up from a legal notepad.

"What's going on?" Ella asked, avoiding his question.

Dad hunched his shoulders, his brow creasing. "Your brother's case has been reopened."

"But I thought you settled out of court?" Ella sat at the kitchen table next to her father.

"Fred Martin, the man that your brother wounded in the accident, committed suicide," said Mr. Bailey. "The Martins are suing your family for five million dollars in damages." Besides a few more lines surrounding his eyes, Mr. Bailey didn't seem to have aged much; he had already been bald and gray when Ella first met him.

"Can they win?" Ella asked in shock.

"It's not likely," Mr. Bailey replied. "But they found a judge who is willing to hear the case. Luckily for us, the burden of proof is on them."

"Will I need to testify?" Ella asked, gripping her stomach.

"Most likely," Mr. Bailey said. "I'll coach you through all of the questions. Nothing for you to worry about, assuming you follow my advice."

Ella couldn't pretend she didn't know what Mr. Bailey was hinting at, having intentionally sabotaged Jordan's first trial by going off script from what Mr. Bailey had advised.

"Does Jordan know?" Ella asked her father.

"Yes." Dad sighed. "We are trying to delay the case as much as possible, so Jordan can finish his year in law school."

How ironic, Ella thought, Jordan being slapped with a lawsuit while in law school. Still, she did feel a little sorry for him; neither of them seemed able to put the accident behind them.

Ella decided she would be of no use to Mr. Bailey or her parents tonight and proceeded upstairs to take a shower. Her thoughts were already burdened with the flask fiasco—now old memories of the first trial swept through her head. This evening was going from bad to worse.

The warm shower soothed Ella enough for her to snuggle into her childhood bed where she felt safe and at peace. She read a few chapters of a novel she had checked out of the library and dozed off, hoping for nice dreams since the evening had not produced memories worth keeping.

"Will Gabriella Sage Heart please come to the witness stand?" a voice called. Ella walked to the stand and was sworn in. Her brother was in the defendant's seat, staring at the wall, Mr. Bailey by his side.

"Would the witness please tell the court about the events of the evening of May the 22nd?" said a woman with short, russet hair.

"My brother was driving me home from my graduation party," Ella began. "I could tell he had been drinking."

Mr. Bailey wagged a warning finger at Ella before calling out, "Objection, speculative."

"Sustained," the judge said.

"You're doing fine, sweetheart," said the plaintiff's attorney. "Please continue."

Ella went on, "Jordan went through a stop sign, then ran a red light. I told him not to."

"May I have a word with the witness?" Mr. Bailey said, clearly unhappy with Ella's performance.

"No, you may not, counselor," the judge said firmly. Mr. Bailey gave Ella a stern look but sat back down.

"You said you thought your brother was drinking. Why is that?" the plaintiff's attorney, Mrs. Green, asked Ella.

"He smelled like beer and was acting like a jerk," replied Ella.

Her mother shook her head, her face pinched. Her father placed an arm around her shoulders, drawing her close. His sad, conflicted eyes pleaded with Ella to behave.

"It is clear you knew exactly what was happening," said Mrs. Green.

"Objection," Mr. Bailey said. "Leading the witness."

"Sustained," the judge said, then pointed at the plaintiff attorney. "Mrs. Green, only ask questions; do not make comments."

"Do you feel your brother has learned from his mistake?" Mrs. Green asked, making sure to keep her comments in question form.

"Mr. Bailey has suggested this was a single lapse of judgment—do you feel the same?"

Ella looked at her brother and then at her cane against the wall. "No," Ella said, her green eyes blazing. "I don't think my brother has learned anything."

"No further questions, Your Honor," Mrs. Green said, a triumphant look on her face, practically skipping to her seat. The judge turned to Ella. "Miss Heart, you may step down."

Ella's cane was brought to her by one of the bailiffs, and she hobbled down from the witness stand. She stumbled, falling face-first onto the thinly carpeted floor.

Ella awoke with a start. She remembered her father saying that her testimony was so damning that they had to settle out of court or risk paying the Martins the ten million dollars in damages they were asking.

Do I want to see Jordan suffer now? Do I still want revenge? Ella didn't have the answer to these questions. She wasn't sure she ever would. But the question was in her life, where it would always be. All because of a few drinks Jordan had at a party.

# CHAPTER 15

THE WEEKEND HAD been a complete disaster as far as Ella was concerned. Jordan's second trial was an unexpected bomb. She was not sure she could endure another trial, and she worried she had ruined everything between her and Brandon forever. The only good to come out of the weekend was James's public humiliation. Students were still singing "wolves fly" in James's face in the hallway, getting a good laugh at his expense.

When Ella reached American Literature, she noticed James had moved his seat. He now sat next to Samantha in the second row. Ella was quite happy with this new seating arrangement; having James next to her was uncomfortable. She saw Nicole's notebook there instead. The bell rang, and Nicole slipped into her seat before Mrs. Salter could mark her tardy.

"Hi, Nicole," Ella said.

"Hi, Ella," Nicole whispered back. She took out a pom-pom pen, the bottom a fluffy pink and blue. Nicole was by far the nicest one in Brittany's clique, but nice was a relative term.

Mrs. Salter cleared her throat and started class. She wore an intricately-patterned sweater, and her peasant-gray skirt swished as she bustled around the classroom, returning papers.

"I have to say, I am not pleased with many of you," she said.

"Laziness is not a virtue I consider tolerable. And some of you described scenes that were not in any of Shakespeare's plays; you relied solely on the movie adaptations." Mrs. Salter looked directly at Stefan. Stefan slouched in his seat, not looking back.

"James, I would like a word with you after class," Mrs. Salter said as she handed him back his paper, her lips pressed into a reedy line.

James squirmed. His hair was dyed brown again. Perhaps someone had tipped him off that he wasn't rocking the bleached look as well as he thought he was.

Ella looked down at her paper. She had scored a ninety-eight. Mrs. Salter had written at the top, Well done—next time, do not agree to write the paper for your partner. Ella smiled. Mrs. Salter had always been sharp.

When Mrs. Salter was done handing back papers, she taught the best way to outline an essay, writing the steps on the board. Ella's mind wandered. Fall grades were coming out soon. She was excited to see her report card, and pleased with her success. Her lowest grade so far was an eighty-nine from a French test. Well, that was not entirely true—Woodshop wasn't going well. She had failed the toolbox test and botched their cabinet-building assignment. Ella could not fathom why she understood chemical equations with ease, but manual tools eluded her.

The bell rang, and school was out for the day. Ella walked with Nicole to her locker.

"So, you decided to give the front row a try?" Ella asked.

"It was that or be next to Mr. Slick," Nicole replied. "I can't stand James. He talks about nothing but his upcoming concert."

"Brittany seems to enjoy it," Ella pointed out.

"She enjoys being Mrs. James," Nicole said. "I'd take a sweet guy like Max any day."

As if he had been called, Ella's Woodshop classmate appeared in the hall with a fellow wrestler from the team. Nicole gave him a wink. Max's cheeks turned pink as he did a double take.

"Bye," Nicole called as she made her way to the gym for cheerleading practice.

"Bye," Ella called back, wondering if she should express her thanks for making seventh period manageable.

As Ella approached her driveway, she thought about the fight with Brandon. She had to apologize—that was all there was to it. She mustered her emotional strength and cautiously approached the stables. When Brandon saw her, he handed her Dusty's reins, turned away, and continued his work in silence.

"So, this is how it's going to be from now on?" Ella asked, flinging up her arms in frustration.

"I'm sure your pa wouldn't want you talking to a hick like me. Might teach you some bad habits," Brandon said with an exaggerated drawl.

"This is not the 1800s, and you know I didn't mean it," Ella shot back.

"Some things never change," Brandon muttered, continuing to clean out one of the stalls.

Ella sighed as she climbed onto Dusty's back and rode off towards the meadow. I'm done apologizing, she told herself. I have every right to fear drunk driving. Her fears mattered too.

Ella sat on a rock and watched the sunset. The red and orange rays merged together, lighting up the sky as the sun descended below the clouds. This is all you need, she thought. She didn't need Brandon, or any boy for that matter.

The familiar tune of "Chattahoochee" drifted to Ella's ears. Brandon had turned on the radio in the barn. Dusty began shuffling back and forth like he always did to Alan Jackson songs. Ella laughed as she watched her horse dance. She wanted to shout, "Brandon, come see this," but then she remembered they weren't speaking. She didn't need Brandon in her life, but she sure wanted him. There had to be a way to make things right.

"All right, talk," Maria demanded. They were at their usual spot in the lunchroom. Ella wasn't eating, a telltale sign of her unhappiness.

"I've ruined my life," Ella replied, hunching her shoulders, distractedly tearing the crust off her bread.

"I thought you and Brandon were hitting it off?"

"You didn't see the fight we had? We were practically shouting at each other."

"Dez and I went to get some air," Maria said, her olive skin coloring as she took a sip of water.

"You went to make out."

"Basically. So, what happened next?"

"I called him a hick," Ella murmured.

"That's not very nice."

"I'm an awful person," Ella said, laying her head down on the table.

"Why did you call him that?"

"Because he implied I don't know how to have fun."

"I tell you that all the time," Maria countered.

"Exactly why it hurt so much to have him say it," Ella replied. "He's not supposed to know I have flaws . . . yet."

"Glad you're being logical," Maria said, biting her lip and trying not to smile.

"What should I do?" Ella sighed. She lifted her head off the table.

"I've never known a guy to refuse a piping-hot pizza," said Maria.

Pizza, Ella thought. That could work.

Max strutted by, Nicole by his side. It seemed things were developing in that area.

"Shoot, the toolbox test." Ella groaned. She had forgotten Mr. Geller gave her lunch to retake the test she had failed.

"How is Woodshop going?" Maria asked.

"Terrible. I'm supposed to know how to build a bookcase, but I don't have a clue. Plus, I always get the tools mixed up."

"Wish I could help," Maria offered. "But the only thing I'm good at building is my character, which reminds me, did you buy tickets yet for the school play? I can't believe it's next week. Feels like I've been practicing for ages."

"Bought tickets the first day they came on sale," said Ella. "Mom and Chelsey will be joining me."

"Is your mom going to insist on taking a million pictures of me?" Maria said, looking worried.

"Please, Maria, you have to ask?"

"At least it's better than those awkward comments."

"Now Mom is channeling all her annoying behavior into picture-taking," Ella said as she looked down at her sad sandwich. "Maria, can I have some of your pasta? I'm not really feeling my lunch today."

"Have the rest," Maria said, handing Ella the container. There were still plenty of noodles left. Ella took a bite of chili mac and cheese and chewed happily.

"Maria, you know your mom is the best cook ever?"

"I'm lucky," Maria replied, munching on avocado salad.

Ella finished the pasta. "Time to face the tools," she said. She handed Maria back her container and packed up her things.

"Good luck," said Maria. "Or how they say it in Woodshop, break a box."

"Don't worry," Ella called back. "I will."

The next morning came quicker than Ella anticipated. Her alarm buzzed, and she rubbed her eyes and got out of bed; this morning there was no time for dawdling. Ella had decided a pizza was a good start, but not enough. She would also give Brandon a clean barn.

She went down to the stables and cleaned out the horses' stalls, loaded the feeding buckets, and did any other job she could manage. It seemed to take forever. She ignored her leg, determined to get through it all. The horses had left some massive piles of manure, making Ella wonder what they had eaten the night before. She sucked in her breath, only exhaling when her lungs demanded.

When Ella was done shoveling odorous piles of poop, she checked her watch. It was half past seven. Time certainly flies when you're busy. Ella would be late for school if she didn't leave soon. She put down the rake and hurried inside.

"Ella, you will never guess who is coming to visit," Mom said as Ella reached for her backpack on one of the barstools.

"Not now," Ella said, rushing to the garage door.

"Ella, your boots," Mom called.

Ella looked down and shrugged. She would just have to embrace the grunge look.

Ella drove as fast as she could without getting pulled over. Screeching into her designated school parking spot, she rushed out of the car, the bell ringing as she entered the building. Cursing her leg, Ella entered first period seven minutes late. Her French teacher was already at the dry-erase board, writing down new vocab words.

"Tu es en retard—you are late," Mr. Durand scolded Ella and wagged a finger.

"Oui, Monsieur Durand, pardon," Ella said, trying to catch her breath.

"What is your excuse?" Mr. Durand asked. He narrowed his eyes over his horn-rimmed glasses.

"J'ai nettoyer après le cheval," Ella replied, telling the teacher about cleaning up after the horses.

"Caca?" Mr. Durand said. The whole class burst into laughter at hearing the very classy French teacher say the word for poo.

"Oui, Monsieur Durand," Ella replied, her face reddening.

"Well, tell the horses to poop a little earlier next time," Mr. Durand said with a small smile. He turned his back to the class and resumed writing on the whiteboard.

"Did you dress in the barn this morning?" Samantha asked Ella, glancing down at her boots.

"Bite me," Ella said.

Samantha looked taken aback. Ella had never talked back to her before. Well, she had better get used to it, Ella thought as she made her way to her seat. She was no longer taking crap—from people.

After school, Ella rushed home to finish washing and brushing the horses. She scooped up any horse droppings the horses had "gifted" her since she left them that morning and refilled their food buckets. When Brandon arrived thirty minutes later, Ella was just finishing brushing Glenn. It was a job she never wanted to do again; the horse acted like Ella had tried to shave him.

Brandon looked around at the stalls and at the horses' shiny coats.

"You cleaned the whole barn?" Brandon asked in shock.

"Yup," Ella said proudly.

"Why?" Brandon asked.

Ella was about to answer when she heard a car pull into the driveway. She rushed out as fast as her leg would allow.

"Pizza with extra cheese and mushrooms?" the delivery man said, holding out her order.

"That's mine," Ella said. She pulled out some cash and paid the delivery man, making sure to give a large tip.

"What's the occasion?" Brandon asked as he eyed the pizza.

"It's my way of apologizing," Ella said, trying to hold the box steady. She took a breath, closed her eyes, and began the speech she had prepared. "I wanted to say I'm sorry for judging you unfairly and for calling you a name I didn't mean. You are wrong about one thing, though; I don't think I'm better than you. In fact I respect you more than you will ever know." She handed the pizza to an astonished-looking Brandon.

They both stood there for a moment while quiet stretched between them. Ella took Brandon's silence as a sign that he had not forgiven her, and she started dejectedly towards the house.

# CHAPTER 16

"YOU'RE GONNA LEAVE me to eat a whole pizza by myself?" Brandon called.

"I wasn't sure you wanted me to stick around," Ella replied, her heart fluttering with hope.

"Well, I do," Brandon said. He motioned to the bench a few feet away—the bench Ella's father and Paul Lowell had put in a few years back.

Brandon sat down and placed the pizza box between them. He took a slice, steam rising from the crust. "Damn, that's good," he said, his expression one of complete joy. He took another bite. "How did you know I was starving?"

"Took a gamble," Ella replied, taking a slice. The cheese was so fresh, it nearly fell off the pizza. Ella swallowed. "So, do you forgive me?"

"I thought I made that clear when I invited you to eat pizza with me," Brandon said. He had polished off the first slice and headed into the pizza box for another. "You didn't have to clean the stables," Brandon said before taking another bite. "Now I won't get paid for today."

Ella hadn't thought of that. She felt a twinge of sadness at costing Brandon money.

"My father doesn't have to know I cleaned the stables," Ella offered hastily. "Besides, the horses still need exercise, and Glenn needs a bath."

"I wish I could have seen you pick up the horse crap," Brandon said, his smile wide. "Bet you have never done anything so nasty in your life."

"Are you implying I'm a spoiled princess who can't get her hands dirty?" Ella scoffed.

"You said it, not me," Brandon said, finishing off his third slice.

"Well, proved you wrong," Ella said proudly. "Want to hear something funny?"

"Sure."

"Dusty dances to Alan Jackson songs."

"Just Alan Jackson, or anything country?"

"Just Alan Jackson."

"I don't believe you."

"I'll prove it."

"You'll show me later." Brandon reached into the box. It was empty. "Did we really just eat eight slices of pizza?"

"I guess so," said Ella, clutching her stomach.

"Come on. Let's go work some of it off." Brandon stood, and Ella followed him to the stables, where they saddled up the horses. They rode past the horse pen along the grassy path to the meadow. The meadow was no longer lush; the grass was sallow, the trees barren without leaves to fill the branches—all signs of the approaching winter. Still, the brook rippled with sunshine, and a gentle breeze filled the autumn air.

Ella sat on the grass with her hands around her knees. Brandon relaxed next to her, his long legs stretched out in front of him.

"My brother's case has been reopened," Ella blurted out. She was never good at letting conversation evolve naturally.

"What case?" Brandon asked.

"My brother was sued for injuring a man three years ago. My

parents settled out of court, and the case was dropped. All my brother received was a license suspension and six weeks of community service."

"That's all?" Brandon tilted his head towards her.

"I thought he got off easy, too."

"I can see you still hold the accident against him," Brandon observed, picking at a blade of grass.

"Jordan drove drunk. He ruined my life."

"So that's why you spazzed about the flask," Brandon said. A look of understanding crossed his face.

"That's what I was trying to tell you," Ella said, working to keep her voice even. "I would give anything for the accident never to have happened." She hugged her knees tighter to her chest and blinked hard against the forming tears.

"Are you sure about that?"

"Why wouldn't I be?" Ella didn't understand why Brandon would say such a thing.

"My brother was injured on his second tour," Brandon said, sliding his thumb across the node at the grassroot. "One of the men in his unit had awful aim, and the bullet hit Chris square in the back. He was given an honorable discharge, but the injury could have been prevented. What I'm trying to say is," Brandon went on, "I'm sure Chris would love to walk again, but if he had a choice between the accident never happening and losing his family, he would choose the accident."

"Why would he lose his family?"

"Cindy wanted him to retire from the military. The long tours were hard on her. Heard the word divorce thrown around a couple times. Now she has Chris around day and night. A little more than she bargained for." Brandon grinned.

Chris is a handful, Ella thought. She looked across the pond, watching a bird perch on an empty tree branch and chirp as if to ask where all the leaves had gone. Could there have been some reason for all this? Ella had never been a religious person. Her eyes drifted to the horses. She spotted a giant, gray animal creeping towards Dusty. The animal's ears were pointed up, its long snout sniffing the air.

Brandon reached down, his fist closing around some loose pebbles.

"Get away." He hurled them at the animal.

"Wait, Brandon," Ella shouted, waving her arms.

"Ella, the coyote could hurt the horses," Brandon replied and reached for more pebbles.

"It's not a coyote!" Ella cried. "It's my neighbor's dog, Otis. Otis, come here," Ella called. The wolfdog bounced over, his long, yellow leash whipping the ground. He must have run off during a walk.

Brandon cocked his head. "That is the biggest dog I have ever seen."

Ella pulled out her cell phone and dialed the number listed on Otis's dog tag.

"Hello, Mrs. Lowell, it's Ella."

"Ella?" Ros replied. "What a surprise. Is everything alright?"

"I have Otis."

"I didn't even know he was missing," said Ros. "He must have pulled out of Shane's grip when he was walking him earlier. Otis is a beast, albeit a friendly one."

"I'll bring him over," Ella offered.

"No need," Ros said. "I'll come by."

Ella and Brandon headed back towards the stables. Otis barked and tugged at the leash when he saw Mrs. Lowell walking up the driveway.

"Thanks, Ella," Mrs. Lowell said, patting him on the forehead. "I still don't know how Shane lost control of him. He has walked him dozens of times. Oh well. Come on, Otis." Otis trotted next to her as they made their way down the driveway.

How did Otis get all the way to the forest? Ella wondered. Maybe the dog saw a rabbit and ran off.

Thinking of the forest brought her Woodshop project to mind.

She had an exam tomorrow, and Mr. Geller had given her a practice piece to study on.

"Brandon, can I ask a favor of you?" Ella said.

"Sure," Brandon replied, placing Dusty's saddle on a hook on the wall.

"The thing is, I'm in Woodshop this year and I'm not quite as handy with a hammer and nails as I thought I would be."

"Shocker."

"Why is that a shocker?" Ella asked him. "You think women can't handle construction?"

"Women can handle construction," Brandon replied. "My sister-in-law, Cindy, can build almost anything in an hour or less. I have full confidence in women having carpentry skills. You, not so much."

"Are you going to help me or insult me?" Ella asked, crossing her arms and scowling.

Brandon held up his hand. "Wow. If you want my help, you can start by not being so sensitive. Now, where is this wood project of yours?"

"This way," Ella said, leading him into the spacious three-car garage.

Ella felt like she was throwing her parents' money in Brandon's face with the two new cars blinding them with their shine. Ella led Brandon past a lawnmower and over old ski equipment to the project Ella had been working on. Tools were spilled out over a wooden table, and the beginning of a small bookshelf stood in the center. One of the shelves hung awkwardly.

"Now, I'm not trying to be nasty when I ask what it is," Brandon said.

"It's a bookshelf," said Ella. "Can't you tell?"

"If you say so," Brandon said. He eyed the tools scattered on the table. "You need to make a bookshelf by tomorrow?"

"I need to know how to make one," Ella clarified.

"Okay, I need a Phillips-head screwdriver and the vice grip."

"Don't we need a hammer?"

Brandon let out a deep sigh, clearly holding back laughter. He leaned over the table and donned a more professional expression. "First, we are going to have a lesson on the difference between a nail and a screw." He held up a small piece of metal. "This is a nail. See how it's smooth with no ridges on the side?"

He placed the nail down so Ella could get a better look. "See how the top of the nail is smooth?" Brandon ran his thumb over the nail head. "This is a screw," Brandon went on, holding up a piece of metal with lots of ridges. "The project you are working on only requires screws. Repeat after me: never hammer a screw."

"Now you're mansplaining," said Ella. She would not be talked down to.

"No, I'm explaining and having a bit of fun while I'm doing it," Brandon replied. "Now, is this your first time screwing something, or would you like me to show you how it's done?"

Ella put her hands over her mouth and laughed. She knew it was immature, but she couldn't help herself.

"You have a dirty mind," Brandon said, shaking his head and breaking out into a grin. "Seriously, do you need me to show you how to use a screwdriver?"

"Maybe," Ella squeaked, trying to make herself stop laughing.

"Let's see how you do first." He gestured for Ella to begin.

Ella took the screw and placed it on the slab of wood, then began turning the screw with the screwdriver. Immediately, something didn't seem right; the screw wasn't going in straight.

"Try to hold the Phillips-head a little straighter," Brandon coached her. "See how the screw is starting to curve towards the side?" He pointed to the screw jutting out of the wood. "And you don't need to use so much force. The screw is meant to fit inside the hole."

Ella burst into laughter, clutching her side.

"You are worse than my brother's friends, and they are sailors." Brandon shook his head. "Come on, now; try and concentrate."

Ella tried focusing, but between Brandon's comments and his close proximity, she wasn't able to concentrate all that well. As Ella tried gripping a screw with the Phillips-head, she slipped and stabbed Brandon's hand.

"AHH!" Brandon yelled, clasping his injured hand.

"Sorry," Ella said, mortified. "Do you want ice?"

Brandon breathed out. "I think I'll live. Come on, try again."

"Really?" Ella asked in disbelief.

"My hand was too close to the wood, a mistake I will not make twice—come on, now; practice makes perfect."

Ella tried again, and soon she got the hang of it. She learned how to place the screws at just the right angle, using just enough force. In no time at all, the bookshelf was completed, looking exactly as it should. Thanks to Brandon, she would earn an A tomorrow instead of the F she had feared.

"You're not as bad as you think," Brandon said, looking over the bookshelf. "I'm only good at carpentry because I've been helping my dad build things since I was eight. Anything takes practice. Just try not to break off any fingers in the process. Blood makes it harder to treat the wood."

Ella smiled. Brandon always made her smile.

"Els," a voiced called.

Ella turned to see a boy with copper hair and navy slacks standing by the open garage door. It was Matt.

# CHAPTER 17

"SURPRISED?" MATT BEAMED. "I was sure your mother would spill the beans."

"Yeah," Ella choked out. The conversation she'd had with her mother this morning faintly came back to her.

Matt looked at Brandon, and Brandon stared back at Matt.

"Matt, this is Brandon," Ella said. Her hands grew clammy, her stomach feeling like a pack of frogs had invaded. Matt stuck out a hand. Brandon shook it.

Matt was the first to speak. "Do you go to Dellpine Academy?"

"No," Brandon replied.

"Hey, Gabriella," boomed Matt's father as he came up behind them. "Haven't seen you in ages. Still love to study?" Mr. Granger was the only one who used Ella's full name, and she didn't find it endearing.

"Alright," Ella answered, taking a step away from Mr. Granger, wondering why he felt the need to speak so loudly when they stood less than two feet apart.

Brandon crept backwards and headed towards his truck. The visitors seemed to make him uncomfortable.

"Matt," Ella's dad cried, stepping into the garage. "How are you?"

"Good, Mr. Heart," Matt replied.

"Elias," Dad muttered. He cleared his throat and begrudgingly stuck his hand out to Mr. Granger.

"Sam," Mr. Granger replied, slapping Dad on the back. Dad grimaced and rubbed his shoulder.

Ella heard an engine start as Dad and Mr. Granger made small talk. She watched Brandon's blue-and-white truck leave the driveway. A part of her wanted to run after him and tell him he had the wrong idea. Instead, she followed Matt and his father inside the house, where she smelled roast and potatoes.

"So, I had this woman come into the dealership the other day wearing a snake-skinned skirt and a God-awful hat covered in bird feathers. Looked like Tarzan's mistress." Mr. Granger hadn't stopped talking since dinner began. Most of his stories were about his sports car dealership.

"The woman says she wants to buy a Ferrari, the best one. I tell her the 488 GTB has 660 horsepower. The woman replies, 'That's too much horsepower. I want less.'" Mr. Granger chuckled while Dad gave a faint smile and sipped his wine. Mom sighed, her cheeks pinching.

As Mr. Granger looked around, his own smile wavered. "So, how is Jordan?" he asked, deciding to talk about something other than cars.

"His grades are excellent," Mom boasted, her face shining with pride.

"I heard he is going to be a lawyer," Mr. Granger said. "With all the legal trouble he's in, I think he chose the right profession."

Dad drew in his lips, tightening his hold on his wine glass.

"Dad," Matt hissed.

"Sam and Pattie don't mind," Mr. Granger replied. "They're like family."

Mom glanced at the wall clock. The clock showed it was ten past seven. Too early for the evening to be over.

"When are you visiting Vanderbilt?" Ella asked Matt.

"Tomorrow," Matt replied, taking some more roast.

"You promised to bring an open mind," Mr. Granger reminded his son.

"I promised I would visit," Matt said back.

"I'll get dessert," Mom said, gathering up the plates.

Mr. Granger looked down at his own plate, the food barely touched. He began herding the food into his mouth.

"Oh, please don't rush," Mom said. "It's just that it's a school night and Sam and I have an appointment with the accountant tomorrow. And I'm sure you want to get an early start."

"Pattie," said Mr. Granger. "I know Gabriella is your little girl and all, but at seventeen I think she has earned the right to stay up past eight o'clock, don't you?" He bellowed at his own joke. Matt's face turned pink.

Mom's green eyes hardened, and she snatched the plate away from Mr. Granger just as he was about to dip his fork into a potato. Mom bit back a smile and made her way into the kitchen, leaving Mr. Granger's mouth hanging open, his fork midair.

"Ella, do you still have those ghost stories we used to read in middle school?" Matt asked.

"Yes," said Ella.

"Can I see them?"

Ella nodded, getting up. Matt pushed back his chair.

"You will miss dessert," Dad called after them.

"We'll have it later," Ella said as they made their way to the stairs.

Dad stared after them, his hands grasped tightly together on the table. He looked like he would rather be anywhere but next to Mr. Granger, alone.

As Ella climbed the stairs, her leg dragged, making each step painfully slow. Matt reached the top before Ella was halfway through. Matt looked down to her, but Ella averted her eyes, not wanting to see his face contract into sympathy.

Finally, she reached the landing and walked Matt to her room.

"See." She indicated the rows and rows of horror stories they used to share. She rarely gave away her books, even the ones she never read.

"Has it gotten any better?" Matt asked, motioning to her leg.

Ella bit her lip and looked away from him. "Not really."

"Is there nothing that can be done?" Matt asked. "I heard of a guy who was hit by a six-wheeler, made a full recovery with positive thinking and determination."

"I've tried everything."

"Everything?"

"I see your father is rubbing off on you."

"Don't say that." Matt paled. "I'm nothing like him. And after this week, I won't ever have to see him again."

"What if you like Vanderbilt?" Ella pointed out.

"I'm not going to Vanderbilt," Matt said defiantly. "And just because my father has suddenly realized he has children doesn't mean I've forgotten all the crap he put my mom and us through. I know we share DNA, but that is where our relationship ends." Matt shoved a hand in his copper hair, pushing his bangs out of his face. Then he glanced down at the dresser, picking up a picture of Ella and Maria.

"I remember her," Matt said, tapping the frame.

"She's my best friend," said Ella. "And one of the only people I can stand at Pines."

"Are Brittany and Stefan still causing trouble?" Matt asked.

"They have a new member in the party, James Jude."

Matt made a choking noise and stuck out his tongue. Ella laughed, meeting Matt's eyes. They were dark like his father's, but his nose was long and thin like his mother's. Matt joined Ella on the bed, making her heart race. Memories of them talking while ice cream cones dripped in their hands came flooding back. Could that old spark be rekindling?

Matt's cell buzzed. He pulled it out of his pocket and touched the screen, and then tilted his head back, laughing.

"What?" Ella asked.

"Look what my girlfriend, Madison, sent me." Matt held up his phone.

Ella saw a picture of a lizard wearing a flat cap.

"It's an inside joke," Matt explained. "I have a hat just like the one the iguana is wearing." Matt put his phone back in his pocket. "So, what's with you and that boy I met in the garage?"

"His name is Brandon," Ella said. "He helps with the horses. We're friends."

"Are you sure about that?" Matt asked, stretching his neck in Ella's direction. "I felt like I was interrupting something earlier."

"You weren't," Ella replied.

"Are you going to wait three years, like I did, to come clean about your feelings?" Matt joked.

"Look at me, Matt. It's not like I have much to offer."

"I will admit your leg does take a little getting used to," Matt confessed. "But I'm over it now, and I bet that Brandon guy is as well."

Matt's phone buzzed again. He looked down and laughed. "Look what Madison just posted." Matt showed Ella a picture of him and the lizard side by side, both wearing a flat cap with the caption reading, Who wore it better? "So far the iguana is winning," Matt said.

But Ella wasn't looking at the post, eyeing Madison's profile picture instead. Her golden hair was pulled back into a low ponytail, and she sported a canvas baseball cap, her eyelashes coated with mascara, her lips shimmering in a pink hue. Pretty was the first word that came to Ella's mind; cool was the second. Ella studied Madison's sweatshirt—there were some words printed across in French.

"Did you give Madison the sweatshirt?" Ella asked.

"How did you know?" Matt lifted a brow.

"It says, 'I love you, my dear.'"

"I thought French was your worst subject," Matt said, snatching back his phone, his cheeks red.

"So, how is soccer going?" Ella asked.

"Great. Our team is in the state semifinals." Matt beamed. "If we win this next match, we have a real chance of competing in the state finals."

Ella didn't know much about soccer. She knew that Matt's position was the striker, although Ella wasn't entirely sure what that meant.

"Matt," Ella's mother called up the stairs.

"Can I stay here?" Matt pleaded. "My dad has statues of buffalos in the guest bedroom—like, big ones."

"Weird," Ella agreed. "When do you fly back?"

"Tomorrow night," Matt said. He looked down at his phone. "I do not have a lizard nose." Matt scoffed at the screen, rubbing his own nose in defense.

"Matt!" Mr. Granger boomed.

Matt sighed, getting up from the bed and walking with Ella down the stairs. Mr. Granger waited at the bottom, telling Dad some blond joke. Ella was glad Chelsey wasn't there or she would have clipped Mr. Granger's ear off with a nail clipper. Mr. Granger mumbled his thanks to Mom and nudged Matt to do the same.

"Thanks, Mrs. Heart, for dinner," Matt said.

"Anytime," Mom said, giving Matt a big hug, ignoring Mr. Granger completely.

Matt turned to Ella. "Don't be a stranger, alright?"

Ella nodded.

"And give that boy a call sometime. Or better yet, tell him he looks like Dusty."

"Who looks like Dusty?" Mom asked, sounding confused.

"No one," Matt replied and winked at Ella.

Ella and her parents followed Matt and Mr. Granger out to the gleaming silver Maserati. The headlights blinded Ella with their glare as Mr. Granger turned the car around.

"Well, you did your part," Dad said to Mom as they waved goodbye.

"I don't feel right about sending Matt off with Elias," Mom said, wrapping her cashmere sweater tighter around her shoulders. "Florence has been worried sick about him."

"Elias is insensitive, but I doubt he is dangerous."

"I don't know what Florence ever saw in him." Mom shivered, the autumn wind beating her hair about. "At least she's with someone nice now. That's all that counts."

They went inside, and Mom and Dad cleaned the kitchen while Ella got ready for bed. After she brushed her teeth and changed into pajamas, she pulled out an old album and turned to a photograph of her and Matt sitting together at a picnic table, their baskets piled high with chocolate eggs. Ella's hair was in two long braids dangling over her shoulder while Matt's copper hair was longer than ever, covering his forehead.

It had been nice to see Matt again, although the spark would never be reignited. Ella found she could live with this. Her prince wore jeans and riding boots, not dress pants and flat caps. Ella decided she wouldn't want it any other way.

# CHAPTER 18

THE WEEKS FLEW by, and before long it was December 24. A traditional Christmas feast was underway, and so was the usual madness that went with it. Jordan had flown home a few days before, setting everyone on edge with his fluctuating moods. Lucky for Ella, he spent most of the time out of the house with his friends.

"Yams, where are my yams?" Mom cried, searching the counters. "Oh, I'll just have to go buy more." Mom threw up her hands in defeat. She grabbed her car keys and headed out the door. Chelsey, who was making mashed potatoes, moved ingredients around the counter.

"Found them," she called, heading after her mother, holding the bag of yams.

"Oh, good." Mom sighed with relief. "I was not looking forward to braving the supermarket."

They heard a car pulling into the driveway.

"Is that a Ferrari?" Chelsey said, squinting through the window.

Mom stopped peeling the yams and Ella put down the piping bag she was using to decorate a gingerbread man. They gathered at the window, watching as Jordan got out of the front seat of the sleek, shiny black sports car.

"He better have won that car in a raffle," Mom said, her mouth pinching at the corners.

The garage door opened and in came Jordan, wearing a leather jacket, his chestnut hair dangling in his eyes. He waved a brisk hello before heading toward the stairs.

"Jordan, where did you get that car?" Mom called, hurrying after him.

"I can't believe he has a Ferrari," Ella said. She craned her neck to get a better look through the window.

Jordan came down the stairs a few moments later. "Mom, relax. I told you it was Blake Miller's Ferrari. I'm just babysitting it for a couple of days."

"You haven't thought this through," Mom protested behind him. "What if you get into an accident?"

"Mom, Blake trusts me, and I haven't been in an accident since . . ." Ella looked at Jordan. Jordan didn't finish his sentence. Instead, he swiped a gingerbread man from the baking sheet.

"Hey, those are for tonight," Ella complained.

"Chef's privilege," Jordan replied. He stuck the remainder of the gingerbread man into his mouth.

"That only applies if you made them," Ella grumbled, batting at Jordan's hand as he tried and succeeded in taking another.

"I can't believe Blake is even letting you drive the car," Chelsey said as she added butter to the potatoes.

"The whole family is going to Spain for Christmas," Jordan explained. "Blake said there is no point in the Ferrari sitting in the garage. Which reminds me, you need to move your car out of the garage, Chelsey. It's not safe for the Ferrari to be parked out in the open. Someone could steal it."

Chelsey rolled her eyes as she continued mashing the potatoes. "It's not going to be stolen, Jordan, unless I take it for a drive."

"Don't even think about it." Jordan waved a finger at Chelsey. "I will be sleeping with the keys in my pocket just in case you get any ideas."

"Jordan, you shouldn't be driving the car," Mom insisted. "You are tempting fate."

"Mom, stop worrying. If anything happens, I will pay for it," Jordan said. He eyed the baking sheet. Ella tugged back the tray of cookies, keeping them out of Jordan's reach.

The phone rang, and Mom went to answer it. "Florence," Mom said happily when she heard the voice on the other line. "How are you? Is Matt applying to Vanderbilt? Oh . . . I'm not surprised."

"What's everyone getting Mom and Dad for Christmas?" Chelsey asked, disrupting Ella's eavesdropping.

"Well, Mom really wants grandchildren," Jordan said as he opened the fridge and took out a can of soda.

"Well, you better get busy then," Chelsey replied.

"I'm not the one with molding eggs," Jordan shot back, popping open the soda.

"Molding eggs?" Chelsey said, her voice full of outrage. "Well, me and my molding eggs will never visit you in jail."

Jordan's face reddened. "It's a civil case, bimbo. I'm not going to jail."

"If it were up to me, you would be," Chelsey yelled back.

Ella's shoulders tensed. With Jordan's bad mood and her sister's tenacity, there was going to be a lot of fighting over the holidays.

Mom moved the phone away from her ear. "The two of you knock it off or I will turn on my Frank Sinatra Christmas album and sing every word—loudly."

Jordan and Chelsey froze in horror. Everyone loved Ol' Blue Eyes, but their mother could not reach any of the high notes he sailed through. It would be an hour of screeching. Jordan finished his soda and headed upstairs.

"Why couldn't he have gone to Vail for Christmas?" Chelsey muttered to Ella when Jordan was out of earshot. "He is like a more selfish version of the Grinch."

"Why would he go to Vail?" Ella asked.

"Because that's where Shelby's family is for Christmas."

"I didn't know he and Shelby had gotten back together." This was juicy news.

"It's a recent thing," Chelsey replied. "If you ask me, Shelby should stay as far from Jordan as she possibly can."

That afternoon, Chelsey offered to go riding with Ella. It was the first time in a long time they had ridden together, with Chelsey usually having to work long hours at the salon. They walked down to the stables, chatting about what they looked forward to eating at Christmas dinner. Dad had let Brandon off for the holidays, so Ella wouldn't see him till after New Year's. It was only a couple of days, and Brandon deserved the time off. Still, she missed seeing him. She wondered if she should drop by. Her heart went into a sprint every time she thought about it.

"How's my Glenny?" Chelsey cooed. "You are looking so handsome today." She rubbed his spotted nose. Chelsey went to get his saddle and stumbled over something in the hay. She knelt down and moved the hay around to reveal several glass bottles. She picked one up, smelling the top. "Someone's been drinking beer," Chelsey concluded. "Go throw these away. I don't want the horses stepping on them." She handed Ella the bottles.

Ella took the beer bottles to the garage and placed them in the recycle bin. *Who has been drinking in the barn?* she wondered. Ella had a good guess, but it turned her stomach to think it. Is Jordan back to his wild ways? With Blake in the picture, it was more than a farfetched idea.

Ella returned to the stables to find Dusty saddled and Chelsey talking to Glenn in the annoying motherese she liked to use with him. "I'm so glad my Glenny is all right. Wouldn't want your little hoofsies to get a cut, now would we?" Chelsey shook her head, rubbing her nose against his. Glenn neighed in agreement.

"Here." Chelsey handed Ella Dusty's reins.

"Thanks," Ella said. She hoisted herself up, but her right leg wasn't cooperating, and she fell into the hay.

"Ella, are you okay?" Chelsey said, rushing to her.

"I'm fine," Ella said. She accepted her sister's hand and stood up, brushing hay from her jacket. She grabbed the horn of the saddle, and this time she was successful in mounting the horse.

"I'm going to kill Jordan," Chelsey said. "My horse could have hurt himself." She gave Glenn's fur a little rub, easily mounting him with one nimble lunge.

"I really don't think Jordan would do something this stupid. I mean, he is on trial for drinking," said Ella as they made their way to the horse pen.

"He did this," Chelsey said with conviction. "Once a partier, always a partier. It's why I ended things with John."

Ella wondered who John was. Chelsey rarely talked about her love life, and Ella couldn't remember the last guy Chelsey introduced to the family. They usually didn't make it to that stage.

"Can Glenn still jump?" Ella asked, looking down at Glenn's burly limbs.

"He hasn't in a while," Chelsey said. "Our last competition was three years ago. I'll see if he will clear the log fence over there." Chelsey marched Glenn to the edge of the horse pen. She commanded the horse to trot, then to canter. Soon Glenn and Chelsey were airborne, flying over the fence. They landed gracefully on the other side.

"Who's my best jumper?" Chelsey said, patting Glenn's head. Glenn practically beamed, almost as if he understood Chelsey was complimenting him.

"You still got it," Ella agreed. They trotted in silence for a while.

A gust of frosty air blew through Ella's hair, biting at her neck. They hadn't been out long, but she was beginning to lose feeling in her fingers. "Let's go in, Chelsey," she suggested.

"Good idea. Besides, I have some choice words for Jordan."

"Do you have to?" Ella pleaded. "It's Christmas."

"This is the problem," Chelsey replied. "No one ever stands up to him—but I will."

As soon as they reached the house, Chelsey stomped up to Jordan's room. The halls echoed with shouting, sounding like a brawl had broken out upstairs. Ella closed the door to her own room and took a shower to block out the noise.

After Ella showered, she dressed in her Christmas finest—a gray worsted wool dress with a jeweled collar. She made her way down to the kitchen. The smell of candied yams and honeyed ham filled the air. There was going to be a feast tonight.

"Who's ready for Christmas dinner?" asked Dad when he entered the kitchen, rubbing his hands together in anticipation. Dad was wearing his red snowflake sweater that Mom had given him a few Christmases back.

"The ugly sweater isn't mandatory," Jordan said. He stood near the kitchen doorway, looking handsome in a navy suit.

"Neither is your attitude, son," Dad said, patting Jordan's back.

"Don't you look dashing, Sam," Mom said. She put an arm around Dad's waist. She looked lovely in a maroon dress with bell sleeves.

"Not as wonderful as you, my dear," Dad said, placing a kiss on her forehead.

"And how do I look?" Chelsey asked as she entered the kitchen in a white blouse and a black, box-pleated skirt.

"Nailing the overaged schoolgirl look," replied Jordan. Chelsey's eyes narrowed in fury.

"Let's eat," said Dad.

Everyone took a seat around the festive table, Jordan and Chelsey at opposite sides. The table had been set with the good china, the china Mom only brought out for special occasions. The glasses sparkled, linen napkins hanging over the brims. Candles flickered in the candelabra at the center. There were platters of roasted Brussels sprouts and honeyed ham, bowls of fluffy mashed potatoes, and a citrus salad with fresh spinach leaves. And the best dish of all, candied yams, the marshmallow peaks browned to perfection.

"Aren't candied yams a Thanksgiving dish?" Jordan asked, taking a giant spoonful.

"Dad requested them," said Mom.

"I did," Dad admitted. "Now pass them here."

Dishes and trays clunked around the table until everyone's plates were heaping with food. Ella loaded up on ham and mashed potatoes, wondering what Maria was eating now that she had shunned meat.

Dad raised his wineglass. "I'd like to thank my beautiful wife, Pattie, for this delicious meal and going out of your way to make dishes that we all enjoy."

Mom raised her glass in return. "Thank you, Sam. I'm so grateful that we can spend another Christmas together as a family."

"I'd rather be in Vail." Jordan scowled, spooning mashed potatoes onto his plate.

"We would also rather you were there," Chelsey said. She poured herself wine.

"I hear Chelsey has some news for us," Dad interjected.

"I am officially the co-owner of the salon," Chelsey said proudly.

"That's great," said Ella.

"Wonderful," Mom said, but her smile seemed to fumble at the corners.

"You had Mr. Bailey look over the agreement between you and your partner?" asked Dad.

"I don't need Mr. Bailey. I went to business school, remember?" Chelsey defended herself.

"You didn't finish," Jordan pointed out.

"Like you can talk, Jordan," Chelsey huffed. "You only finished college because Mom and Dad bought you out of prison."

"And you are just one step away from being a dog groomer," Jordan countered.

"Jordan had a booze party in the barn," Chelsey blurted out.

"What?" Mom cried, her green eyes growing wide, reminding Ella of a toad with mascara.

"Is this true, son?" Dad asked, his eyes growing sad.

"No," Jordan said, but he blinked faster. He was lying—Ella could tell. Why can't they?

"Chelsey, this really isn't the time for this discussion," Mom said, sipping her wine.

"Well, since Chelsey brought it up," Jordan said, "I have seen the farm manager drink from a flask."

"It's water," Ella said quickly, remembering the dance.

"Oh please." Jordan snorted. "You're so innocent, Ella. Bet you wouldn't know what alcohol smelled like if someone spiked your drink."

"I can't believe this," Mom said, shaking her head. "Brandon is such a nice boy."

"Willie did say he had a bit of a wild streak," said Dad. "I never thought he would do something like this."

"Jordan is distracting you all," Chelsey insisted. "He is not the prince you want him to be."

"That's enough, Chelsey," Dad said, his mouth puckering, lines sprouting on his forehead the way they always did when he was stressed. "Now, no more talking about Brandon or drinking or dog groomers. We will sit and enjoy our food and talk about some ideas for my garden."

"What garden?" Mom asked.

"The one I am planting," replied Dad.

The rest of the dinner passed in silence, no one offering up ideas for Dad's garden. Ella was all too happy to go to bed, not wanting to be around Jordan. She was mad at her brother for selling Brandon out. She was mad at her parents, who seemed all too willing to believe Jordan. Will they fire Brandon? The thought filled her with grief.

# CHAPTER 19

"I CAN'T BELIEVE I'm eating again," Mom said as she placed a small bowl of maraschino cherries next to the toppings bar she had created. She always made little comments like these. Still, Mom took a plate like the rest of the family and piled it high with waffles.

Ella's waffles were about to topple over with toppings. Chelsey stood next to her, adding mostly fruit. Mom put a hand on Chelsey's shoulder. "I know you didn't mean what you said about Jordan last night. I was thinking—"

"Oh, I did," Chelsey replied. She dusted her fruit with powdered sugar.

"Chelsey, we all have to be a bit more sensitive. Jordan needs our support."

"Then maybe he shouldn't have called me a dog groomer," Chelsey said, placing the sugar shaker firmly on the counter.

Mom sighed and glanced at Ella. Ella glanced away. She would not be asking Chelsey to apologize to Jordan, not when he deserved the acid remarks he received.

"Who's going first?" Dad asked when they were all seated in the living room enjoying their waffles.

"I will," Mom said. She never got to go first. Mom looked for presents under the tree with the words Mom or Pattie scribbled on.

Chelsey had given Mom a voucher from the salon she worked at and now co-owned. Dad had given his wife gold earrings, and Jordan gave her a Christmas CD with several of Mom's favorite singers singing the classics. Ella got her mother a new address book, as her old one was falling apart.

"I love all these," Mom said happily, giving them each a kiss.

Chelsey went next. She received a big check from Mom and Dad, and a purse from Ella. Chelsey was in shock when she opened Jordan's gift. "The hair dryer I always wanted!" she exclaimed, examining the box like a treasure. "How did you know?"

"I listen to you . . . occasionally," Jordan said, taking a bite out of his whipped cream–covered mountain of waffles, the berries like red rocks around the bottom. "Just remember the blow-dryer isn't a magic machine," Jordan pointed out. "Can't make you desirable or anything."

Chelsey threw a Christmas ornament at him.

"Ouch." Jordan clutched his heart, pretending to be wounded.

"Knock it off, the both of you," Dad insisted. "Let's adopt a more generous spirit, shall we?"

Chelsey and Jordan scowled at each other.

"Your turn, Ella," Dad said, trying to put the focus back on the giving spirit of the holiday.

Ella put down her plate and took out the various-sized gifts bearing her name. She received a pretty cashmere sweater from Chelsey and the Dirty Dancing DVD from her parents. She had completely worn out her other copy. "It comes with footage never seen," Mom said, pointing to the special features on the back cover.

"And this is from me," Jordan said, handing Ella a heavy book covered in newspaper wrapping. She ripped open the paper. It was Harrison's Principles of Internal Medicine. "How did you find this?" Ella asked in complete surprise, turning over the book. The bookstore was out of stock when she had asked to buy a copy, and the websites she checked were asking a fortune.

"I have a friend who is a med student," Jordan replied. It was one of the most thoughtful gifts anyone had ever given her. Jordan was usually sullen and selfish, not generous and thoughtful. Ella muttered a thank you; she still hadn't forgiven him for implying Brandon drank on the job.

"My turn," Dad said, rubbing his hands together in anticipation.

He pulled out a small square box. "The Godfather DVD box set?" Dad cried. "Thanks, Chelsey! I know what I'll be watching later today." He pulled out Ella's gift. It was a book called How to Improve Your Golf Game. "Are you hinting at something, Ella?" Dad teased.

"Just thought you might like it," Ella said, smiling back. Jordan had given Dad a bag for his golfing gear.

"Thanks, Jordan," Dad said, patting his shoulder. "How did you know my cart bag was worn out?"

"Because it split open the last time we played," replied Jordan.

"I guess that would do it." Dad grinned.

"This is for you," Mom said, handing Dad a card.

Dad opened the card and unfolded the piece of paper inside.

"It seems I am signed up for cooking lessons," Dad read. "How nice of you, Pattie." Dad's smile turned into a grimace.

"Maybe you will cook me a romantic dinner," Mom offered.

"Don't count on it," Dad muttered, sticking the paper back into the envelope. Ella noticed her mother bite back a smug smile. She guessed her mom was tired of doing all the cooking.

"Your turn, Jordan," Mom prodded. Jordan went to the tree to pull out the remaining presents.

He opened an envelope. "Bet I know what this is," Jordan said, pulling out a check. "Thanks, Mom and Dad." He opened the watch Ella had given him and pulled out a couple of CDs from a gift bag.

"Thanks, Chelsey," Jordan mumbled.

"Mom made me," Chelsey replied. "If it were up to me, I would have gotten you lipstick."

"Enough," Mom cried. "You are ruining Christmas."

"I'm going to call Shelby," Jordan said, standing up. "Thanks for the watch, Ella."

"I'm going to the salon," Chelsey said, grabbing her handbag.

"I'm going to watch The Godfather. Ella, want to join me?" Dad asked.

"I think I need to study," Ella replied. She gathered up her gifts. She loved her father but didn't feel like watching the demise of the Corleone family. Instead, she went to her room with the medical book Jordan had given her. It was a thoughtful gift; she had been wanting this book for some time. Ella plopped down on her bed and looked through the index, wondering what to read first.

Dad knocked on her door. "Ella, can I talk with you for a second?"

"Tired of The Godfather already?"

"Never started, actually," Dad said, sitting next to Ella on the bed. "It's not as fun watching alone."

"Jordan might join you," Ella offered.

"Good idea. I'll ask him." Dad rubbed his knee, looking nervous. "Something doesn't seem right about this whole barn drinking story," he began. "Brandon has always been responsible and courteous. The horses seem to take to him. It would be a shame to let him go."

"Don't fire him, Dad," Ella pleaded.

"Here is the problem," Dad said as he clasped his hands together. "If he didn't do it, who did? Jordan swears it wasn't him, and I'm afraid the only other option is Brandon."

Ella didn't think before blurting out, "It was me."

"You?" Dad asked, looking skeptical.

"I have to let loose somehow," Ella said. "I mean all the studying and the pressure to get into a good college—"

"You believe this performance?" Jordan interrupted from the doorway.

"Not one word," Dad answered.

"Jordan, tell the truth," Ella begged. "You know you did it."

"The thing is, I didn't do it," Jordan replied.

"We have to face facts," Dad said gently. "It seems Brandon is the culprit. No use denying it."

Ella was shaking. Jordan was lying, and her parents were buying it, like they always did.

Dad turned towards Jordan. "I was going to make a sandwich out of leftovers and watch The Godfather. Want to join me?"

"Sure, Dad," Jordan replied. "Be down in a second."

"You know you did it," Ella seethed, when her dad was out of earshot.

"Look, Ella, I didn't do it," said Jordan. "And not that it's any of your damn business, but I don't drink beer anymore, only wine on occasion. I know you're crazy about 'horse boy,' but he is guilty."

"He is not," Ella insisted. "And I'll prove it."

"Go on, Miss Marple," Jordan replied. "But when you realize I was telling the truth, I want a full apology plus a triple sundae." With that, Jordan shuffled out of the room, calling down the stairs, "Leave me some candied yams." Dad tended to be a candied yams hog.

Ella sat on her bed, bringing her knees to her chest. She would prove that Jordan was lying and exonerate Brandon. And like Miss Marple, she would use the clues people overlooked, while pretending to be not looking for clues at all.

Ella started by going down to the kitchen. She found Jordan and Dad stuffing their faces, mayonnaise oozing out of their sandwiches.

"I'm going to ride Dusty," said Ella.

"Have fun," Dad said, wiping his mouth. "I may join you later."

Ella went down to the stables, the frosty air lashing at her back. She pulled her knit hat over her ears. Dusty greeted her with a loud "mumm" as she entered the stables. Ella patted his caramel-colored forehead. "Tell me what happened, boy," she said, looking into Dusty's big brown eyes. "Who drank the beer?"

Dusty just stared back at her.

"A lot of help you are," Ella said, rubbing his nose.

She looked around the barn but saw nothing but piles of straw.

We should put cameras in the barn, Ella thought. Shane might be on to something. Most mischief happens at night, she told herself. Ella would be back at nightfall and every night until she caught the drunkard in the act.

Ella waited in the stall, her finger ready to hit record at the slightest hint of action. She had come out to the barn every night for the last five, hoping to catch the mystery beer-drinker. Ella stayed in the empty stall next to Dusty. His snoring was as loud as a leaf blower. If the question ever came up about horses snoring, Ella could answer in the affirmative. Dusty's snoring aside, the barn was usually quiet and boring. Then again, Ella never made it very late before the house with all its cozy comforts tempted her back inside. She checked her phone. It was 10:30. Ella quivered. So many hours left, and she was freezing. Tonight, she wouldn't cave to comfort, determined to make it till midnight.

Ella scrolled through her phone, tissue in hand. Catching a cold was one of the hazards of staying out night after night in the frigid air. The other was cracked and bloody lips. Ella wiped at her dripping nose, glancing at a picture Maria had sent. She was standing by a lookout point, the view of city life behind her. Maria and her mom were in Chile for winter break, visiting family.

Ella scrolled through her Facebook feed. She saw a post of Matt in his soccer uniform, his foot angled towards the ball, ready to make a goal. He occasionally tagged her in something he thought would amuse her, like posts about horror stories. Ella would tag Matt in pictures of lizards in funny costumes. They would never have the closeness they shared before; time and distance had seen to that.

She debated sending Brandon a text, asking how his Christmas had been. She had his number, but something held her back. Was it fear? She didn't know. All Ella knew was every time she thought of texting him, her fingers tensed up and her heart raced. Her fingers rested above the keys, thinking of how to begin. Hi, hey . . . howdy?

Then she heard crunching straw, drawing her attention towards the stable entrance.

"Did you get it?" a voice rasped.

"Fresh from the fridge," another voice answered, the outline of a bottle in the crook of his arm, red hair flopping over his face. It's Shane!

Ella pointed the camera at their faces and pressed record. Shane drank from the bottle before handing it to a boy wearing a watch cap. Shane's friend finished the bottle and tossed it on the ground. Then he pulled out a badly rolled cigarette and torched the end of it with a lighter, smoke traveling up in small, hazy clouds.

"You sure no one will notice?" the boy with the watch cap asked, letting out a giant white puff.

"Not a chance, Troy," Shane said back, reaching for the stick of smoking paper. "My neighbors are about the most clueless people I have ever met. Wouldn't notice if a whole fraternity streaked across their yard."

"You promised me a glimpse of that Chelsey girl." Troy elbowed Shane. "Which room is hers? I see a light on the second floor."

"I have a better view from my window," Shane replied. "Too bad she usually does most of her changing in the bathroom."

"Gross," muttered Ella as she zoomed in on the deviant pair. She would be instructing Chelsey to keep her blinds down from now on. She felt a cough trying to escape her throat. She held her breath, covering her mouth with her gloves. To think, she was endangering her whole spy mission because of a stupid winter cold!

The urge to cough subsided. Then Ella's phone rang. She fumbled, struggling to turn the volume down, but her gloves got in the way.

"Damn, someone left their cell phone," Shane swore. "Troy, let's go before they come looking for it."

The pair ran from the stables. Ella tried to video them as they ran past her, working hard to keep her cover. But her phone screen jammed, causing the recording to stop. At least I have some footage of when Shane first entered the barn, Ella thought, making her way back to the house. She had done it, caught the hoodlums in the act, and Brandon's good name would be restored once more.

# CHAPTER 20

"IT'S SHANE!" ELLA shouted, waving her phone in front of her parents. They were watching some Lifetime movie in the den.

"What are you talking about?" Mom said, sitting up.

"I have it recorded right here," Ella said. She played the video for her parents.

"I don't see anything," Dad said. He squinted at the dark images.

"I think I see an outline of someone." Mom blinked, taking a closer look.

"We can take videographer off Ella's resume," Jordan said, leaning between Mom and Dad.

"But there are two figures in the video," Ella insisted. "I saw them with my own two eyes."

"Ella, we know you have never gotten on with Shane, but we are not about to start accusing him of trespassing and drinking," Mom said.

"Your evidence is questionable, not to mention possibly illegal," Dad added. "I wouldn't show this video to anyone."

"I believe it is legal," Jordan interjected. "The Recording Law would most likely support Ella. Furthermore, Shane's crime of trespassing and underage drinking is the real issue a prosecutor would care about. It reminds me of a case I studied in class—"

"Jordan, how many times have I asked you to use a napkin?" Mom moaned and pointed to the dusting of yellow crumbs on the white carpet.

Jordan shrugged, taking another napkin-free bite, finishing the cookie.

Mom glared at Jordan, her shoulders hunched in defeat. She turned to Ella. "Paul is a good man, and I've known Ros for years. I'm sorry, Ella, I just don't believe that the Lowells would have a son that would act this way."

"Why won't you guys believe me?" Ella cried before descending into a coughing fit. There seemed to be a correlation between how much she talked and how much she coughed.

"Ella, you have made yourself sick," Mom scolded. "And I really don't think Shane could get away with acting so reckless. I'm sure Ros wouldn't allow it."

"I believe you," Jordan said quietly.

"But you said Brandon was the one who was drinking?" Mom said to Jordan, her lips pursed in confusion.

"I said, I saw him drink from a flask," Jordan countered. "Which Ella assures me contains only water."

"It's water," Ella insisted. "Just ask Brandon the next time he's here."

"Ella saw something," Jordan concluded. "She tried to tape it. I think you should believe her."

"Are you sure you saw Shane?" Mom pressed.

"I'm positive," said Ella, sick of repeating herself.

"I'll call Ros." Mom pushed herself off the couch.

"I wouldn't bother," Jordan said. "Instead, I would put up a no trespassing sign in the stables and a video camera. You don't even have to plug the camera in. The sight of one should be enough to scare the rascal away."

"But if he is drinking?" Mom asked.

"And smoking weed," Ella added.

"I have to call Ros." Mom searched for her cell phone.

"Well, at least I won't have to fire Brandon," Dad said, relaxing his shoulders into the couch. "But I will have to build a fence to block out our pesky neighbors. What joy."

"And someone owes me ice cream," Jordan said, glaring at Ella.

"I'm sorry, Jordan," Ella said.

"That was an apology?" Jordan tilted his chin towards her. "Come on, put in a little effort; look up some quotes, read some psychological journals. I want the apology double-spaced."

"Yes, teacher," Ella huffed.

"Stop rolling your eyes or I will send you to your room." Jordan wagged a finger at her, staying in character. "And tomorrow night, we will dine at the ice cream parlor down the street, your treat."

"But tomorrow night is New Year's Eve," Ella pointed out.

"Sorry, will I be ruining your highly anticipated evening of stuffing your face with popcorn and watching whatever crappy movie is on TV?"

"Fine, but only if we go in the Ferrari."

"Like I would let you drive," Jordan replied, pulling out his cell and turning his attention to the screen.

Ella looked forward to a nice hot shower and clearing her stuffy nose. She was glad the beer mystery was finally solved. And while she would never admit it to her brother, she was glad Jordan was not the culprit. In some ways he was the jerk she always knew him to be, but Ella saw a change in him, a change she hoped would remain permanent.

Jordan and Ella sat in Blake's Ferrari, eating ice cream. Ella wiped the edges of her cone, not wanting to be shouted at again after a wayward sprinkle landed on the dashboard. There were no seats left in the ice cream store, and Jordan and Ella were too wimpy to sit out in the cold.

"To think I could be by a warm fire, enjoying a steaming cup of hot cocoa with Shelby now." Jordan sighed as he placed a giant spoonful of chocolate fudge brownie ice cream into his mouth. A few drops spilled onto his navy sweater. Jordan jumped, breathing out when he realized the ice cream had landed on him instead of the car.

"Why didn't you go to Vail?" Ella asked.

"I wasn't invited," Jordan said quietly, his teal eyes on the steering wheel. "Shelby's parents aren't thrilled we're back together. You know, once a villain, always a villain sort of thing."

Ella licked her mint chocolate ice cream. She had three napkins wrapped around the bottom of the cone, not taking any chances. "Well, you still act like a jerk sometimes," Ella pointed out. "Like calling Chelsey a bimbo and implying that I'm a loser who does nothing on New Year's Eve."

"Hey, the truth hurts," Jordan said, taking another bite of his ice cream, carefully placing the spoon in his mouth.

"See, right there. Do you have to make comments like that?"

"I do." Then he paused and leaned his head back against the leather seat. He turned towards Ella. "Look, I wasn't intentionally trying to get Brandon fired, but it sucks being blamed for other people's mistakes simply because I made a similar one. I just wish people would believe me, that's all."

"Mom and Dad believed you."

"Yeah, well, it would have been nice if you also believed me."

"I said I was sorry. And I bought you ice cream. What more do you want from me?"

Jordan shrugged, polishing off his last spoonful. "Hey, want to go somewhere? It's too early to be at home."

"Want me to look up movie times?" Ella asked, taking out her phone.

"How about we go visit your boyfriend?" Jordan gave her a wide grin. "It's high time I had the whole brotherly 'I'm going to break your legs' talk with him."

"I don't have a boyfriend."

"Ella, stop being impossible."

"Should I say it in French?" Ella shouted. "Brandon is not my boyfriend! Besides, we weren't invited to his house."

"It's New Year's and I'm driving a Ferrari. Do we really need another reason to come over? Now, what is Brandon's address?"

Ella slumped her shoulders, muttering, "288 Landcork Drive."

Jordan plugged the address into the GPS on his phone. "Estimated driving time is forty minutes," he said, sounding like a pilot getting ready for takeoff. "Current temperature is freeze-your-balls-off cold. We expect a smooth ride and an on-time arrival."

The car handled like a dream, almost like gliding on water. Jordan turned up the radio and the sound of an electric guitar filled the car. The forty minutes went by too quickly for Ella. Before she knew it, they were on Landcork Drive. Brandon's truck was in the driveway. The Ferrari rolled smoothly over stray pebbles in the road. Chris was in the front yard; a young man Ella didn't recognize stood alongside him.

Chris paused and studied the Ferrari. He said something to the other man before rolling over to them, moving his hand towards his back.

"Jordan, lower the window," Ella commanded.

"Ella, what's the problem?"

"Now!" Ella yelled, seeing Chris's eyes narrowed at the car. She reached over Jordan and pressed the window button down. "Hi, Chris," Ella called.

Chris removed his hand from his side. "Ella?" His brows connected in surprise.

"This is my brother, Jordan," Ella said, waving her hand in her brother's face.

Chris rolled up to the car and put a hand out to Jordan. Jordan returned the handshake.

"What year?" Chris asked, glancing inside the car.

"My friend got it from the dealership a few weeks ago," Jordan replied.

"And he's letting you drive it?" Chris gaped.

"He's been leasing Ferraris since he graduated from high school," said Jordan. "This car is nothing special to him. Money literally grows on trees at his house."

"Can they plant one here? I'd sure love to have one," said Chris.

"Wouldn't we all," Jordan replied.

Chris chuckled, revealing a small dimple in his right cheek, damping his tough guy image.

"Ella, can you tell Brandon to come up?" Chris asked. "He is going to want to see this."

Ella got out of the car and went inside. She found Paulina in the kitchen, arranging food platters. Is it just me, or is Paulina always in the kitchen? Something didn't seem right about it.

"Hi, Ella," Paulina said as she dumped salsa into a bowl. "What a nice surprise. Wish Brandon had mentioned you were coming; I would have saved some of that blueberry pie you like."

Ella flushed, mentally kicking Jordan for the insane idea of just stopping in. "That's okay; it was kind of a last-minute decision." Ella glanced around for familiar faces. "Where are Cindy and Holley?"

"Cindy's asleep on the couch with Graham," Paulina replied, opening a big bag of tortilla chips. "Graham wore her out something awful at the park this afternoon. Holley is around here somewhere. I know she would love to see you."

Right on cue, Holley bounced into the kitchen. "Ella!" she shrieked, throwing her thin arms around Ella's neck.

"Hi." Ella hugged her back.

"I have to show you something," Holley said. She pulled out an old, battered cell phone and scrolled through some pictures. "Look, it's me and James!" Holley squealed, pointing at the guy with gelled hair standing next to her. Holley's smile was so wide, Ella could see all her teeth, even the molars in the back.

"He told me he thinks I'm cool," Holley gushed. "I told him we are getting married."

"What did he say to that?" Ella asked.

"He said if I'm still single in ten years, he would seriously consider it. I'm officially changing my last name to Jude."

"Sounds like the beginning of a Beatles song," Paulina teased.

Holley rolled her eyes, sticking her phone back in her jean pocket as Paulina began singing, "Hey Jude."

"I wouldn't go changing your name yet," Ella advised. "You should give some of the other boys a chance. Tastes change as we age."

"Never," Holley said and clutched her heart.

"Is Brandon around?" Ella said, remembering Chris was waiting to show him the sports car.

"He's downstairs," Paulina said. She motioned towards the basement steps with her head, since her hands were knuckle-deep in avocadoes.

"Thanks," Ella replied as she went to the basement steps. She held on to the side rail and slowly made her way down. Her boots had a tall heel; the last thing she wanted to do was make a memorable entrance. As Ella neared the landing, she heard Brandon's voice.

"Ranny, come on, we are about to start the fireworks."

"Just a few more minutes," a girl answered. "We never get a chance to be alone."

Ella's hands flew to her face in shock, leaving the rail. She lost her balance and tumbled down the last three stairs, landing with a painful thud on her bottom. Looking up from the floor, she saw Brandon and a pretty blond girl staring back at her. Brandon's arms were around the blond girl's waist; their faces were almost touching. Ella had never been so embarrassed, but that feeling was quickly overwhelmed when she realized what she had just interrupted. In that moment, all of Ella's hopes went up like a firecracker, sailing high into the dark night sky, exploding into teeny-tiny pieces and falling onto the cold pavement.

# CHAPTER 21

"ELLA, ARE YOU alright?" Brandon asked as he rushed to give her a hand.

"I'm fine," Ella said, wishing the fall had knocked her into a coma. She didn't want to see Brandon looking at her with pity or the beautiful blond girl staring at her with a mixture of shock and annoyance.

Ella took in Ranny's appearance—how her short, blond hair jutted out to her chin, how tight jeans defined her toned legs. Ella's heart sank. There was no way she could compete with the girl standing before her. In a beauty contest that included Nicole, Samantha, and Brittany, Ranny would win. It seemed Ella had a reason to fear Ranny all along.

Brandon helped Ella back into a standing position.

"Ella, this is Ranny," Brandon said, breaking the awful, tension-filled silence.

"Hi," Ella said quietly.

Ranny gave a half-smile back, biting her nails. Ella noticed they were all square and nibbled to the core. There was also a small mole by her left ear, almost unnoticeable unless you were looking. Ella gave a sigh of defeat. Ranny was perfect, chewed-up nails and all.

"Brandon, you coming?" Chris called from upstairs.

"In a minute," Brandon called.

"But there's a Ferrari in the driveway."

Brandon's eyes dilated to saucer size.

"He's lying," Ranny said. "And you just fell for it."

"There is a Ferrari," said Ella, hoping her tone didn't sound too forceful, like she had something to prove.

"How do you know?" Ranny shot back, still biting at her nails.

"Because my brother drove it over here," Ella said.

Ranny's mouth fell open.

"Come on," Brandon said as he and Ranny began hurrying up the stairs. Brandon paused on the third step, turning to Ella. "You joining us?"

Ella glanced at Ranny. It was clear by the narrowing of her gray eyes that she didn't want Ella to come.

"It's okay, I've already seen it," Ella said, shrinking back.

Brandon and Ranny continued up the stairs and out of sight.

Ella looked around for something to do and saw the light on in Brandon's room. She knew etiquette dictated that she be invited to enter, but then again, Brandon had told her Ranny was "just a friend."

Brandon's room was cleaner than she expected. His bed was made, his clothing in a hamper by the wall. There was no smell of musty socks or pictures of girls on the walls. There was only one poster—one of a man in a uniform, saluting the American flag.

A signed Reggie Jackson baseball card sat next to some pictures on his dresser. Ella ignored the baseball card, more interested in the photos. There was one of him as a small boy, pointing a rifle at a dinged-up metal target. His light-brown hair was long, dangling down his neck. There was a more recent picture of him in camping gear, his father standing next to him. They both wore giant, blue hiking bags on their backs. Brandon's strong arms looked tan.

His closet door was ajar, and she peeked in. Brandon's closet was just as Ella expected, with rows of blue jeans on hangers, his shoe rack lined with boots. There were a few white dress shirts and a pair of khaki pants. A black suit was stuffed in the corner. Ella guessed it hadn't been worn since his brother's wedding.

Ella closed the closet door and sat on the bed, wondering what to go through next. She saw a small bookshelf filled with spy novels and yearbooks. Ella took a yearbook off the shelf and leafed through it. She found Brandon's junior photo. His hair was short, his grin wide. Ella flipped to the back of the yearbook and read the comments.

One inscription caught her eye, from a girl name Lori Shirly.

*Brandon, it was so fun being in science together. I would never have discovered the hole in the wall leading to the basement if you hadn't shown me. It was sooo worth the detention we got. Every moment spent with you is worth the world to me.*

Ella quickly looked up Lori's picture. She was shocked to discover that Lori had mousy hair and thick glasses. Her smile was sweet, with large braces covering her teeth. Ella suspected this was probably a case of unrequited love. There was another note from a girl name Morgan, saying how nice Brandon was to give up being homecoming king to a guy named Bert. Ella tried to look up who Bert was, but there was more than one.

Ella put the yearbook back and browsed through the rest of his book collection. She pulled out a spy novel, peering at the back cover. A piece of paper dropped to the ground, a brochure. Ella read the words printed at the top: Do you have what it takes? The picture showed two men with windblown hair, dressed in military gear, paddling through rapids in a raft. The words Sea, Air & Land, America's Navy were printed underneath.

The basement steps abruptly squeaked. Ella shoved the brochure into the book and placed the book back on the shelf just as Brandon entered the room.

"We're starting the fireworks now," Brandon said. He was wearing a green, military-style jacket, his cheeks red from the cold.

"Okay," Ella stammered, embarrassed to be caught in his room.

"You can borrow the book if you want," Brandon offered.

"Book?" Ella asked, confused. Then she remembered she had been going through his bookshelf. "Yeah, I'm not really into spy novels."

"Your loss." Brandon shrugged.

The sound of crackling filled the air.

"Come on," Brandon said. "The fireworks are starting."

Reluctantly, Ella followed Brandon upstairs. They joined the crowd at the end of the cul-de-sac.

Sizzle, crack, pop went the firecrackers into the air, bursting into wide, wonderful colors in the sky. Ella saw Chris and Cindy holding hands, enjoying the show. Paulina laid her head on Gary's shoulder, their hands intertwined. Ella peeked in Brandon's direction. His arms were wrapped around Ranny's waist. Her head rested against his chest. They looked like an ad for winter clothing.

Jordan was talking with the young man they had seen earlier in the front yard.

"This is Charlie," said Jordan to Ella.

Ella shook his hand, and Charlie and Jordan resumed their conversation. After about ten minutes, Ella couldn't take it anymore. She was cold, tired, and alone. No one to talk with, no shoulder to rest her head on.

"Let's go," Ella said to Jordan.

"But we just got here," Jordan replied.

"How about you wait a few minutes more?" Charlie said to Ella. "The best fireworks are at the end."

Ella gave Jordan a look.

"All right," Jordan sighed. "We'll go."

Ella walked over to Brandon and tapped his shoulder. "We're leaving now."

"Now?" Brandon asked in surprise. "But we just got started."

"My parents want us home," Ella lied, not thinking up a better excuse.

"Tell them to come next year."

"Ranny . . . it was nice to meet you," Ella forced the words out.

Ranny nodded, turning her head back to the sky.

"See you around," Ella said to Brandon. "Happy New Year."

"Happy New Year," Brandon replied, their eyes meeting.

With that, Ella and Jordan made their way to the car. Ella gave one last look towards Brandon. Ranny whispered in his ear, and they both laughed. We should have gone to a movie, Ella thought, slumping into the Ferrari. This had been the worst end to a bad holiday season. Why is life so unfair?

Winter break ended, and Ella had to get used to waking up early and wearing normal clothes, her comfy pajamas not conforming to the dress code. The day seemed to drag by as teachers piled on homework and assignments under the mistaken impression the students had come back to school eager to learn.

Ella slogged through the day solemnly, while Maria, on the other hand, was unusually chatty. She couldn't stop talking about her trip to Chile and bringing out her phone in between classes. Maria showed Ella pictures of Santiago, where her mother had grown up, and Easter Island and the monolithic sculptures. She also saw photos of Maria's baby cousin Florencia, who had almond eyes and raven hair, like a miniature copy of Maria.

Ella let Maria talk endlessly. She enjoyed hearing about Chile, and it saved Ella from having to tell about her awful Christmas. Mom had invited the Lowell family over for "talk and tea" New Year's morning, where she brought up the barn-drinking incident. Shane denied he was ever in the stables, and not surprisingly, the Lowells took their son's side. Ros went on to write the number of a counselor who specialized in PTSD on a piece of paper and handed it to Mom. She insisted that Ella might benefit from speaking to someone. When the Lowells left, Mom ripped up the piece of paper and threw it in the garbage, muttering something about a black kettle. Later that evening, Ella informed Chelsey about the show she was putting on for Shane and his posse every evening. Chelsey went online and ordered curtains, paying extra for expedited shipping.

"Did I show the pictures of me at the beach?" Maria asked, scrolling through her photos.

"Yes," said Ella. She opened a packet of crackers. It was only third period and she was famished.

"Well, I guess I have shown you everything." Maria shrugged, putting away her phone. "Hey, did you hear about Brittany's mom? She skied headfirst into a tree. Rumor has it that she is having vision problems."

"That's nice," Ella replied, not really listening.

"Ella!" Maria cried.

"What?" Ella snapped back to life.

"You just said 'it was nice' that Brittany's mom slammed into a tree."

"I did?"

"Yes, you did."

"Is she alright?"

"You really weren't listening, were you?"

"Well, is she?"

"No, she is having problems seeing."

Ella looked down, auburn hair falling into her face. She pushed it back. It was strange feeling sympathy for Brittany. Ella didn't like it.

Maria changed the subject. "I have an audition for Syball in a couple weeks. Got my letter over the break."

"No way," Ella said, beaming at Maria.

"You will help me practice, won't you?"

"Wouldn't dream of letting you have a Syball audition without my input," Ella said, knowing full well Maria didn't need her help.

"So how was your winter break?" Maria asked.

"Brandon has a girlfriend." Ella sulked.

"How did you find that out?" Maria asked.

"I caught them mid-kiss."

"Well, that sucks."

"Yeah, it does."

The bell rang, signaling the end of break. AP Calculus was next. For the first time in Ella's school career, she thought about going to the nurse and feigning the flu.

# CHAPTER 22

MARIA AND ELLA spent the next few weeks perfecting Maria's routine, which allowed Ella to forget all about Brandon and Ranny. Rumors of snow days drifted through school, but the flurries didn't stick, and sadly no school was missed. January passed by, and before Ella knew it, it was the beginning of February. The time for Maria's audition had arrived.

"I'm going to bomb," Maria wailed.

Ella gripped Maria's shoulders and shook her. "Maria, stop the panicking. You will be great."

"You don't know that," Maria countered.

"Hey, I'm the smart one, remember? Now, stop this worrying. You are about to give the best performance of your life, and I will be in the auditorium to witness the moment."

"Should I put back in the time step?"

"No, the time step didn't go with the other choreography." Ella looked down at her watch. "It's time, Maria."

Maria's brown eyes seemed stuck in wide oval shapes; she looked like she was going to lose it. Ella shook her again. "Maria, repeat after me: you got this."

"I got this," Maria repeated back.

"Like you mean it."

"I got this," Maria said louder.

"Good, now go get changed," Ella commanded.

"You really think I can do this?"

"Go!"

Maria hurried off while Ella made her way to American Lit.

After school, Ella went to the auditorium. An audition was already in progress. A girl from French class named Alley was imitating Adelaide from "Guys and Dolls." Ella looked around for a place to sit. She noticed Denzel near the back. He looked nervous, his fists by his chin. "Where were you?" he whispered as Ella sat next to him. "Maria's audition is coming up."

"American Lit ran late," Ella replied. They watched Alley belt out the last note of "Adelaide's Lament."

"If this is Maria's competition, then she is going to kill it," Denzel said confidently. Alley had hit all the notes, but there was no spark in her performance. It seemed more like Alley was making fun of Adelaide, imitating her nasal voice rather than bringing the character to life.

"Maria will kill it like a stroke," Ella said, punching the air for emphasis.

Denzel arched an eyebrow at her.

"No good?" Ella asked.

Denzel chuckled and shook his head.

A few rows down, Ella saw strands of sandy-colored hair protruding from a seat back. Barry was here. She remembered Maria had mentioned something about Stanley Harris auditioning. Ella wondered if Barry was hiding or simply slouching.

Ella's eyes continued to wander and landed on a man with large glasses sitting in the center of the auditorium. The man turned his head, giving Ella a view of his profile. Most of his hair lined his chin and upper lip; not much was left on his head. His nose took up too much room on his face, his glasses taking up the rest. Ella pictured Syball's representative to be more flamboyant; with a goatee, suspenders, or at the very least a cool hairstyle. This man had none of those things.

However he looked, the representative held the power to make or break her best friend's dreams. Ella hoped he would make them.

"Stanley Harris," the Syball representative called.

Stanley entered from stage right, his dark hair parted, and he wore a 1920s-style shirt and black trousers. "Something's Coming" began playing from the speakers. Stanley started off strong, hitting every note, his dance moves keeping with the theme of the song. Then it happened—he tried a free spin and fell. He paused for a few seconds, but it felt like an hour.

He continued with his performance, but the enthusiasm was gone. Some of his notes were off-key, and his jumps seemed jerky, the landings unplanned. Ella saw Barry wringing his hands, his mouth twisted into apprehension. When Stanley was done, he all but moped off the stage, utterly shattered.

While Ella knew it meant less competition for Maria, she couldn't help but feel sorry for Stanley. He looked deflated, like every dream he ever had was gone.

The Syball representative wrote something in a notepad before calling, "Maria Garcia."

Maria entered the stage. It was unclear by her expression whether she knew about the disastrous performance before her.

"Begin when you're ready," the man instructed.

"Come on, Maria," Ella said under her breath. This performance had to go well. It just had to!

Ella saw Maria take a quick breath, gathering up her nerves. Her makeup was subtle yet elegant, her shiny raven hair up in a high ponytail, hoop earrings in her ears. A leather jacket completed the outfit. Ella saw Maria don her stage presence and relax her body. The music came on: "One Song," from Rent. Maria's voice held just the right amount of emotion as she belted out the first note. Ella felt the message of the song come alive, and Maria's choreography held meaning in every step. Maria became the song. It was Maria's chance to make some glory.

Ella couldn't take her eyes off Maria; she was riveting. Maria jumped into the air, her legs stretching out into a perfect line, her toes pointing to the sky. She landed effortlessly into a kneeling position as she sang out the last word, "glory."

Ella bounded out of her seat, clapping. Maria had just given the best performance she had ever seen. Denzel caught her arm and pulled her back into her seat. Ella stopped clapping, hoping she hadn't ruined her best friend's audition with her exuberant outburst.

"I have to say, Ms. Garcia," the Syball representative began. "When I heard the title of your music selection, I was a bit baffled. 'One Song' was written about a male, a dying male." Ella's breath quickened. Does the Syball representative have no imagination? "Your interpretation of the song," the man went on, "to put it simply, was brilliant."

Maria's pretty face lit up, but she was clearly trying to keep her expression natural.

"We will let you know in March if you have been accepted," the man said as he opened his briefcase, placing the pen and notepad back inside. As soon as the gentleman left, Denzel and Ella raced to the stage.

Denzel grabbed Maria into a big hug, swinging her around. "You were amazing."

"You were even better than in practice," Ella gushed. "I knew when you landed that split leap that you had nailed it."

"He said I was brilliant," Maria said. She couldn't contain her joy. "How did I sound?"

"Deevy." Denzel beamed.

"Not a wandering note anywhere in the song," said Ella reassuringly. "I told you everything was going to be alright."

"Let's celebrate," Denzel said. "My treat. We will go to Rome's Pasta House."

Maria squealed with excitement; she loved Italian food.

Off they went for a celebratory meal. Maria was relieved that her audition was over; now all she had to do was wait for the acceptance letter to come in. Ella didn't see how Syball could refuse her after her stellar performance. Maria was born a star, and Syball was just the beginning.

# CHAPTER 23

ELLA TILTED HER head back, struggling to keep her concentration on the microscope at Dr. Taylor's lab. The hospital had called that morning. It seemed Nia was no longer responding to treatment. All Ella could think about was Nia's sweet amber eyes and charming smile.

Thunder shook the room, the windows tinted with fog. Ella felt trapped inside the gloomy lab on this rainy day, sick of recording tumors that seemed to grow and grow. She tapped her cheek and tried to regain her concentration, steering herself from the emotional cliff she was plunging towards. She peered into the microscope lens. Something seemed different about this tissue sample. It didn't look like the other samples that Ella had observed. The usual clumps of black cells were missing.

"Barry, can you come here for a second?" Ella asked.

"What's the matter, lionhead? Discover you are going blind?"

"Barry, get over here," Ella shouted at him.

"Jeez, no need to roar, lionhead." Barry stepped away from his own microscope and dragged himself over.

"Does something look different about this tissue sample?" Ella asked as he peered into the lens.

Barry shrugged. "I would write what you see. It's not our job to make diagnoses."

"I don't think it's cancer."

Dr. Taylor came over then. "Is something the matter? I heard shouting."

"That was Ella getting in touch with her ancestral roots," Barry replied, his beady eyes pinning her in accusation.

"I don't think the person has cancer," Ella said, ignoring Barry's jab.

"All participants have a confirmed cancer diagnosis before entering the study," Dr. Taylor said curtly.

"Look," Ella said, indicating the microscope.

Dr. Taylor's lips tightened. "I do not have to look, Ella," she said.

"But what if you're wrong? What if the patient is receiving improper treatment?"

Dr. Taylor's mouth turned down into a stern frown. "Ella, come with me."

Barry smirked as Ella followed Dr. Taylor past boxes of sterile discs and test tubes to her office. Dr. Taylor took a seat behind a wooden desk. Ella sat across from her teacher, studying the metal bookshelf lined with red binders. A potted fern wilted in the corner and one lonely picture hung on the wall. This place could use some sprucing.

"I'm disappointed in you, Ella," Dr. Taylor said, bringing Ella's attention back to why she was in this dreary office in the first place. "Disrespecting me in my own lab. It's unlike you to be so discourteous."

"I'm sorry," Ella said. "But I just wanted to show you—"

"You, a student in high school, wanted to show the director of a cancer research lab that your opinion is more accurate than a highly trained doctor's?"

Ella hadn't thought about it that way. She guessed she had been a bit presumptuous.

"I'm sorry," Ella said.

"When someone is as smart as you are, they tend to feel they have nothing to learn," said Dr. Taylor. "If you want a sure course to failure, keep that attitude. Great scientists know they are limited in their knowledge; they seek to improve by experimenting. They most certainly do not contradict their senior advisor, or in this case, teacher."

Ella stayed quiet. She felt she knew so much, when in reality her pool of knowledge was just beginning to fill.

"If you would simply write down what you see and save diagnosing cancer for the experts, you may continue your internship at the lab. Do you think you can do that?"

Ella nodded dutifully.

"You may join Barry for the washing up." Dr. Taylor turned her attention to the paperwork on her desk. Ella left the office, her pride crushed.

"Did she fire you?" Barry asked as Ella joined him at the sink.

"No, Barry, she didn't fire me," Ella said, restraining the urge to shove his head under the running water.

"Oh," Barry said. He looked as if he had been promised an action movie and instead got a documentary on the migration pattern of seabirds.

Ella found the cleanup more tedious than usual. She put the clean flasks back in the cupboard, making up her mind to keep her mouth shut in the future. She wanted to keep this internship and would do whatever was necessary.

On Sunday morning, Ella visited the children's oncology ward in the hospital. Ella found Nurse Hellen busy with paperwork at the nurse's station.

"How is Nia?" Ella asked.

Nurse Hellen chewed her lip. "She's not doing too well. You should look in on her."

"Where is she?" Ella asked.

"Room 702," Nurse Hellen said. "I know she will be happy to see you."

Ella started down the hall when a boy with a squeaky voice called out to her, "Ella, come play with me." Arthur shook a wooden box.

Ella was surprised to see Arthur there, attached to an IV pole. His cancer had been in remission thanks to the successful brain surgery.

"Maybe later, Arthur," Ella said.

"Oh, come on, one game . . . please," said Arthur.

"Alright," Ella sighed and walked into his room. She pulled a seat up to Arthur's bed, noticing a half-eaten tray of food on a side table.

"You left your Jell-O," Ella pointed out.

"I'm saving it for later," Arthur replied. "And no cheating this time," he warned as he pulled the lid off the chess box.

Ella bit her lip, knowing full well she would do what had to be done to make this game end in a timely fashion.

"How are you?" Ella asked as they each set up their side of the board.

"Fine," Arthur muttered. "I'm only here because I have a cold. My mom freaks out over every little thing. She's looking for a nurse to discharge us. I hope I get out before the comic book store closes. They are holding this new Spider-Man comic I've been waiting for."

"You didn't want to order the book online?" Ella asked, letting Arthur take her knight.

"I will not be controlled by the internet!" Arthur cried. He took her queen. Ella gaped at him. She hadn't meant to make his path to victory that smooth. Within four moves, he managed to corner her king from all sides.

"You win," Ella said as she laid down her king.

"You cheated," Arthur accused, pointing a stubby finger at Ella.

"No, I didn't," Ella insisted. She had put forth some effort, just not as much as she could have.

"Then you need lessons," said Arthur, pushing up his glasses. She noticed his hair was growing back, his cheeks round and rosy.

"Care to give me some lessons?" Ella teased as she put the chess pieces away.

"No." Arthur shook his head. "You need, like, professional help."

Ella laughed, sticking the lid on the chess box, anxious to see Nia. She stood up. "I have to go now, Arthur."

"Bye," he mumbled.

"Enjoy your comic book." Ella waved as she made her way to room 702.

She found Nia lying in a bed, holding a picture. Her arms were thin, and her legs looked like two poles under the covers. Her parents sat in chairs next to the bed. They looked up at her. Ella had never seen her father before, and had met Nia's mother only once, and in a happier setting.

"Hi," Ella said, as six eyes stared at her.

"Can I help you?" Mr. Burton asked.

"It's the girl who volunteers with Nia." Mrs. Burton elbowed him; she was on the phone. She dabbed her eyes with a tissue before saying, "I can't handle this right now," hanging up the phone.

Ella's heart tugged, sadness filling her. She wouldn't know how to handle the situation either. Did any parent?

"I'm going down to the cafeteria to get something to eat," Mr. Burton said, standing up, stretching his hands over his head. He turned to Mrs. Burton. "Join me, Jayla."

"I can't leave Nia, Benjamin," Mrs. Burton replied, blotting at her eyes once more. Her face was streaked with tears, her eyes puffy and bloodshot.

"I'll stay with Nia," Ella offered.

"Thank you," Mr. Burton said. He offered his hand to his wife.

"No, Benjamin." She swatted his hand away.

"Come, just for a little while." He took Mrs. Burton's hand and led her out of the room. Ella watched them leave, wondering how long they had been in the hospital room hoping for their daughter's recovery, preparing for the unthinkable.

She sat down next to Nia. "What have you got there?"

Nia handed Ella a picture of her and James.

"That was a fun day," Ella mused.

"Do you think James will come again?" Nia whispered, too weak to project her voice.

"I can see," Ella offered. She and James were not on speaking terms. Maybe his agent would talk with her, but Ella didn't care to speak to him either.

"Do you think angels fly?" Nia said softly, her eyes closing as she spoke.

Ella tried to think of a response. None came to her.

"I'm going to be an angel," Nia said. "I'd be happier if I knew I could fly."

Ella brushed away a tear. She couldn't stand the thought of little Nia leaving the world. It just didn't seem fair. But then again, fair wasn't a word used often in a cancer ward.

Ella placed an arm around Nia's shoulders. "You're not going to be an angel; I won't allow it."

"You sound like my mother," Nia replied, her eyes opening wider, her voice gaining strength. "And if I were five, I might believe you, but I'm ten years old. I don't believe in the tooth fairy, or Santa Claus, but I believe in angels. I will make a pretty angel. I have dimples." She pointed to her cheeks.

Ella held Nia, unable to speak, her tears falling on Nia's head.

"You're raining on me," Nia said. Her eyes were like two crescents as she fought to keep them open.

Ella wiped her eyes with the back of her hand. "Want to play Scrabble?"

"No, I'd rather watch something," answered Nia.

Ella pulled out her phone and brought up a movie. They sat together, with Nia's head on Ella's shoulder. Soon, Ella heard Nia's even breathing; she had fallen asleep. The Burtons returned.

"I think we should let her rest," Mrs. Burton suggested. It was time for Ella to go. She shifted Nia's small head onto the pillow and stood. Ella mumbled her goodbyes, but Nia's parents were too focused on their daughter to reply.

As Ella pressed the button for the elevator, she thought about what Nia had said. Nia would make a beautiful angel; Ella hoped it would be when Nia was older, much older, but it seemed cancer had other plans.

Ella made her way home from the hospital, Nia's words repeating in her mind. She couldn't bear the thought of losing Nia. She turned on the radio, treating her pain with music. Thinking of all the schoolwork awaiting her at home made her want to take a detour. All she felt like doing was climbing into bed and finishing the ghost story she began the night before. Ella pulled up the driveway and found Chelsey waiting at the top.

"Good, you're home," Chelsey said, pouncing on Ella the moment she stepped out of the car. "Mind if I try a new hairdo on you?" She gave Ella big puppy eyes.

"Alright," Ella said, "but make it quick. I have a test to study for."

Chelsey followed Ella to her room. She pulled out a brush and some hair ties from the top drawer of Ella's dresser and began brushing her hair.

Ella flipped to the chapter she needed to review, highlighter in hand.

"How was the hospital?" Chelsey asked.

"Hard," Ella replied. "One of the patients I have been visiting is dying. I just keep hoping for a miracle."

"I would get comfy with death," said Chelsey. "As a doctor, you're going to have to get used to it."

"Can we talk about something else? You're depressing me."

"How about we listen to some music?" Chelsey put on Ella's iPod.

Ella relaxed into Chelsey's hands and closed her eyes, feeling like a doll.

"I thought you completed the hairdo course," Ella pointed out, remembering she had been Chelsey's guinea pig last summer, with Chelsey arranging her hair into a million different styles. But when Chelsey had offered to cut her hair, Ella refused. And after the debacle that became her mother's current look, Ella was glad she never let Chelsey near her with a pair of scissors.

"I'm practicing this complicated hairdo that a client of mine requested for her upcoming wedding."

"Oh," Ella replied, trying to refocus on the chemical equation she had highlighted.

Chelsey sang along to the song playing, flipping her golden hair side to side. She had the family curse; her voice wasn't even close to being on key. Jordan was the only one who could carry a tune.

"Did I tell you I was scolded in the lab yesterday?" Ella said, feeling the need to vent and to stop Chelsey from singing.

"What happened?" Chelsey asked.

"I questioned a slide and told Dr. Taylor I didn't think the tissue sample contained cancer."

"That's why you were scolded?" Chelsey tied one of the braids she had made with a hair tie.

"Yes." Ella leaned forward slightly to move away from Chelsey's knee, which was pressing into her back.

"Sometimes you do act like a smart-ass," Chelsey said, taking a bit of Ella's hair and yanking her back towards her.

"Ouch," said Ella.

"I'm hurting you?" Chelsey asked, sounding concerned. She prided herself on being gentle.

"Your knee is digging into my back."

Chelsey shifted her knee away from Ella's back and tied the end of the second braid. She pivoted Ella towards the mirror. "What do you think?"

"I think I look like I'm twelve." Ella craned her head so she could see the back.

"We will start over." Chelsey began to undo her braids.

Ella didn't mind—in fact, she enjoyed the sensation; it was like a massage for her scalp. As Chelsey weaved her hair into plaits, Ella read the chapter, paying close attention to the highlighted sections.

A knock on the door interrupted her reading. Ella turned to see Mom in the doorway, clutching the house phone. Ella wondered why they still had a landline, with everyone using their cell phones nowadays.

"Ella, can I speak with you?" Mom asked.

"What is it?" said Ella, her skin prickling. Mom didn't look right, her mouth turned down, her green eyes moist.

Mom came and sat down on the bed. "The director of the hospital called," Mom began, taking Ella's hand. "Nia passed away."

"No." Ella shook her head as tears filled her eyes. She dragged her hand from under her mother's, wrapping her arms around her shoulders in an effort to keep her sorrow at bay.

"The director said she went peacefully," Mom went on.

"They don't know what she felt," Ella said bitterly. She hated these cliché phrases. No one knew what it felt like to die, and it never made hearing the bad news any easier.

"The family is having a small funeral tomorrow," Mom said. "The hospital will hold a memorial service for her; they'll let you know when."

"I'll go to the funeral."

"The family has requested the ceremony be kept to family," Mom said quietly. "We must respect their wishes."

Ella leaned against the pillow. It wasn't fair. She had to be there, to say goodbye. Nia would have wanted that.

Mom put her hand around Ella's shoulders. "I'm so sorry, sweetie."

"We'll practice the hairdo some other time," Chelsey said, gathering up her things. "I'm sorry, Els." Chelsey bent down and gave Ella a kiss on the cheek. "I'm always here for you if you want to talk."

The phone rang in Mom's hand. She answered it, stepping out

into the hall. Ella sat on the bed and stared at the picture of her and Nia. She reached for her cell phone, wiping her eyes as she dialed the number.

Maria gave her usual greeting. "Well . . . hello."

"Maria," Ella choked.

"Ella, are you alright?"

"No, I'm not. Can you . . ." Ella wondered how to finish that sentence without being overdramatic.

"I'm coming," Maria said, hanging up. Best friends never needed big hints.

Ella put her phone down and rested her head against her bedframe, tears soaking her pillowcase. About ten minutes later, Maria was there.

"Your mom told me about Nia," Maria said. She joined Ella on the bed.

"She was like a little sister to me," said Ella, making space for Maria. "And I'm not even allowed to go to the funeral."

"Tell me about her," said Maria gently.

Ella told the story of how she met Nia four years ago, when Nia had asked if Ella could read a book to her from the Land of Stories series. They would dream of becoming rich by thinking up brilliant inventions such as edible shoelaces and mirrors that gave fashion advice.

Maria just listened, letting Ella cry on her shoulder. Soon it was dinnertime, and Maria joined the family for lasagna. Mom made sure to leave out the ground beef since Maria was a vegetarian.

That night, as Ella got ready for bed, she thought about the new beautiful, brown-eyed angel above, wondering if she had learned to use her wings.

# CHAPTER 24

THE NEXT WEEK brought the dreaded holiday Valentine's Day. The school hallways were littered with Valentine notes and chocolate wrappers. The day began with Brittany throwing candy at Ella's feet, saying, "Have it. No one sees your thighs anyway."

Ella just stood in shock, not knowing how to respond. Brittany had been particularly nasty since the fall dance. Ella couldn't tell if Brittany was mad that Brandon had shamed James or jealous that he hadn't fallen for her charm.

"No one wants to see her thighs either," said Nicole after Brittany had flounced off.

Ella turned to her in surprise.

"What?" Nicole replied, tossing back her blond hair.

"It's just—"

"You think because Brittany is my friend, I have to agree with everything she does?" Nicole shot back. Nicole and Ella had been talking more since she joined her in the front row.

"Is Brittany's mom really blind?" Ella asked.

"That's the rumor," Nicole answered.

Ella saw Max in his varsity jacket standing by the lockers across from them.

"Gotta go," Nicole said.

Ella watched them walk off as she processed the new information.

French class was no better, with Mr. Durand teaching them the meaning behind the love song "C'est Si Bon (It's So Good)." The other teachers went along with the love theme, making the next few periods about as awful as the first. Ella had to pass ooey-gooey couples holding hands and talking about their plans after school all morning.

Finally, lunch came, and Ella discovered a little cupcake inside her lunch bag with a note attached from her mother. At least someone is thinking of me, Ella thought, placing the cupcake to the side.

"Be my valentine?" Maria asked, dangling a box of chocolates in Ella's face.

"Ooo, thanks," Ella said. She opened the box filled with assorted truffles. She had given Maria candy hearts the day before.

"Where is Denzel taking you this evening?" Ella asked. She offered Maria a truffle.

"Some Italian place," Maria replied, popping a round piece of chocolate into her mouth.

"I wonder where Brandon is taking Ranny," Ella muttered.

"Oh, don't be a sour apple. Be proudly single. You don't need boys; they need you."

Ella's shoulders slumped. She was not in the mood for a motivational speech.

"You will find your prince," Maria assured her. "He is probably working in one of the Johns Hopkins labs, waiting for you to come rescue him from his dreary life as a rat killer."

"People come before animals, always," Ella replied, grimacing.

"It's that kind of thinking that has polluted our water, caused global warming, and destroyed our rainforests," said Maria, in full-blown activist mode.

The bell rang, and lunch was over.

"Save me the caramel truffle," said Maria as she grabbed her school bag.

"I'll try," Ella replied, packing up the remainders of her lunch.

A squeal echoed from across the lunchroom. Ella turned to see Samantha jumping up and down holding a tennis bracelet, Stefan by her side. Three more hours, she told herself. In just three more hours she would be home, riding Dusty, and the holiday would be over. With this happy thought, Ella made her way to her next class.

Ella found Brandon sweeping out Dusty's stall. His cheeks were splotched with red patches; the day had been unseasonably cold. Brandon wore the green military jacket she had seen him in on New Year's, his short brown hair sticking up slightly in the front.

"Hey," he said when he saw her.

"Hey," Ella replied, her boots crunching the hay as she walked towards him.

"Are you alright?" Brandon asked. "You seem kind of down lately."

"Someone close to me passed away," Ella replied, her eyes growing watery at the corners. She brushed the tears away before they could slip down her cheeks.

"I'm sorry," Brandon said sympathetically. "Was it sudden?"

"No, the person had cancer."

"Cancer sucks," Brandon said. He placed the rake against a wall.

"It sure does. So, doing anything for Valentine's?" Ella asked, trying to keep the conversation in motion.

"I'm watching some chick flick with Ranny later," said Brandon. "Honestly, I can't stand this holiday. It feels fake, you know?"

"Tell me about it!" Ella patted Dusty's forehead, shooing away a fly by his ears. "Brandon, can I ask you something?"

"Alright," Brandon replied, filling a bucket with water. Ella noticed his hands were chapped.

"Why did you tell me Ranny was just a friend?"

"We are friends."

"Brandon."

"We were at the time," he replied, bringing the water pail to Glenn's mouth. The water in the horse trough had frozen the night before.

"Do you love her?" The question slipped out before Ella could think to stop herself.

Brandon's face held a curious expression; he seemed to choose his words carefully. "I don't know anything about love. I'm not sure I even like what I eat for breakfast. Well, this morning I did enjoy eating Captain Crunch—it was the peanut butter flavor, in case you were wondering."

"I'm guessing that's a no," Ella said, feeling slightly better, speculating why he was going on about cereal.

"I wouldn't say that." Brandon set down the bucket.

"Until something is proven, it's considered unproven and therefore false," Ella said. She was extrapolating from Bertrand Russell's teapot analogy, the one that explained the burden of proof fell on the one making the outrageous scientific claim instead of the burden being on another scientist to disprove it. Ella knew her theory wasn't entirely accurate, but she hoped Brandon wouldn't notice.

"Therefore," she went on with her science babble, "the fact that you do not know you love Ranny means there is room for doubt, and one could argue there are too many variables in your relationship to say if it will prove satisfactory for both parties involved. So, my suggestion would be to terminate the relationship as soon as possible."

Brandon studied the bucket of water, shifting his mouth from side to side. Then he flung the remainder of the water at Ella.

"Ahh!" she cried as the cold water numbed her legs, her riding pants dripping at the bottom.

Ella stared at Brandon. He stood with his back straight and chest out, like a man who had won the battle. Coming out of her momentary daze, Ella picked up the garden hose lying next to her and held it up like a pistol, glaring at Brandon. A one-sided duel was about to ensue, with Ella holding the only available weapon: an upmarket hose that could shoot at different speeds and distances with variable pressure settings ranging from soft raindrops to high-pressure waves. Ella placed her boot on the waterspout. All she had to do was turn it slightly and Brandon would be drenched.

"Now, Ella, let's think about this," Brandon said, fear written across his handsome face. The weather was an icy forty degrees, and Brandon was about to be drenched.

"Never start a fight you can't finish," Ella said, her smile growing wider. "It's combat strategy 101." With that, she turned on the spout and squeezed the trigger. Brandon yelped and jumped backwards, the blast of water soaking him within seconds. Ella dropped the hose, claiming victory with a thump.

"You want a fight, I'll show you a fight," Brandon said, determination in his hazel eyes. Ella tried to run, but Brandon was too quick, catching her around the waist and wrestling her to the ground playfully. Ella grabbed wildly for the hose; it was her only hope. Brandon pinned her hands on either side of her. Panic ran through her—how was she going to get out of this jam? Brandon leaned back, gloating. He thought the war was over.

"Ouch, my leg." Ella grimaced in pain. Brandon moved off her instantly, looking worried. Ella was free once more. She took the hose in her hand and shot him clear in the face, proud to be back in control.

"Truce," Brandon yelled as Ella continued to pelt him with water.

Ella let go of the trigger, blowing across the nozzle like cowboys did with their pistols in westerns.

"You fight dirty, Ella." Brandon panted, his eyes bright. His short hair was wet, dripping down his cheek. He looked incredible.

"You started it, bucket man!"

"You wouldn't happen to have a change of clothes, would you?" Brandon asked, his breath returning to an even speed.

"My brother might have some," Ella offered. "We can check his room."

"I don't trust you enough to follow you inside," said Brandon. "You might have a pet tiger waiting to eat me or something."

Ella waved her hand. "We got rid of the pet tiger years ago. Besides, my mother made cookies."

"Fresh?"

"Baked yesterday."

"For cookies I'll do just about anything." Brandon stood.

Ella led him inside, Brandon dripping as they made their way to the stairs. Mom would fume if she saw her precious floors taking a hit like this. Brandon's eyes went wide as they passed the living room with the giant TV and updated stereo system. His expression was similar to the one he wore when they were in the garage, surrounded by her parents' luxury cars a few months ago, working on the bookshelf.

Ella was glad to find Jordan's room neat, his bed made, the blinds drawn. Ella noticed a poster of a woman in a skimpy bathing suit sitting on a rock by the beach. Does Mom know Jordan has that? Ella remembered how her mother had asked her to remove her Dirty Dancing movie poster because she felt it was too suggestive. There is always a double standard when it comes to Jordan, Ella thought irritably. Jordan probably got this poster when he was seven.

Ella opened the walk-in closet and perused the rows of dress shirts and pants. How different Jordan's metro style was to Brandon's casual ruggedness.

"Here," Ella said at last, pulling out a navy dress shirt and khaki pants.

"Are we going to church?" Brandon asked, looking down at the clothing in Ella's hands, his face scrunched with distaste.

"I'll keep looking," Ella said quickly. She found a gray sweater.

Brandon grimaced as Ella handed him the sweater, but said nothing.

"I'll let you change," Ella said. She went to her own room and closet and changed out of her wet pants, putting on a pair of jeans. Then she flopped onto her bed and flipped through a magazine as she waited for Brandon. A few minutes later he appeared at the door, looking like a preppy schoolboy. The look didn't suit him, and he seemed uncomfortable in the clothes, but he was holding Jordan's guitar, which suited him just fine.

"Mind if I have a go?"

Ella nodded. "Jordan never touches it anymore."

Brandon sat on the edge of the bed and played a few notes.

"Your room looks different than I imagined," he said, strumming a melody Ella didn't recognize, something folksy.

"You thought it would be a science lab or something?" Ella joked.

"A lava lamp at least. Your room seems so . . . normal. There aren't any glow-in-the-dark stickers on your ceiling, even." Brandon looked around. "Wait, what's this?" He held up a glass tube with floating spheres in multiple colors. "It looks like floating eyeballs. You are Dr. Frankenstein. Don't try to deny it."

"You got me," Ella said. "Now would you like to hear the real answer?"

"Sure."

"It's a Galileo thermometer." Ella tapped the glass. "Do you see the numbers attached to the bottom of the spheres?" Ella pointed to the gold-colored tags. "The temperature is indicated by the spheres floating closest to the surface."

Brandon put down the thermometer. "Would have been more fun if it were eyeballs." He picked up a picture on her dresser. Ella was at Disney World, waiting in line for the Expedition Everest ride, a hat covering most of her face.

"You look different," Brandon observed.

"I should hope so. I was thirteen in that picture."

"No, I meant you looked relaxed."

"Well, I thought I had it all figured out at thirteen. I was going to be one of the few Broadway stars with a medical degree."

"Well, I was going to be a rodeo star. I had a great name picked out too—Handy Brandy."

"That is quite a name," Ella said, suppressing a giggle.

"It sounded cool at seven," Brandon defended himself. He

stopped strumming, turning to Ella. "You play?"

"No," Ella said firmly.

"Let me teach you the chords," Brandon offered, holding out the guitar.

"I don't think that's a good idea. I'm hopeless at learning music." Ella pushed the guitar back towards Brandon.

"If you can quote me theories in physics, you can learn a few chords," Brandon said. He inched closer to her, placing her right hand up at the guitar neck and her left hand on the strings.

Brandon showed her the keys C, E, G, D, F, A. Ella missed a few notes at first but quickly got the hang of it.

Ella's cell rang, startling her. Reaching for the phone, she whacked Brandon in the chin with the neck of the guitar. Her hands flew to her mouth as Brandon's hands went to his chin.

"I'm so sorry," she said, horrified.

Brandon took his hand away, revealing a small trickle of blood. Ella flew up.

"Do you want ice?" Ella asked.

"I think I'll live."

Ella inspected the wound. It was shallow, but a bruise was forming on his chin.

"I'll get ice," Ella said. Brandon caught her arm.

"It's all right. I'll be fine." He pulled Ella back down.

"I'm a bit of a klutz." Ella's cheeks flushed pink.

"A bit?" Brandon arched a brow. "Your hands work independently of your brain."

Ella deserved that; her hands did whatever they wanted most of the time. Brandon's eyes fell to hers, and Ella noticed he was still holding her arm. Her spine tingled. Very slowly, Brandon leaned forward, and the tingle in her spine exploded into flames. His nose was inches from hers.

"You're right, Ella," Brandon whispered. "I don't love Ranny."

Brandon inched his mouth closer to hers. Ella closed her eyes and waited for the sweetest kiss she could ever imagine.

"Ella," her mother called. Ella jerked her head up, and Brandon pulled away. "Ella!" her mother called up the stairs. "Chelsey is trying to reach you."

Ella picked up the phone, seeing three missed texts from Chelsey.

She dialed her sister, snapping, "What?" when she answered.

"Wow, did I catch you during Nova again?" Chelsey replied, sounding a bit taken aback. Little did Chelsey know she had just interrupted something way more exciting.

"What do you need?" Ella asked, impatience in her voice.

"I still need to perfect that hairstyle for my customer's wedding. Can you come by the salon?"

A hairdo? I just missed the greatest kiss of my life because of hair?

"Chelsey, I'm not your play doll on call 24/7," Ella muttered.

"Please, I really need to impress this client. Besides, what's so important that you can't spare an hour of your afternoon?"

Ella sighed, all the oxygen sucked out of the moment. "I'll be there soon."

She turned back to Brandon; his eyes were on the floor.

"I'm sorry, I have to go," Ella said.

"I should get back to the horses," Brandon said. "Still have to brush Glenn. Wish me luck."

"You'll need it," Ella replied.

There was silence between them.

"I'll get these clothes back to you on Monday?" Brandon said.

Ella nodded.

Brandon hurried out of the room. Ella heard the back door open, and the crunch of gravel as Brandon made his way back to the barn. She placed a hand on her lips. Why did Chelsey have to call and ruin everything?

Ella drove to the salon, thinking of how close Brandon had been to her. There was no denying it—there was something between them.

# CHAPTER 25

IT WAS MARCH Madness at Dellpine Academy, and not just because of NCAA basketball championships. College acceptance letters were coming in. Students were constantly checking their emails. No one was surprised to hear Barry had been accepted into Harvard, but everyone was surprised to hear Stefan was accepted to Yale. A great accomplishment, considering he only turned in half of his assignments.

Ella was studying in the library when she heard shrieking out in the hall. The library door swung open and Maria waved her phone at Ella, her face glowing. Ella pushed back her chair and rushed to Maria as fast as her leg allowed. She threw her arms around her best friend.

"Will you please take your fête outside?" The librarian hissed, glaring at the pair. The girls left the library and resumed their celebration.

"I knew you could do it," Ella said, giving Maria another big hug.

"They offered me a full scholarship," Maria said. Ella grasped Maria's hand, squealing even louder.

"I just hope you'll still talk to your common friends after you become famous," Ella joked.

Maria pushed Ella. "Of course I will!"

Denzel came down the hall, carrying his blue duffel around his shoulder.

"Denz!" Maria shouted as she ran to him. She whispered something into his ear.

"No way," Denzel cried, spinning her around.

Ella smiled as she watched them. If anyone deserved to hear such good news, it was Maria. Ella remembered how the girls had snubbed Maria when she first joined Dellpine in middle school, counting her out. Now Maria was going to Syball.

As Ella made her way to her locker, she saw Brittany taking out books. James stood behind her. Neither of them looked happy.

"You told me you would apply to Tulane," Brittany wailed, her shoulders hunched in disappointment.

"I never said I was going to college," James defended himself. "My latest album went platinum. I'm going on a world tour this summer."

"Well, you will be going alone." Brittany slammed her locker door shut.

"Like you can't be replaced," James hissed, his eyes like two frozen peas. He had gelled his hair into spikes again; it reminded Ella of a bulldog collar. Ella knew better than to think they were having the final fight. James and Brittany were always threatening to break up with each other. They would be making out by their lockers at the end of the day, like always. Some relationships ran on trust, but James and Brittany's relationship ran on drama.

Ella waited for an email from Johns Hopkins. She received acceptance letters to all her backup schools—schools Ella didn't want to attend. Would they be her only choice?

Another week went by, and still nothing. Ella received an email from Willie. He sent a picture of himself and Amanda standing by a sparkling riverbank surrounded by greenery. They were in Missouri Headwaters State Park in Montana. The pair had succeeded in traveling to over twenty state parks so far. Their goal was to see them all.

At least someone is living their dream, Ella thought. Each passing day, Ella's hope sank further and further down the drain. John Hopkins should have posted their admissions decisions. Maybe she was just waiting to hear bad news.

That evening, her mother made a family favorite, fried chicken with mashed potatoes. Chelsey had called to say she was missing dinner. Ella knew it was a matter of time before Chelsey got her own place. Mom and Chelsey were always bickering, and Chelsey made more and more excuses to be absent from the house.

"Well, tomorrow is the big day," Dad said, taking some fried chicken.

"Big day?" Ella asked.

"Jordan's court case starts tomorrow," Mom said as she spooned mashed potatoes onto her plate.

"Are you picking up Jordan from the airport, Dad?"

"No," Dad replied. "Richard said defendants do not have to be present in civil cases. We see no reason for Jordan to interrupt his schooling."

"Will I be testifying?" Ella dreaded the answer.

"I'm afraid so," Dad said, reaching for his glass of water. "Mr. Bailey will be by this week to discuss your testimony."

Lucky me, Ella thought bitterly, the fried chicken suddenly dry and gritty in her mouth. This trial is really happening. It brought back all kinds of repressed thoughts Ella didn't wish to have.

Was she still mad at Jordan for causing the accident? Could she let the past go? Maybe Brandon was right; maybe there was a reason for all this. Maybe it was time to let the pain of the past be buried once and for all.

"Repeat after me," Mr. Bailey said. "Keep it to yourself. Never give effusive answers. This is a courtroom, not a talk show." Ella and Mr. Bailey had been sitting at the kitchen table for what felt like hours. Mr. Bailey was determined that she wouldn't sink the trial a second time.

Ella looked out the kitchen window, distracted by the pretty sunset covering the sky. A whole Sunday wasted thanks to this stupid trial.

"Ella, did you hear me?" Mr. Bailey asked.

"I'll only say what you tell me to," Ella groaned.

"Good," Mr. Bailey said, glancing over his yellow notepad, sliding a hand over his balding head—an old habit, Ella guessed, from when he had hair. "You will be asked about the events of the accident," Mr. Bailey went on. "Do you remember how to respond?"

"I say the facts as I remember them and do not add any theatrics," Ella said in a monotone.

"Very good," Mr. Bailey said. "Now, we will practice a new question. Please tell us how your life has been since the accident?"

Ella pursed her lips before giving the rehearsed answer. "I am able to participate in most activities."

"Most?" Mr. Bailey questioned.

Ella glared at him.

"Good enough," Mr. Bailey replied, seeing her stony expression. "Well, Ella, I think you are ready." Mr. Bailey clicked open his briefcase and stuck the yellow notepad inside.

"Do you think we will win?" Mom asked as she placed fudge brownies on the table.

Mr. Bailey helped himself to a brownie. "If I were a gambling man—which I am—I would say, most assuredly."

Mom relaxed her cheeks and smiled. "I'm glad to hear it."

Ella took a brownie. It was chewy with small chunks of mint chocolate. Just what she needed after the grueling afternoon with Mr. Bailey.

The following week, Ella learned that Jordan would be coming home after all. Mr. Bailey told her parents that Jordan's absence was creating a sense of distrust amongst the jurors. It was decided that Jordan would be present for the rest of the trial.

Ella found she was looking forward to seeing him. They had gotten closer after New Year's, sharing emails and the occasional picture. Ella spoke with Jordan more in the last few months than she had spoken with him in the last three years.

When Jordan arrived home, he plopped his suitcase on the kitchen floor and headed straight for the couch.

"How was the flight?" Ella asked, taking a seat next to him.

"I sat between a man who snored like a motorboat and a mother holding a crying baby. How do you think it went?" Jordan rested his head against the wall, his arms lifeless at his side.

"Were the pretzels decent at least?"

"The crackers they gave us were okay."

"How is Shelby?"

"She's good—looking after the dog."

"The dog?" Ella raised a brow.

"Yeah, a little West Highland terrier named Sashie."

"Mom's first grandchild," Ella cooed.

"Stop it, Ella," Jordan said, not bothering to open his eyes.

"Do you have a picture of Sashie?"

"Yeah, on my phone."

"Can I see it?"

"Maybe tomorrow. I'm going to bed." Jordan slid off the couch, his chestnut hair limp from the plane.

"Tomorrow I want to see pictures of my niece pup!" Ella hollered after him.

The next day, Ella found Jordan eating cereal in his pajamas.

"You're up early," Ella observed. "Having jet lag?"

"Haha," Jordan replied, taking a bite of his cereal. He swallowed. "Did you see what Chelsey's date did to the front gate?"

"No."

"Reversed into it, made a big dent, broke a couple of the bars."

"Geez." Ella winced. "I bet Mom and Dad aren't too pleased."

"I could hear Mom complaining about it to Dad last night," said Jordan. "How did you miss the sound of crunching metal?"

"I'm a sound sleeper," Ella answered.

She looked at the wall clock. Seven thirty; she had to get going. "I'm off," Ella said, placing her bowl in the sink.

"Bye," said Jordan, glancing at the morning paper. Ella reached in the fridge for her lunch, then gave Jordan a kiss on the cheek. "Save your kisses for your boyfriend," he said, rubbing off her kiss with the palm of his hand.

"I don't have a boyfriend."

"You do," Jordan insisted. "Mom tells me how you and Brandon hang out all the time. Oh, and warn him that I have a clear shot of the stables from the kitchen and nothing to do all day but watch the two of you."

Ella rolled her eyes, placing her lunch in her bag. "Send me a picture of Sashie," she commanded as she headed out the garage door. It was sweet, Jordan feeling the need to protect her. The old Jordan had never cared.

"You ready for the trial tomorrow?" Maria asked, standing next to Ella by the lockers.

"No," Ella groaned. She placed her French vocab book into her bag.

"Well, have no worries because I will be in the audience to support you," said Maria.

"You will?" Ella said happily.

"Yup," Maria replied. "The school granted me special permission to attend the trial."

Ella hugged Maria, feeling her worries disappear. But by the end of the day, Ella was nervous again. Maria was acting sluggish, not her usual peppy self. Worse, she was complaining of a headache. Ella hoped Maria would feel better by tomorrow. She really needed her best friend.

At the stables, Ella helped Brandon wash the horses. Glenn was not cooperating. He kicked over the bucket of soapy water Brandon had prepared. Dusty let Ella wash him, taking the sponge bath like a champ.

"You know, the front of your gate is broken," Brandon said, refilling the bucket Glenn knocked over.

"Chelsey's date hit it with his car," Ella replied. "Mom is trying to find a repairman to fix it."

Brandon grinned. "I'm guessing there was no second date."

"I doubt it."

"Hear anything from West Point yet?" Ella asked, rubbing down Dusty's hind legs.

"No," Brandon said, but his mouth twisted to the side, making Ella wonder.

"Have you thought of a backup plan?" said Ella. The brochure in his room came to her mind.

"If I don't get accepted, I'm still planning to enlist. I just won't be an officer."

"Any interest in the Navy?"

Brandon turned to her, looking puzzled. "Why do you ask?"

"I was just wondering." Ella shrugged. She didn't want to give away the fact she had gone snooping in Brandon's room.

"Ah!" Brandon shouted, jumping away from Glenn. Ella looked to see Glenn relieving himself in the hay, nearly hitting Brandon's boot. "You just won't give me a break today, now will you?" Brandon shook his head at Glenn.

Ella laughed. Glenn sure knew how to be impossible when he set his mind to it.

Brandon raked up the pile of urine-soaked hay and went to get a fresh batch. Ella continued washing Dusty, making sure to clean his belly. A burst of hay flew into her face, making her sputter and spit. She pulled straw out of her mouth, her hair covered in golden stubble. Brandon whistled as he tossed hay on the ground, acting like nothing happened.

Ella thought of ways to get revenge. She gauged the distance between her and the garden hose. As if he had read her mind, Brandon leaped towards the hose, guarding it with his back. She kicked herself for being too slow.

Then she saw the bucket of soapy water in the corner and made her way towards it. Brandon caught her around the waist. "Don't even think about it," he warned. Ella wasn't sure what to do now; she couldn't pull the leg trick again, could she? Thinking fast, she reached for Brandon's stomach and tickled him. Brandon released her instantly and Ella darted away. But she didn't see the stool in front of her. Tripping, Ella landed on her face, her hands stretched out in front of her.

"You deserved that," Brandon called down.

Ella looked around, deliberating how to get back up. She pushed away from the ground and felt something furry beneath her right palm. Scared to think of what she was touching, Ella removed her hand. A small ball of brown fur scurried across the barn, headed for Glenn's hooves. Ella froze as Glenn thrashed around her. A white hoof lashed out in her direction. She covered her head with her hands, waiting for the painful blow. But instead of pain, Ella felt a strong tug on her legs dragging her back to safety.

"Did Glenn get you?" Brandon asked, clearly worried.

"Nope, just missed me," Ella said. She sat up. "I could have been killed." Ella's heart thumped loudly. Can he hear it?

"We're both lucky," Brandon said, offering her his hand.

They finished working in silence. As they were about to leave the barn, a giant gray dog jumped into the freshly strewn hay, rolling around by Ella's feet.

"I see the wolf dog is back," said Brandon.

"What are you doing here, boy?" Ella asked, petting Otis's head.

"Otis!" Ella heard Mrs. Lowell call.

"Here he is," Ella called back, bringing him out of the barn.

"Your gate is broken," Mrs. Lowell said, her arms crossed over her neon sports top.

"Yeah," Ella replied. Why do people feel the need to state the obvious?

"Tell your father to drive slower," Mrs. Lowell advised. "Come on, Otis." She reached out for Otis's leash without a word of thanks.

"And tell your dermatologist that plumb-sized lips aren't good for making sour faces," Ella muttered when she was sure Ros was out of earshot. The Lowells had been nothing but nasty since Mom spoke to them about Shane.

"Dinner," Mom called from the garage door.

Ella walked back towards the house, wondering if it was kidnapping to take a dog that willingly came into their yard. She saw Brandon at his truck.

"You're going?" Ella asked.

"It seems to be supper time," Brandon replied.

"Stay for dinner. My mom made sweet and sour meatballs. You'll be sorry if you miss them."

"I don't know . . ."

"You saved my life. The least I can do is invite you to dinner."

"I didn't actually save your life. Glenn was farther away than I realized."

"It's the thought that counts. Now, are you coming, or do I need Glenn to give you a kick?"

Brandon laughed and followed Ella through the garage door into the kitchen.

# CHAPTER 26

"MOM, BRANDON WILL be joining us for dinner," Ella said.

"Wonderful," said Mom, glancing up from the stove. "Ella, get an extra place setting from the cupboard." Mom brought the pot of sizzling meatballs to the table while Ella handed Brandon silverware and a plate.

"These smell really good," Brandon said, digging a fork into a meatball after he'd taken a seat.

"Glad you like them," Mom replied. "There's also rice and salad. Ella, pass Brandon the rice bowl."

"You don't eat meatballs with spaghetti?" Brandon whispered to Ella.

"They're sweet and sour meatballs," Ella whispered back. "They go better with rice."

"Hey, Brandon," Jordan said as he joined them at the table.

"Hey," Brandon mumbled, his mouth full. He swallowed and repeated the greeting in a clearer voice.

"You didn't send me a picture of Sashie." Ella waved a fork at Jordan.

"Who is Sashie?" Mom asked, ladling meatballs onto a plate.

"My dog," Jordan replied before taking the outstretched plate from Mom.

"When did you decide to get a dog?"

"Shelby's good friend got her before she knew her boyfriend was allergic. So, she had to give it away. Shelby always wanted a dog and so we decided to take Sashie in."

"I would love a dog." Mom sighed. "But instead I have horses." She glared at Dad as he joined the dinner table.

"There's no reason we can't have both," Ella pointed out.

Mom shook her head. "Too many animals."

"Brandon," Dad said, shrugging off Mom's jab about the horses. "What a nice surprise. I bet you came for the meatballs. They're the best in town." He winked at Mom.

"They are, sir," Brandon replied.

Mom blushed. "Please have more." She held out a hand for Brandon's empty plate. He passed her his dish for a second helping.

"Oh, and Brandon," Dad said, spooning salad onto his plate, "I haven't forgotten about our discussion. I wrote Rick an email this morning."

"Thank you, sir," Brandon said before taking another bite.

"Call me Sam," Dad replied. "This isn't the 1800s, you know."

Brandon and Ella's eyes met. They both laughed.

"What?" Jordan asked, looking between them.

"Inside joke," Ella replied.

"So, why do you need my father to talk to the governor?" Jordan said to Brandon.

"Jordan, keep your eyes forward," Dad ordered.

Jordan turned his face down to his plate. The table was quiet, except for the sound of chewing.

"How's Chris?" Jordan asked Brandon.

Ella exhaled, glad her brother had thought of something to say.

"Good," Brandon said. "At least he was this morning."

"Chris and I talked about having a shooting lesson when I was at your house," Jordan said. "Do you think he has any spare time this week?"

"He's at the shooting range until 9," Brandon said. "I'll ask him if he has any cancellations."

"Let's go after dinner," Jordan offered. "If he can't teach me, I'm sure you can show me a few pointers." He turned to Ella. "Mind if I borrow your car?"

"You're not coming?" Brandon asked in surprise.

"I have a Calculus test to study for," Ella said, wishing she could go.

After dinner, Brandon thanked Mom as Jordan grabbed the car keys from a hook on the wall.

"My pleasure," Mom answered, spooning the leftover meatballs into a container. "You know you can join us for dinner any time you wish. And, Jordan . . . don't stay out too late. We have to be at the courthouse at 8 AM tomorrow."

"What am I, five?" Jordan muttered to Ella.

Ella laughed. Her mother would never see them as anything but her helpless children. Ella wished Brandon a good night before making her way up the stairs. Even though she couldn't go, she liked the idea of her brother spending time with Brandon. It had been nice having Brandon sit next to her at the table, like he was a part of the family. Something was happening between them—Ella could feel it. If only Ranny would get out of the way, they could be together.

That night Ella tried hard to get some sleep, but her body trembled every time she thought of taking the witness stand the next day. Brandon had helped push the trial from Ella's mind for a while, but anxiety brought it back.

She thought long and hard about the accident. Do I forgive Jordan? Did I want to sabotage his trial for the second time? Ella stared at the clock; it was past midnight. She heard Jordan on the phone talking to Shelby in his room.

"Hey, Shells, how's the dog? No way. I can't wait to see her roll over on command." Ella thought of a little white dog rolling over in the grass. The image was too precious for words.

"I went out with Ella's boyfriend this evening."

He is not my boyfriend, Ella wanted to shout down the hall.

"Total badass," Jordan went on. "He can shoot almost any kind of rifle and reload his magazine in, like, two seconds." There was a pause. "The magazine is where bullets are kept," Jordan explained. "No, not Chelsey. I said E-l-l-a; it's Ella's boyfriend . . . Ella can so handle badass. She is much tougher than people give her credit for."

Ella wondered why Jordan kept calling Brandon her boyfriend. She had told her brother several times that he wasn't. It just wasn't sinking in.

Still, Ella had heard all she needed to hear. She finally rested her head on the pillow, at peace with the coming day. She hoped for sweet dreams about horses and her stable boy. Instead, she dreamed of twelve stern faces and words leaving her mouth she never intended to say.

The courtroom seemed so stiff and condemnatory. Ella was nervous; she was worried about saying too much; she was worried she might cry. Jordan looked no better than she felt. His freshly pressed navy suit was not able to hide his pale face and trembling hands.

Ella took her place next to her parents in the pews behind Mr. Bailey and Jordan. Mr. Bailey looked distinguished in a sharp green suit and a crimson tie. He joked with Jordan, offering him Valium to calm his shaking. The jokes slid off Jordan's back. He looked like he was waiting to be executed.

Ella felt her own hands start to quake. She craned her neck to see if Maria was at the courthouse yet. Ella's cell phone rang.

Maria sounded terrible. "Ella, I'm so sorry, I can't make it. My throat is on fire and my head feels like someone's trying to get out of it." Ella's heart sank. She had hoped her friend would bounce back; she had been really counting on her support, but she knew Maria would be here if she could.

"Feel better," Ella said.

"Thanks," Maria croaked.

"No cell phones allowed during court," said a stern voice. The Honorable Judge Foxworth had arrived and was taking her position. She had a severe face—so severe Ella was sure it could send the Grim Reaper running. Ella put her cell phone away, the day already off to a bad start.

The judge looked down at her papers and gripped a pen with her bony hand. She wore no makeup, her hair pulled securely into a bun. Ella looked for a ring on the judge's left hand and was surprised to see a large and stylish diamond sparkling in the fluorescent lighting of the courtroom. The judge was someone's sweetheart, which made Ella relax a little.

"Would the plaintiff like to call their first witness?" the judge asked, placing down her pen with a thud.

"We would, Your Honor," said the Martins' lawyer, getting to his feet. Mr. Kaufman had sandy gray hair and a wide nose. He looked like most of his authority came from his designer suit. "We would like to call Mrs. Sandra Martin to the stand."

Mrs. Martin walked slowly to the stand. The first thing that Ella noticed was how glamorous she appeared. She was in a suit the color of eggplants, with matching pumps, looking like a talk show host with her dark hair perfectly blow-dried and her garnet studs sparkling boldly in her ears. She took the oath and sat.

"Mrs. Martin, please tell the court what happened the night of August the 25th," Mr. Kaufman said.

"I had just come home from the pottery class I teach at the rec center," she began. "I have also started a pottery line called Make Your Own—"

"Objection, relevance," Mr. Bailey squawked.

"Sustained," said the judge. "Mrs. Martin, please only give details relevant to the case."

Mrs. Martin looked affronted but went on. "I came back from

my pottery class and found my husband lying on the kitchen floor."
She took a tissue from her pocket, her voice increasing a few octaves.
"I found Fred lying on the floor. He was unconscious. He had taken
pills—arsenic trioxide they were called. I knew he was unhappy, but
suicide? I never thought."

"Did your husband ever express feelings of depression?" Mr.
Kaufman asked gently, his tone sympathetic.

"My husband was a strong man, a proud man. He never
complained. The accident ruined him. He was never the same after
it. It was like a cloud of despair hung over him. My husband loved to
cycle; he was training for a triathlon at the time of the accident. After
the accident, he became helpless. Like a mother, I had to do everything
for him. He could not handle this new life. Always being in pain."

"Do you believe, Mrs. Martin, if the accident had not occurred,
your husband would still be alive?" Mr. Kaufman asked.

"Yes," Mrs. Martin said confidently. Then she turned to Jordan.
"You are a murderer. You should be rotting in jail. You should have
never been allowed your freedom."

The judge banged her gavel. "Mrs. Martin, I will ask you to
restrain yourself."

Jordan looked like her words had thrashed him, his teal eyes wide
and frightened.

"No further questions," Mr. Kaufman said, taking his seat.

"Would the defense like to cross-examine the witness?" the judge
asked.

"We would, Your Honor," Mr. Bailey said, rising. The jury looked
like they had just seen a documentary about abused children. Some
gave Jordan disparaging glances.

"Mrs. Martin," Mr. Bailey said. "Let me first give you my
condolences. You have suffered a great loss, and you have my deepest
sympathy."

"I don't want your sympathy, you slug!" Mrs. Martin cried. Mr.
Bailey looked to the judge expectantly. The judge looked back at him.

It seemed she was going to let Mrs. Martin's comment slide.

"You said your husband died of arsenic trioxide poisoning?" Mr. Bailey went on.

"Yes, I've already said that. Pay attention."

"Were you aware, Mrs. Martin, that the drug is only available in injectable form and can't be administered orally?"

"I was not aware," Mrs. Martin said simply.

"So, your husband could not have taken arsenic trioxide pills," Mr. Bailey pointed out.

"Pills, bottles—the point is, I found my husband dead."

"Can you explain to the court how your husband obtained a vial of arsenic trioxide when his doctor never prescribed it?" Mr. Bailey asked.

Mrs. Martin did not miss a beat. "The doctor did prescribe it, and I think he should lose his license."

"I have spoken to your husband's doctor and the ER doctor who serviced him. He was not dead when you found him, as you stated—your husband died at the hospital, approximately three hours after being admitted. Both doctors informed me you have tried to sue them as well—unsuccessfully, I might add. They would never prescribe arsenic trioxide, because it is a drug used to cure patients with acute leukemia, cholera, and cardiac arrhythmias. All diseases your husband did not have."

"Objection, speculative," Mr. Kaufman said. "Mrs. Martin is not a doctor and should not have to discuss her husband's medical history."

"Overruled," the judge said.

Mrs. Martin shimmied her shoulders before replying, "I don't know what to say. I was never asked a question; I was rambled at."

Mr. Bailey wiped his damp forehead and let out a deep sigh. "Mrs. Martin, your husband had four times the recommended dosage of arsenic trioxide in his postmortem toxicology report. Records show your son was put in jail just a few months ago, and the charges were for drug possession. It seems he was selling prescription drugs just like the one found in your husband's body. Do you think it is possible your son was the one who gave Fred the vials of arsenic trioxide?"

"How dare you!" Mrs. Martin screeched, her eyes blazing with anger. "My son's case is being appealed—he will be found innocent!"

"There was evidence found in your son's home. Over twenty boxes of prescription drugs in both pill form and in vials."

"Objection. Mrs. Martin's son is not the one being tried," Mr. Kaufman said.

"Sustained," the judge replied.

"Your Honor, I feel it is imperative that we establish a reason why the Martins were in possession of arsenic trioxide," Mr. Bailey pleaded.

"Then ask your witness," the judge hissed, her red eyes looking like they would burst into flames at any moment. Ella wondered how the lawyers could remain so calm with a judge looking like the devil.

"Mrs. Martin, why would your husband be in possession of arsenic trioxide?" Mr. Bailey asked. "Did he have cancer?"

"He did not," Mrs. Martin replied.

"You mean to tell me you didn't notice vials of arsenic trioxide in the bathroom or bedside table?"

"Objection," Mr. Kaufman said. "Calls for speculation."

"No, it doesn't," Mr. Bailey thundered at Mr. Kaufman.

"It does," Mr. Kaufman fired back.

"Gentlemen." The judge banged her gavel. "I will decide what is acceptable and what is not. Mr. Kaufman, your objection is sustained."

Mr. Bailey looked frustrated but undeterred.

"I see your granddaughter died of a heart disorder in the summer of 2016," he said, moving to a different topic. "Your husband was very close to this granddaughter, was he not?"

"Yes," Mrs. Martin said. "Very close." More tears came to her eyes.

"Did you and your husband take your granddaughter on a trip to Disney World, a trip her doctors advised you not to take her on?"

"Sally deserved some happiness before she died," Mrs. Martin protested.

"Your granddaughter died two weeks after the trip, the cause being heart failure due to taxation."

Mrs. Martin wept openly. "I tried to tell Fred not to take her, but he wanted to make her happy. He loved Sally so much."

"Perhaps your husband's depression was caused by the loss of his granddaughter," Mr. Bailey said gently.

Mrs. Martin didn't respond, tears of mascara falling down her cheeks.

"No further questions, Your Honor," Mr. Bailey murmured. Mrs. Martin started sobbing like a baby on the stand, her hands covering her face.

"The witness may step down," the judge said. Mrs. Martin dabbed at her eyes with a tissue before standing up. She was decidedly less composed than when she first ascended the stand.

"Does the plaintiff have any more witnesses they wish to call?" the judge asked.

"We do, Your Honor," said Mr. Kaufman, jumping to his feet. "We would like to call Miss Gabriella Heart."

# CHAPTER 27

ELLA'S HEARTBEAT QUICKENED. For a moment she thought she would get away with not testifying. It seemed she wouldn't be so lucky. The jury looked passive as she made her way to the stand. After she had been sworn in, she sat in the witness box. Jordan looked like a scared guppy, his cheeks clenched, his face conveying sheer discomfort.

"Please state your relation to the defendant," Mr. Kaufman said. Ella looked at Mr. Bailey. He nodded in encouragement.

"Jordan is my brother," said Ella.

"Can you please tell the courts what happened the night of May 15th, 2014?"

Ella took a breath. "My brother ran a red light and a car slammed into my side."

"Was Jordan drunk at the time?" Mr. Kaufman asked.

Ella hesitated before replying with the rehearsed answer. "I don't know."

"A breathalyzer test was taken at the accident and Jordon was found to be over the limit," Mr. Kaufman said, addressing the jury.

"Objection," Mr. Bailey said.

"Overruled," the judge bellowed. Mr. Bailey's mouth pursed as he sat back down.

Mr. Kaufman tried to swallow his grin. He turned back to Ella. "Ms. Heart, how does the accident your brother caused affect your daily living?"

"I am able to manage most activities independently," Ella answered in the same monotone she had practiced. Mr. Bailey gave her a nod of approval.

"You were registered for dance camp the summer you were injured," Mr. Kaufman went on. "Your friend Maria Garcia took your spot instead. I understand that Maria did so well that the manager of the camp helped her receive a scholarship for further lessons."

"Objection, relevance?" Mr. Bailey said loudly.

"Sustained," the judge said.

Mr. Kaufman smoothed the front of his suit, composing himself. Ella wondered how long he had been practicing law. His thinning hair indicated decades; however, his temples were damp, and he was nibbling on his index finger. Ella had never seen an experienced lawyer eat at his fingers in a courtroom.

"How did it feel when your classmates nicknamed you Mr. Peanut and Mr. Scrooge because of your walking stick?" Mr. Kaufman asked.

Ella felt her cheeks redden. How did he know?

"Objection, badgering the witness," Mr. Bailey called out.

"Overruled," the judge said.

Ella froze. Her heart felt like it was trying to sprint out of her chest, deserting her in her time of need.

"Would you like me to repeat the question?" Mr. Kaufman asked her. Ella noticed his confidence had returned.

"It was painful," said Ella honestly.

"Your brother narrowly escaped a ten-year jail sentence," Mr. Kaufman went on. "Do you really feel justice was served? A man was crippled with arthritis, your right leg shattered—two severe injuries while your brother walks free and fit. Deep down, you know your brother will never change. Neither will your ability to live the life you were meant to."

"Objection!" Mr. Bailey said angrily.

"Sustained." The judge wagged a firm finger at Mr. Kaufman. "Watch yourself."

"Miss Heart has not answered my question," Mr. Kaufman reminded the judge.

Ella's hands trembled. The moment of truth had arrived. She turned towards Jordan. He looked in agony. Ella knew he had been punished enough. Guilt could be a cage, and it seemed he would be forever trapped within its bars.

"I forgive you, Jordan," Ella blurted out.

"That was not the question," Mr. Kaufman said sternly.

"But it is your question," Ella said. She felt her family's eyes on her. "And the answer is—I forgive him. He made a mistake, a terrible one. But punishing him more will not bring Mr. Martin back or fix my leg. It will simply take another life. Jordan has changed, and at least one of us should be able to live the life they were meant to have."

The judge banged the gavel. "No one asked you to give a sermon, Miss Heart." She turned to Mr. Kaufman. "Do you have any further question for the witness?"

"None at this time," Mr. Kaufman grumbled, his lips puckering. The trial seemed to be slipping away from him.

"Mr. Bailey, your witness." The judge waved her hand in Ella's direction.

"Miss Heart, how has your brother's behavior changed since the accident?" Mr. Bailey asked.

"He is more cautious when he drives," Ella answered, glad the difficult part of her testimony was over.

"Isn't it true he has not had one beer since the accident?"

"To the best of my knowledge."

"Do you feel your brother has learned from his mistakes?"

Ella looked directly at Jordan. "Yes."

"No further questions, Your Honor," Mr. Bailey said.

"Very well," the judge said, following up with the words Ella had longed to hear ever since she entered the courtroom: "Miss Heart, you may step down."

"How did you think we did?" Dad asked Mr. Bailey as they walked out into the lobby.

"I think we are closer than ever to securing the not liable verdict," Mr. Bailey crooned. "Ella, I have to hand it to you. You said exactly enough. Thanks to your testimony, I foresee this trial being over in a matter of days. The opposition has nothing left."

On the way home, Ella sat next to Jordan in the backseat of their father's Jaguar. Dad turned on some soft rock. Mom looked at her cell phone, checking for missed calls.

"Is Brandon coming over today?" Jordan asked Ella.

"Not today," Ella replied. "Why do you ask?"

"I had a question for him about one of the rifles Chris showed me," Jordan replied. "I still can't believe you're dating such a badass. I always thought you would be into a nerdier type."

"I'm not dating him," Ella said, hoping this time Jordan would get it.

"Yeah, yeah." Jordan didn't look convinced. Then his expression became serious. "Did you mean what you said?" Jordan asked, his eyes an ocean of sorrow. "You forgive me?"

"Yes," Ella said.

"I don't deserve your forgiveness."

"Don't be a drama queen."

Jordan smiled, turning back to the window. Dad sang along with the radio—loudly. Clearly Ella got her singing inability from both parents.

Jordan covered his ears. "Jeez, Dad, I'm getting a headache."

"Can't hear you, son," Dad said and turned up the music, singing louder. Mom turned down the volume to make a call. Ella was grateful to not have to shout over the music.

"Jordan, please listen to me," Ella begged. "You are not responsible for Fred Martin's death." She needed Jordan to believe her.

Jordan didn't respond; he just looked out the window. Perhaps he hadn't heard her.

"Jordan," she tried again.

"I heard you, Ella," Jordan said, his blue eyes darkening. "The problem is—I am guilty."

"No, you're not. How many times can you be punished for the same mistake?"

"Some mistakes can't be undone," Jordan said. "I can be sorry all day that I ate the meatballs left out last night. Won't change the fact that my stomach is in agony."

"Why would you do that?" Ella asked in astonishment. "You can get salmonella poisoning, and I suspect you already have malaise."

Jordan winced in pain. "What else do you want to quote me from the medical book I gave you?"

Ella grinned. "How much time do you have?"

"Dad," Jordan said, clutching his stomach. "I think we need to stop the car."

Dad got off at the next exit and pulled into a gas station. Jordan hopped out and rushed to the restroom. He came back a few moments later, his face less green.

"Success?" Ella asked.

"Yup, I just hope there are no more meatballs to discard."

When they reached the house, Ella had an overwhelming desire to see Brandon. He had told her she could come over anytime she pleased, and Ella wanted to tell him about the trial and how she had forgiven Jordan. She changed out of her gray suit and into more casual clothing. Then she drove to Brandon's house.

When she arrived, the blue-and-white truck was absent. Ella knocked on the screen door anyway. Maybe someone else was using the truck. Holley opened the door.

"Ella," she said happily, greeting her like an old friend. Ella hugged her back. She loved how happy Holley was to see her. But then again, Holley was a happy kid in general.

"Where's Brandon?" Ella asked. "I noticed the truck's gone."

"He's out with Ranny," Holley said. Ella's heart squeezed uncomfortably, her conscience yelling at her to leave with her dignity intact. But she ignored her conscience and decided to stay.

Little hands caught around her leg. Ella looked down to see Graham staring up at her. She scooped him up.

"Did you come to play with me?" Graham asked eagerly, his eyes hopeful.

"What do you want to play?" Ella asked.

"I got a new ball from the store. Let's play catch." He took her hand and led her out to the front yard. A red, plastic ball with a white star was on the porch swing. Graham picked up the ball and ran to the grass, and Ella followed him.

He threw the ball up, and Ella reached backwards and caught it. Graham squealed with delight. Back and forth the red ball went. A half hour later, Brandon pulled into the driveway. The windows of the truck were rolled down, and Ella saw Ranny pouting in the passenger seat. Brandon looked upset. "I know what I saw," Ella heard Brandon say to Ranny.

"You know what you think you saw," Ranny shot back.

Brandon got out of the car, not looking at Ranny. He went to Graham. "Hey, buddy, you playing catch?"

"She's playing with me." Graham motioned to Ella. She waved awkwardly.

"You can't just walk away from me. It's childish," Ranny said as she slammed the door of the truck. She was wearing her cheerleading uniform, looking painfully perfect. Ranny spotted Ella.

"What is she doing here?" Ranny pointed at Ella, fuming. Ella looked down, not knowing what to say.

"Graham, what did you do?" Brandon yelled, the cuff of his pant leg suddenly wet. Graham looked embarrassed. His own corduroy pants were soaked.

"Come on, let's take you to Momma. Uncle Brandon doesn't clean up wee." Brandon took Graham's hand and led him inside.

Ranny stomped over to Ella, her expression truly frightening.

"Why are you stalking my boyfriend?" she demanded.

"I'm not stalking him," Ella said. "I just came over to—"

"It's not enough that you have a big house and horses? Now you want my boyfriend?"

Ella didn't know what to say. She hugged herself, seeking comfort in this very uncomfortable situation.

Ranny took a breath, closing her eyes and opening them slowly. "Please go."

Ella wanted to protest, but she couldn't ignore the pleading in Ranny's gray eyes.

"Tell Brandon I'll see him at the stables," Ella said as she turned and headed for her car. She pulled out of the driveway just as Brandon returned to the yard. Ranny looked pleased with herself as she tried to distract Brandon by tugging on his shirt. Ella felt those hazel eyes watching her as she drove down Landcork Drive and away from the Cunninghams' home.

# CHAPTER 28

THURSDAY STARTED OFF on a positive note. Ella had received a ninety on a particularly challenging Calculus test. She also received a one hundred on a French paper she had written. During American Lit, Ella learned that she had scored the highest grade on the practice AP exam with a five out of five on all questions and essays.

Ella made her way to her locker, thinking of all the ways to celebrate when she got home. Brandon would be in the stables. Maybe she could think of a reason to invite him inside or perhaps join Jordan the next time he had a shooting lesson with Chris. Then Ella felt guilty, remembering what happened with Ranny earlier in the week. Brandon and I are just friends, Ella reasoned to herself. There was nothing wrong with being friends, right?

Ella found Brittany and Stefan smooching, blocking her locker. Brittany's hands were wrapped tightly around Stefan's back. Stefan's hands were not visible. Ella grimaced and wondered if she had missed the memo that Brittany and James had finally called it quits.

A furious James rounded on Brittany and Stefan.

"You bitch," James said, his face twisted with fury. It seemed James hadn't received the breakup memo either.

"Go away, James," Brittany said. "I told you it was over. I can kiss whoever I want now."

"I hope you are happy together," James said coolly. "You two losers deserve each other."

"I pity the next girl who goes out with you," Brittany shot back. "You are all wrapper and no treat."

"Like you're a picnic," James shot back. "Wish I could ski into a tree—then I wouldn't have to see your bird face scowling at me in the halls."

Brittany's mouth dropped in horror, and Stefan socked James in the stomach, knocking him to the ground.

"Go for the hair!" Brittany called, smirking from the sidelines. Stefan grabbed at James's hair, and his hand slid right off. He looked at his slimy hand and mouthed a soundless "eww." It was distracting enough for James to wrestle him to the floor.

"Never touch the hair," James warned before giving Stefan a good punch in the stomach.

"Break it up, boys!" It was Dr. Taylor. It was the first time Ella had ever heard Dr. Taylor shout. Stefan and James got to their feet and slowly backed away from each other, their eyes still locked in battle. Dr. Taylor turned to Ella. "May I see you for a moment?"

Ella followed her to the science room and took a seat, but Dr. Taylor remained standing, leaning against her desk.

"You were right, Ella," Dr. Taylor said. "That tissue sample you checked a few weeks ago was not cancerous." Ella exhaled. She had been summoned for a positive reason. With Dr. Taylor, it was hard to tell.

"I stand by what I said," Dr. Taylor went on. "You are young and have a lot to learn. However, I feel I must give credit where credit should be given. I passed by Mrs. Pierce's office. It appears the John Hopkins admissions decision site is up. Shall we take a look together?" She indicated the classroom computer.

Ella's veins turned to ice. The moment of truth had arrived. Ella went to the website and shut her eyes.

"Go on," Dr. Taylor encouraged. "Open your eyes. Read it."

Ella blinked at the screen and in just one word she had her answer. "I got in!" she shrieked. Her hands shook from the rush of the moment.

Dr. Taylor put her arm around Ella's shoulders. "I'm so proud of you."

"Maybe I can do this; maybe I can be a doctor," Ella said, her head soaring to cloud nine.

"I have no doubt," Dr. Taylor said reassuringly.

"What about my leg?" Ella said, anxiety suddenly taking hold of her. "Will I be able to keep up with all the walking up and down the hospital wards? What if people don't want a disabled doctor?"

"Calm down, Ella," Dr. Taylor instructed. "People were not always keen on having an African-American scientist work in their lab. I had many internships fall through when they saw I was a black woman. I had two choices; I could let them win and pick a different profession, or I could look them in the eyes and tell them to stuff it. Guess which option I chose?"

Ella smiled at hearing her teacher, one of the most intelligent people she knew, use the words "stuff it."

"There will always be people telling you what you should do," Dr. Taylor said. "You have to learn to push back, and politely tell people to—"

"Stuff it," Ella finished Dr. Taylor's sentence.

"Now you're getting the hang of it," Dr. Taylor said, a smile lighting her naturally stern face.

"I'm not good at confrontation," Ella said glumly.

"The only way to improve is to practice," Dr. Taylor replied. "Now, run on home and make your parents ecstatic with the good news."

Without hesitation, Ella rushed straight to her car, turned up the volume as high as she could bear, and drove home to share her announcement.

"Mom, Mom," Ella shouted as she burst through the garage door. Her mom was on the phone.

"I'll call you right back, Janet," Mom said, seeing Ella's happy face. She hung up. "What is it?" she asked expectantly.

"I got in! I got in!" Ella tried to jump, but her legs wouldn't let her. She pulled up the Johns Hopkins website on her phone. Her mother looked at the screen and began jumping for her. Then she leaned over and scooped Ella up into a big hug, nearly choking Ella with the intensity.

"Where's Jordan?" Ella asked, looking around. She wanted to tell the world.

"Riding Dusty," Mom replied. "I'll let him know when he comes back. Now, go tell your father. He's in his office."

Ella went downstairs to her dad's office. "Dad, I got into Johns Hopkins!" Ella said, but he was not there. Ella sat in his chair and swiveled around. Catching her breath, she considered where to search for him next. The computer screen caught Ella's attention— there was an email from the governor, Rick Forrest. She knew she shouldn't read the email, but her nosiness got the better of her.

Sam,

I'm anticipating beating your golf score of 97 and ask you to forget my abysmal 130. I had a headache that day. I hear you're telling people you're a better golfer than I am. One or two wins doesn't prove anything. Besides, being Governor means less time for golfing. I have a state to run after all.

I will beat you one of these days, you just wait!

Yes, I have received your request for writing a letter of recommendation on Brandon Cunningham's behalf. After reviewing his school records as well as his physical examinations, I have come to the conclusion that I cannot recommend the boy for West Point.

Yes, I did make a note of 2000 SAT score. And while he meets all the physical requirements, his lack of interest in his studies makes him an unfit candidate for such a prestigious Military Academy.

I appreciate all the good work he has done for your disabled daughter, Ella, but it is not enough.

Since I have recommended other students for acceptance into West Point, my recommendation must be taken seriously. Therefore, I'm afraid I cannot recommend Mr. Cunningham at this time, or risk losing the credibility that allows me to offer up recommendations in the future. I hope this will not impact our friendship.

Sincerely,
Rick Forrest


The fluffy cloud Ella had been floating on vanished. The good work Brandon has done for me? She reread the words "your disabled daughter." Her father referred to her as disabled? What is going on here? Her heart and mind raced. Was she just a pawn, being used for a second time by a boy who saw her as simply a means to an end? Had Brandon been pretending? Of course he was, the cynical part of her mind whispered. She was damaged and that was all any boy would ever see.

Dad sauntered in, then tensed immediately when he saw Ella in his chair.

"Ella, are you alright? You look pale."

Tears spilled down her cheeks. Her dad looked from her to the computer screen.

"You read the governor's email," Dad said quietly, his forehead creasing, unable to hide his sheer embarrassment.

"Did you pay Brandon to be nice to me?" Ella asked.

"Now, sweetheart, I know how this looks."

"Did you?" Ella shouted.

Dad bit his lip before replying. "Willie gave me the idea. He thought Brandon could be a friend for you. I only asked him to pay you a little attention."

Ella covered her face with her sleeves, the tears pouring out faster than her hands could hold them. She stood up and walked out. Her dad called after her, but Ella didn't heed him. She struggled up the basement steps, down the hall and out of the back door. She knew exactly where she was headed next.

# CHAPTER 29

BRANDON WAS IN the barn, filling up Dusty's food pails.

"Hey, Ella, I have the funniest story to tell you," he said when he saw her. "Chris was giving your brother a lesson and—"

Ella took the pail he had just filled and threw it on the ground, little brown circles scattering in the hay. He turned to her in complete shock.

"I know everything," Ella said. "Your deal with my father, how you were promised a recommendation letter if you would be nice to me. Telling me that Ranny was just a friend. All you ever wanted was to go to West Point, and it seems me and my family were your ticket in."

Brandon hung his head.

"How could you?" Ella shouted at him. "You made me think I had a chance, a chance that you might want me."

Brandon looked at her, saying nothing.

"I thought James Jude was good at playing people, but it seems you could give him a few pointers." Ella was shaking and so angry it was hard to control her speech. She turned away, not wanting to see Brandon's face confirm all her worst fears—that none of it was real, just a wonderful delusion.

Brandon caught her wrist and turned her to him. "You think you have it all figured out. That you know why everything's the way it is. Well, your conclusion is wrong. Yes, your father told me that you might walk a little funny. So what? My brother would love to limp—he would give anything to limp! You think I wanted to impress your father by spending time with you?" Brandon's eyes blazed like emeralds on fire. He was still holding her wrist. "Coming here each day felt dishonest, like I was cheating on my girlfriend. That's how it feels every time we are together. I don't see your leg, Ella. I see you!"

Ella's breath slowed down a little. She stopped shaking. But she did not see tenderness in Brandon's eyes; she saw fury.

"You think I'm a phony?" Brandon continued, letting go of her wrist. "You live for the approval of others. If that's not being fake, I don't know what is."

Ella whipped around and stomped back to the house.

"Wait, Ella, come back," Brandon shouted after her. "I'm sorry. I didn't mean that."

"Take a long walk off a short pier," Ella called behind her, throwing open the back door.

She climbed the stairs and slammed her bedroom door shut, flopping onto her bed and putting a pillow over her head, silencing the world. She was so tired of people telling her what to do and how to feel, coddling her and treating her like an expensive doll that had been cracked, never to be loved or played with, just to be looked at and pitied.

Her cell phone buzzed. It was a message from Brandon. Ella's heart raced. It was the first time Brandon had ever texted her besides the time he sent her his home address.

She clicked on the text. It read, *I didn't mean to call you phony, it just came out. Please can we talk?*

*I see the pier wasn't long enough*, Ella wrote back.

*Did you mean that to be mean or funny?* came Brandon's response.

*Stop pretending, Brandon, it won't help you get into West Point. Maybe if you tried harder in school.*

*You mean if I were a nerd, like you?*

*I wish I never met you*, Ella wrote back. She slammed her phone down on the dresser. How dare he call her a nerd.

The drama of the day had tired her out, and soon she passed out. She woke to find her sister crouched beside the bed.

"Ella," Chelsey said, brushing hair out of Ella's eyes. "Can you please tell me why on the day my little sis finds out she is going to her dream college, she's in her bed looking like a train wreck?"

Ella turned from Chelsey and looked up at the ceiling. "It was all a lie. Brandon was hired out of pity for me, like charity." The tears picked up right where they left off.

"Ella, I just spoke with him. He looks awful, like someone told him he could no longer wear blue jeans."

"Good."

"Ella, you have it all wrong."

"I don't have anything wrong."

"Ella, you do have it wrong, and if you would stop being such a hothead for two seconds, you would see that—"

"No," Ella said in defiance. She was hurt that her sister was taking Brandon's side.

"Then don't come crying to me when Brandon won't return your calls. You might feel justified now, but you won't tomorrow, I can promise you that."

Ella faced the wall. She didn't need a lecture; she needed to be alone to mourn the relationship that never was. Ella pulled a pillow over her head, indicating the conversation was over.

"Fine, be stubborn," Chelsey said as she left the room. "But when you want to hide your dark circles and uneven skin tone, ask someone else."

"Ella, can I come in?" she heard her father ask only moments later.

Why is my room a freaking train station? thought Ella bitterly.

"Ella?" called her father.

"Go away," Ella said. She didn't want to hear his excuses. She had never felt so betrayed, and by her own father no less.

She heard the door creak open.

"Ella, please look at me," her father begged.

"No," Ella said. She didn't care that she sounded like she was six years old.

"Just listen, then." Dad sat on the bed next to her. Ella kept her back to him. "I knew from an early age my little Gabriella could be anything she wanted. Well, after four years of all your hard work it seems I was right. My little girl can be a doctor, a scientist, whatever she wants. She can be everything except happy. As a father, that is all I ever want for you—to be happy."

Ella's tears stopped flowing, her father's words more comforting than she thought they would be.

"When Willie told me about Brandon, he sounded like someone who could brighten anyone's day," her father went on. "During the interview process, I asked him if he had problems with people with disabilities. He told me his own brother was in a wheelchair. I told him I have a wonderful daughter who might make a good friend. That's all. I never asked him to be kind to you or invite you to his home for a barbecue or take you to the dance. He did that on his own."

Ella felt terrible. The story she had in her head was not the truth at all—just an old tape of her worst fears playing in her mind. And now she had pushed Brandon away, perhaps forever.

"What about the note you wrote the governor calling me disabled?" Ella wasn't going to let her father off the hook so easily.

"I'm sorry for that," Dad said. "I was trying to make the case strong in Brandon's favor. I was wrong to use such a word. It's not how I think of you, Ella. I have never thought of you that way."

"Brandon still used us to get into West Point," Ella insisted.

"Maybe, but can you blame him?" said Dad. "West Point is hard to get into. It is no different than you asking for a recommendation letter from Dr. Taylor. Who just so happens to be one of the most respected scientists in the state."

"She is my teacher," Ella pointed out.

"We pay good money to give you access to the finest," Dad replied. He put a hand on her shoulder. "I'm sorry I hurt you, Ella. I'm sorry for what I said. I would do anything for you to return to that little girl who never had a bad day. Who went out with her friends and invited others into her life. I love you. I guess I was just trying to show you, even if I went about it in the wrong way."

Ella turned to her father and gave him a hug.

"Do you forgive me?" Dad asked, his brows knitted together in hope.

"Yes," Ella said, wiping her eyes.

"Your mother and I have booked a dinner reservation at a fancy restaurant downtown because our Gabriella got into one of the top universities in the country. We would really like it if you came with, but we are prepared to go celebrate without you."

Ella laughed as she pushed her hair behind her ears.

Her dad kissed her on the cheek. "See you downstairs in fifteen minutes?"

Ella nodded.

Her dad got off the bed. "That's fifteen minutes, now, not three hours. Your sister gets those time measurements confused." Ella smiled. It felt good to smile.

"Did I tell you that Denzel got into Duke University?" Maria asked. They were on Ella's bed, listening to some music.

"No way," Ella said, sitting up.

"On a football scholarship," Maria said proudly.

"He could've got in without the football scholarship," Ella pointed out. "I think he has one of the highest GPAs in the school."

"Of course he does. Wouldn't date a dunce, now would I?"

"No, you wouldn't."

"How does it feel to be accepted into your dream school?" Maria asked.

"I still can't believe it," Ella replied, leaning back, looking up at the ceiling.

"I can. You know all sorts of fun facts, like the one where we have enough cabin in our body to make, like, 1,000 pencils."

"You meant carbon."

"No, I meant cabin. You need the wood from the cabins to make the pencils."

Maria met Ella's eyes and they both giggled.

"Did I tell you about my prom dress?" Maria asked. "It's black and poofy and I feel like a princess when I twirl around."

"Bring the dress by and model it for me sometime," said Ella.

"How about I model the dress for you at the prom? Come with Denzel and me. Please?"

"I don't have a date."

"You don't need a date. You can sit with us."

"I think I like my plan of making a big bowl of popcorn and watching Dirty Dancing better."

"You have seen that movie a zillion times," Maria huffed. "Your senior prom only happens once in a lifetime."

"Well, I'll never be an Olympic athlete or run a marathon. I'll just have to add prom to the never going to happen list."

"What happened with Brandon? You haven't spoken about him in a few days. It could be a record."

"I told you about Ranny," said Ella. She was getting sick of repeating that he already had a girlfriend.

"Yeah, I know all about Ranny—she has a killer bod and is a bit possessive. You used to talk about Brandon anyway, but now it's like he never existed. Something else must have happened."

Slowly, Ella told the story of how she discovered the email from the governor and the fight she had with Brandon afterwards.

"I felt like he was only with me because he wanted into West Point so badly he'd do almost anything," said Ella. "I found out later it wasn't the case. He saw me for me, Maria, but I pushed him away when I let my inner lion loose."

"I can see how you would have thought that."

Ella laid her head on Maria's shoulder. "I'll never have anyone. I might as well get some cats."

"You will always have me." Maria placed a hand over Ella's.

"Good, because I don't know what I would do without you."

"I can't imagine what you would do without me either," Maria replied. Ella laughed, feeling a bit better.

"Maybe you can join us after the prom," Maria said; then she frowned. "Scratch that."

Ella's ears perked up. "Why?"

"Because we have plans, that's all."

"You're keeping something from me?" Ella said, crossing her arms.

"Ella," Maria said, giving one of her it's none of your business looks.

Mom knocked on the bedroom door. "Dinner is ready. It's stir-fry. I made sure to add tofu instead of chicken."

"Thanks, Mrs. Heart," Maria said.

"My pleasure, and I have something for you." Mom handed Maria a book wrapped in shiny silver paper. Maria tore off the paper. The book was a biography about a Latin-American singer. Maria looked a bit confused as she flipped through the pages.

"I thought she could inspire you," Mom said. "You also have South American roots."

Ella palmed her forehead, but Maria put down the book and hugged Mom. "Thanks, Mrs. Heart. I will enjoy reading it."

"And I will enjoy listening to your music on the radio one day," Mom replied.

"That was mighty gracious of you," Ella said to Maria after her mother left the room.

"Your mom meant well." Maria shrugged. "I have better things to get upset about than well-intentioned gifts. Now let's go eat." And the two of them made their way down to the kitchen for dinner like sisters in arms.

# CHAPTER 30

AFTER A LONG day at school, Ella pulled up next to a red truck in her driveway. Brandon's old blue-and-white one must have gone to car heaven, Ella thought. Well, it would be a good conversation starter. Ella was still mad at him, but she knew she had to talk to him eventually or be a stranger to her stables.

But Brandon was nowhere to be found. Where could he be? Ella saw an older woman carrying a bucket of water. The woman put the bucket down and stuck out her hand.

"Vicki Reinhardt."

"Ella," Ella said, returning her hand in greeting. Ella noticed the deep lines in Vicky's face, and around her eyes. "Where's Brandon?"

"You mean the young man who used to work here? He quit last week," the woman said, pouring water into the horse trough. "Jeepers," Vicki said. She placed a prune-like hand on her lower back. "I don't know how I'll give the horses a bath. I don't feel much like walking back to the garden."

"There's a hose right here," Ella said, showing Vicki the hose in the corner of the stable.

"Well, thank heavens, or my back would start moaning," Vicki said gratefully.

Ella felt numb. Vicki Reinhardt seemed nice and all, but it would never be the same without Brandon. There would be no more water fights, no more reason to visit the Cunninghams, no more long talks in the meadow about screws and horses and life after high school. There would be no more flirting, no more Brandon. The fairy tale of seeing her prince every day was over.

Vicki patted Dusty's forehead as she hooked his feeding pail around his neck. Vicki seemed like a good farm manager. The horses were calm and their stables clean.

"We will be seeing a lot of each other," Vicki said, breaking into Ella's thoughts. "I'll be living in the guesthouse."

Ella tried to muster a smile. "How nice."

"Your folks are generous people," Vicky went on. "And I know Glenn will warm up to me." Vicki reached out to pet Glenn's spotted forehead. Glenn responded by biting her arm.

"Ouch," Vicki said, pulling back. Ella was shocked. Glenn had never bitten anyone before. The bite was superficial, but Ella saw the outline of teeth marks on Vicki's arm.

"I'll get the first aid kit," Ella said. She hurried to the house and returned to the stables with supplies to treat the wound.

"Thanks, dear," Vicki said as Ella placed some ointment on the bite. "I seem to be losing my touch. Horses usually like me."

"Glenn has always been impossible. I try to stay away from him."

"I won't give up yet." Determination filled Vicki's light eyes. "You don't win the corn bag toss three years in a row without grit."

"What's a corn bag toss?"

"Well," Vicki began, pushing up her sleeves, "our town has a corn festival every year called the Husk Show. There is corn decorating, picking, tasting . . ."

Ella sat on a stool, realizing this was going to be a long answer to what she thought was a simple question. Ella had never seen anyone get so animated about corn. Vicki told stories about the different flavors of popcorn sold and the guessing jar filled with kernels. She told Ella that she held the record in the corn sack toss, being able to throw a twenty-pound bag of corn flour over ten yards.

Vicki was easy to talk to, and Ella opened up about the accident and the fight she had with Brandon. After all the barn work was completed, Vicki invited Ella into the guesthouse to taste her cornbread. Vicki was competing in the corn flour competition this year and testing out different recipes.

Vicki gave Ella a big piece of cornbread. It melted in Ella's mouth, the flavors of corn and butter mixing together on her tongue.

"This is amazing," Ella said. She took another big bite.

"Glad you like it," Vicki said as she poured Ella a glass of fresh lemonade. "And I wouldn't be too hard on yourself. It seems you and that Brandon fella had a simple misunderstanding that led to some colorful words. I would also like to point out that being straightforward isn't a crime."

"I was a little too straightforward," said Ella.

"I think the best thing is to move forward," Vicki said. "Let this Brandon boy know you still value the friendship, and if he wants to keep his resentment fresh and stirred, well, then that is his problem, and you don't need to share in it."

They spent the rest of the afternoon talking and getting to know each other. Ella decided if Brandon had to leave, Vicki was the best replacement.

The next morning, Maria talked about the new facts she had learned about Syball. "Did you know that since Syball is a conservatory, it means I will never have to take math again?"

"But you were getting so good at it," Denzel said, putting his arm around her shoulders. Maria rolled her eyes and nudged him off. Ella looked down at her phone—no new texts.

"Call him, Ella," Maria said.

Ella slumped against her locker. "Brandon's probably glad I'm out of his life."

"Are we talking about that guy from the fall dance?" Denzel asked.

"Yes," Ella and Maria said at the same time.

"I agree with Maria," Denzel said. "Be the bigger person; offer the olive branch."

"Thanks for not telling anyone," Ella snapped at Maria.

"It's Denzel," Maria shot back, waving her arms in her boyfriend's direction. "You know he won't tell."

"If only my father had gotten him that recommendation for West Point." Ella sighed. *If only I hadn't let my inner lion loose.*

"West Point?" Denzel asked, straightening his shoulders. "My father went to West Point. Maybe he can put in a good word for Brandon?"

"Would he?" Ella asked, feeling hopeful.

"Let me call him," Denzel said. He pulled out his cell phone and moved to the corner.

Maria nudged Ella. "Wouldn't it be great if Colonel Moland could help?"

"It would," Ella replied, her palms sweating. She studied Denzel's face as he spoke with his father. He strode back to them.

"He said he would be happy to talk with Brandon," Denzel said.

"Ahh!" Maria and Ella both cried, jumping up and down.

"Ehhh," Denzel mocked them, flailing his arms.

"You're the best," Ella said. She threw her arms around Denzel's neck. "I owe you one."

"No, you don't, Ella," Denzel said as he patted her back. The bell rang, and Ella practically skipped off to class.

Ella drove to Brandon's house right after school. She knocked on the back door, bracing herself for the cool reaction he'd have for her showing up unexpectedly. Cindy answered the screen door in a pin-tuck denim romper that hit mid-thigh, her long, thin arms exposed by the short sleeves.

"Hi, Ella, long time no see," Cindy said, smiling.

"Hi, Cindy, nice to see you," Ella replied. "Is Brandon around?"

"He went to the stables to help his mom."

"Could you tell me how to get there, please?"

"Sure, it's just up the road. Maybe you can stop by on your way back. Graham would love to see you."

"Of course," Ella said. It was nice to feel cared about, even if it was by the wrong Cunningham boy.

Ella pulled her car into a gravel lot. The blue-and-white Chevy was parked by the stables. Ella's right leg locked as she climbed out of her car. Between the long drive and hours sitting in class, it wouldn't budge. Ella dragged it behind her, trying to shake it awake. Finally, her leg awoke, allowing her to walk at a normal pace.

Ella found Brandon leading Ranny on a horse. Ranny was in daisy dukes and a light-blue T-shirt. Her long legs hung on either side of the horse, brown cowboy boots inside the stirrups. Brandon pulled the reins and began running, which made the horse gallop. Ranny screeched for Brandon to stop. But Brandon just ran faster.

Ranny shrieked again for him to stop, which he did this time. He held out his arms and she slid into them, wrapping her legs around his waist. She kissed him. It was not an innocent kiss. This was the kind of kiss that led to other things, things Ella didn't want to think about Brandon and Ranny doing. Ella felt sick, but she had to do this—tell Brandon about the colonel's offer.

The crunch of the gravel gave her presence away. Brandon looked surprised to see Ella, while Ranny looked irate.

"Hi, Brandon, sorry to intrude," Ella offered. Her courage was slipping. Maybe she should have simply texted him the number.

"That's alright. What brings you out here?" asked Brandon.

Definitely should have texted him, Ella thought. But she had wanted to see him so badly she convinced the more sensible part of her brain that this was a good idea. Nothing she could do about it now.

"Well, I was talking about college with my friends today," Ella began. "I learned that my friend's dad went to West Point; long story short, I brought you this." Ella held out the piece of paper.

Brandon took it. "It's a phone number," Brandon said, his tone dubious.

"His name is Colonel Moland. He's Denzel's father," Ella explained. "He graduated from West Point and has some valuable contacts, including friends who are on the board of admissions. He said he would be happy to speak with you."

"Thank you, Ella," said Brandon. He looked like he wanted to say something more but didn't have the words. Ranny wrapped her arms around Brandon's shoulders as she peered at the number. She was marking her territory.

"Good luck," Ella called, heading back to the parking lot. She hoped the number was enough to get Brandon speaking with her again. She climbed into her car and made her way down the road back to the Cunningham's. Ella had promised she would play with Graham and intended to keep that promise.

# CHAPTER 31

THAT NIGHT AT dinner, Dad and Mom talked mainly about the trial. Ella got the sense her parents were not as certain about winning as they were in the beginning. They talked freely, expressing their worries about the case and preparing for all the what-ifs they could think of—something they couldn't do when Jordan was around. Lucky for Mom and Dad, Jordan was at the shooting range with Chris that evening. He seemed to spend a lot of time with Chris and Brandon, discovering his passion for firearms, while not talking much about his friend Blake.

As dinner dragged on, night fell. Ella watched the shadows form on the ground outside by the pool as the horizon swallowed the sun. She finished her plate of lasagna, happy Mom had put in the ground beef. It just didn't taste the same without the meat.

"I'm going upstairs," Ella said, taking her plate to the sink.

"But we have brownies," Mom said. She shoved the platter of fudgy squares over to her.

"I'll have one later," said Ella. She backed out of the kitchen and headed up the back stairs before Mom could offer her more treats. Nothing could entice Ella to stay at the table.

She met Jordan on the landing, her car keys dangling from his ring finger. They shared a car these days.

"Where did you come from?" Ella asked.

"Shhh," Jordan whispered, "I don't want Mom to know I'm here. I missed a meeting with Mr. Bailey today and Mom's pissed."

"You didn't," Ella mouthed. This was a capital offense.

"I did," Jordan replied, his mouth widening to a grin. "Mr. Bailey wants to give me this whole lecture on courtroom etiquette. He says I smirk too much, but I think he's harping because he's afraid we'll lose the case."

"Do you think you'll lose?" Ella asked.

"Mrs. Martin is a drama queen looking for a reality TV show to star in," Jordan replied, jamming his hand into his bangs and pushing them behind his ear. They flopped back out, too short to reach that far. Ella wondered why Jordan didn't cut his bangs to a more manageable length.

"The problem is," Jordan went on, "the jury seems to be sympathetic towards her even though the facts and the law are on our side."

"There is a difference between sympathy and empathy," said Ella. "Most get those two terms confused. They might sympathize with Mrs. Martin, but it doesn't mean they will decide in her favor."

"Thanks for the vocab lecture, wisenheimer. Who needs a dictionary when I have you?"

"Jordan," Mom called up the stairs. "Jordan, are you there?"

"Damn," Jordan swore, rushing to his room.

"Ella, can you come here for a second?" Ella turned to see Chelsey peeking out of her bedroom door. It seemed they all were hiding from their parents this evening.

There was clothing on Chelsey's bed, makeup wipes scattered on the dresser, and only one lonely pair of sneakers on her shoe rack in the closet while the rest lay strewn about on the floor. People might think that Chelsey was a neat freak because she encouraged the perception by looking well groomed and being punctual, but their view of Chelsey would change the minute they saw her bedroom.

"Would you mind putting this necklace on me?" Chelsey held out a strand of pearls.

"You look nice," Ella said, stepping over a pair of blue jeans to get to her sister. "Hot date?"

"No, I'm going grocery shopping," Chelsey replied, patting her neck and moving her perfect blond hair to the side.

Ella placed the pearls around her sister's neck and fastened the clasp. The necklace went well with the red mini dress she wore, her long legs looking toned in black pumps. Her skin seemed to sparkle—not one blemish could be found. Ella knew that Chelsey had a strict skin regimen, following all the skin care rules everyone else ignored.

"So, are you going to tell me about him?" Ella said, shifting the clothing on Chelsey's bed to sit down. Chelsey kept her private life private, never saying much unless she was in the mood to dish. Ella hoped tonight would be one of those nights.

"His name is Mark Winston," said Chelsey, a dumb grin forming on her lips. "My friend Ava married his brother, Steven. I met him at their wedding a few nights ago. We talked all evening."

"Where does he live?"

"Chicago."

"Well, you always did like your space," Ella said, looking curiously at Chelsey.

"It's a first date, Ella," said Chelsey as she sprayed herself with perfume. "If it goes well, we will work out the logistics."

"Fair enough."

Chelsey's face went rigid, the dumb smile gone. Ella followed her angry stare to the window.

"Those creeps," Chelsey fumed, rushing to close the blinds. "It's like I'm a prisoner in my own home." She turned the blinds until nothing could be seen in or out of the window. "Mom's always in my business, asking me if I see myself as a mother one day, and that stupid Shane boy peeps at me any chance he gets. I'm going to move out!" Chelsey declared. "As soon as prom season is over, I'm out of here."

"Just don't move too far," Ella said softly.

"Oh, sweetie," Chelsey said, joining Ella on the bed. "I would never go too far."

"Good." Ella laid her head on her sister's shoulder.

"What's on your mind? You have been quiet lately. You know you can talk to me about anything."

Ella stayed quiet, not sure where to start. She removed her head from her sister's shoulder and leaned back into a cream-colored pillow, feeling her muscles release. While Chelsey's room was the definition of cluttered, nothing was grimy or dusty. Her white pillows and comforter glimmered as if they were recently purchased.

"Is it about college?" Chelsey guessed. "Because I would never dream of sending you off without an updated wardrobe."

Ella decided to confide in her sister; after all, Chelsey had told her about Mark. "Brandon quit," said Ella quietly. "He didn't even tell me. I guess I really didn't mean that much to him." Ella hung her head, the words sounding worse out loud.

"Should have known it was about Mr. J. Crew." Chelsey sighed. "Your obsession with him is at a worrisome level."

"I can't help it," Ella muttered miserably, wondering if she should have kept her thoughts to herself. Chelsey wasn't known for her tact and sensitivity.

"I told you things would end this way if you didn't make nice."

"I tried to make nice."

"You should tell him the truth."

"Which is?"

"The truth. That you are completely, stupidly in love with him."

"But that's just it," Ella said, her eyes dampening at the corners. "He isn't in love with me." Ella brushed away the few wayward tears, taking deep breaths. She glanced at the box of tissues on the dresser but was scared to reach for them, not wanting this to become a full-blown cry fest.

Chelsey circled her arm around Ella's waist, drawing her near. "It's going to be alright, Els," she said gently. "You'll see. Everything will work out."

The doorbell rang.

"Chelsey," Mom called from downstairs.

"Good luck tonight," Ella said as Chelsey strode past her. Ella followed, anxious to get a look at this Mark Winston. Mark stood by the front door in a dark suit and tie, talking with Mom. He was handsome. His caramel-colored hair was thick and groomed to perfection. His sapphire eyes sparkled when he saw Chelsey. It was as if he was seeing the queen. Mom wished them well as Mark led Chelsey out the front door.

"They are so cute together," Mom gushed.

"Like Barbie and Ken." Ella giggled.

"Well, with any luck, I will be a grandmother before I'm ninety," Mom replied. "Oh, I have something for you." She handed Ella a Smithsonian. "Came in the mail today." Ella thanked her mother and took the magazine upstairs, eager to read it.

It was eight o'clock on a Thursday night—too early to go to bed and too late to wear anything other than pajamas. Ella flipped through the magazine, and was reading about an archaeological dig in China when the doorbell rang. Who could that be? Ella thought. She surmised that it must be Mr. Bailey, coming to lecture Jordan. It was too late in the evening to be anyone else.

She continued reading the article until her mother called up the stairs. "Ella, Brandon is here to see you."

# CHAPTER 32

WHAT? CAN'T BE, Ella thought, looking at her PJs and loose ponytail in the mirror. Could I be any frumpier?

"Ella," her mom called again.

When Ella came down the stairs, she could not believe what she was seeing. Brandon, in her house on a Thursday night. This had to be a dream.

"Hi, Ella," Brandon said.

"Hi," Ella said timidly, trying not to gape at him. He was in a navy polo shirt, his jeans ripped at the knee, although it seemed more from wear than a fashion statement. His short, light-brown hair stuck up in the front. Ella had to resist the urge to flatten it back down.

"Would you like something to eat?" Mom offered Brandon.

"No, I'm good, thanks," Brandon said, shoving his hands into his pockets.

Ella led Brandon towards the couch in the living room and sank into the plush pillows. Brandon sat down on the other end.

"I wanted to thank you for giving me Colonel Moland's number," Brandon began, his hands moving to his lap. He clasped them and looked down. "We had a good talk. He will speak with his friends on the admissions board."

"I'm glad," Ella said.

Brandon looked up at her. "Are you still mad at me?"

Ella was quiet for a moment.

"Look, I may have been a bit nicer to you in the beginning than I normally would be to someone I just met," Brandon admitted. "But I wasn't pretending, Ella, honest. I'm no good at it. That's why my grades are so lousy. I can't pretend to care about something I don't."

"I'm sorry for telling you to walk off a pier," Ella said. "I seem to have a shorter fuse than I care to admit."

"It's your hair," Brandon said. "Redheads tend to be fierier. It's in your nature."

"This boy in my class says I'm part lion."

"I can see that."

They both laughed.

"Can we put this behind us?" Brandon asked, his hazel eyes hopeful.

"I'd like that," Ella replied.

There was a pause as they each decided what to say next. Brandon shifted around on the couch like he was sitting on ants.

"I saw you quit working in the stables," Ella said, looking for something to say.

"I needed to start training for West Point," said Brandon. "And Ranny was complaining we didn't spend enough time together. How is the new farm manager?"

"Vicki is nice. She makes the best cornbread I have ever tasted. Dusty seems to like her, but Glenn has been acting up. He bit Vicki the first day they met."

"Glenny, Glenny." Brandon shook his head. "You know, I miss that monster. Can't think why."

"You can have him."

"That's mighty kind of you, but I think I'll pass."

Ella laughed, catching his eye. Brandon held her gaze and the slightest of smiles played on his lips. Then he looked at his watch. "I think I should get going. I promised Cindy I'd help her build Graham's new toy chest." He got to his feet.

"Maybe I should help you," Ella offered. "It would be good

practice for my Woodshop final."

"Cindy has really high standards," replied Brandon. "She wants the box to stand and not fall apart the first time Graham uses it."

"Picky, picky," Ella scoffed, keeping the tone light to mask her despair.

She walked Brandon to the front door.

"Did I tell you the bigots across the street are moving?"

"Really?" Ella asked.

"The 'for sale' sign went up last week." Brandon leaned against the doorframe. "My friend Seth is throwing an unofficial party this Saturday to celebrate. Want to join us? Ranny will be there, along with my friend Marcus."

"I can't," said Ella, looking down. She noticed a hole in her sock by her pinky toe. She crossed her feet, covering it up.

"You're already accepted into college," Brandon pointed out. "So what if you get a seventy on something? Come on, Ella. My mom is making peach cobbler for dessert. You'll be sad if you miss it."

Ella's stomach turned. She could make up a thousand excuses not to come—a paper due, her commitment to working in Dr. Taylor's lab, the golf game her father had challenged her to. But Ella was sick of lies. For her stomach's sake, she had to come clean. She took a deep breath.

"Brandon, I can't do this whole friend thing anymore."

Brandon flinched. "Jeez, Ella, don't hold back. It's not like I have feelings or anything."

"That's not what I meant," Ella said quickly. "I mean, I've always wanted to be more than friends." There, she had said it. She lifted her head to brave a glance in Brandon's direction. He was looking down, picking at a string on his jeans.

"I have a girlfriend," he said, finally.

"I know," Ella muttered, leaning her head on the door.

"Ella, I wish things were different," Brandon said, conflict on his face. Ella didn't want to be the cause of his anguish.

She held up her hand. "You don't have to explain."

Brandon nodded. "Well, goodnight."

"Goodnight," Ella mumbled back.

She watched him walk to his truck. Soon the sound of the loud engine filled the quiet night. Ella went inside, closing the door with her back. She slumped to the floor, her heart in turmoil.

"Was that Mr. Bailey?" Jordan asked. He was perched on the top steps. "I bet he wants to kill me." The words were edged in fear.

"I'm sure he does," Ella agreed.

"I think I'll go to Blake's tonight." Jordan leaped to his feet. "Haven't seen him since I've come home."

"Relax, Jordan, Mr. Bailey isn't after you."

"Was he even here?" Jordan arched a brow at her.

Ella suppressed a giggle. "No." She was enjoying this way more than she should.

"Good." Jordan sighed, relaxing his shoulders. "Hey, want to see a picture of Sashie?" He held up his cell phone and Ella followed him to his room. Seeing the dog would be a nice distraction.

Jordan scrolled through some pictures before landing on a small white dog holding a chew toy in its mouth. A pink bow was clipped to the top of the dog's small head. Shelby knelt beside the dog, her honey-colored hair curling at the ends. The high-end jacket she wore showed off her toned figure, and running shoes were on her feet.

"Awww," Ella said when she saw the picture. She wanted to jump through the phone and give the puppy a gentle squeeze.

"They're at a park near First Avenue," Jordan explained. "Shelby likes to take Sashie jogging there. They don't get very far. Still, Shelby counts it as exercise."

"She is really cute," Ella said.

"I know; why do you think I'm dating her?"

"Haha." Ella pushed a beaming Jordan. He thought he was so funny.

The garage door slammed, making Ella and Jordan both jump.

"What was that?" Jordan asked.

"Not sure," Ella replied. She decided to go see.

Ella found Chelsey in the kitchen, looking like she had been chased by a pack of wolves. Her hair was a mess, her heels were in her hands, and her dress smelled like vomit.

"Worst night ever!" Chelsey said to Ella. "Mark got drunk and threw up all over me. If that weren't bad enough, I didn't think to take my ATM card or my cell phone. So, taking a cab was out of the question, as was calling one of you guys for help."

"Why not use the phone at the restaurant?" Ella asked, sitting on one of the barstools by the kitchen counter.

"Because after what Mark did to me, I didn't really feel like sticking around. I had to mooch a few dollars off a kind stranger and take the bus."

"But the closest bus stop is two miles away."

"Ding, ding," Chelsey said, her voice high with annoyance.

"That does sound like an awful evening," Ella conceded. Chelsey went to the fridge and took out a bottle of beer, popping the top off with a wine opener.

"Wasn't alcohol what got you into this mess?" Ella pointed out.

"This is one bottle of beer," Chelsey defended herself, taking a swig. "I won't drink a whole bottle of red wine like Mark did."

Ella's mouth dropped open. "He drank the whole bottle?"

"Nearly." Chelsey sipped her beer. The drink seemed to calm her.

"Did he offer you any?"

Chesley gave her a look that told Ella to watch herself.

"My night wasn't so great either," said Ella. "Brandon came by. We are no longer friends."

"Why?" Chelsey asked, taking a seat next to Ella.

"Because he has a girlfriend!" Ella shouted.

"That doesn't mean you can't be friends."

"It does if I fantasize about stealing him away from his girlfriend."

"You're too good." Chelsey nudged Ella and drank more of her beer.

"It's a curse," Ella moaned, resting her chin on the granite countertop.

"Don't mope. You did the right thing." Chelsey finished off her beer.

"Have you ever seen Cruel Intentions? Got it yesterday on sale."

"Yeah, a while ago."

"Come on." Chelsey took Ella's hand, leading her to the den. She popped the DVD in and pressed play.

"I think this is the first time we are both having boy problems at the same time," said Ella as her sister plopped down on the couch beside her. "I feel like I'm advancing in the world."

"It's not something to be proud of," Chelsey said, shifting her legs under her. Ella wrinkled her nose.

"Chelsey, I love you and all, but you smell like a bar bathroom," said Ella.

Chelsey pushed her. "Well, get used to it, because I'm not moving an inch."

"What are you guys watching?" Jordan asked. He joined them on the couch.

"Cruel Intentions," said Ella.

"Who puked?" Jordan asked, holding his nose.

"It's my new fragrance," Chelsey replied. "Bastard vomit."

"Geez," replied Jordan, inching away from Chelsey.

Ella relaxed. It was nice, the three of them on the couch, enjoying a movie together. She couldn't remember the last time it had happened. It was just the remedy she needed for a broken heart.

Early the next morning, Ella was called away from French class to the front office. She had a phone call from her mother.

"Mom, is everything alright?" Ella asked nervously.

"I need you to get down to the courtroom," Mom commanded. "It appears the jury has reached a verdict."

Ella got a permission slip from the front office and drove down to the courthouse. Jordan's fate was about to be revealed.

# CHAPTER 33

MOM WAS WAITING outside for Ella when she arrived at the courthouse. Mr. Bailey paced back and forth, talking on his cell phone. Dad turned his watch in circles on his wrist. Did they think Jordan would lose? Would her parents be forced to pay the five million dollars the Martins were asking for if Jordan was found liable?

The Martins' side practically strutted with triumph. They seemed to think today would be the end of their money troubles and the evil Heart family would get what was coming to them. Mr. Kaufman gave Mrs. Martin a confident smile. Mrs. Martin returned the smile, looking radiant in a white suit with a matching white hat.

Ella sat with her parents in the pews behind Jordan. The judge came in, her hair in the same style as when Ella had testified, pulled back into a tight bun on the top of her head. At seeing the judge, Mrs. Martin waved to her family before taking a seat next to Mr. Kaufman. The judge summoned the jury, and twelve passive faces filed into the jury box.

"Will the defendant please rise?" the judge instructed.

Jordan rose, Mr. Bailey by his side. Ella saw her brother's hands trembling.

"Has the jury reached a verdict?" the judge asked.

A tall man with a ponytail stood up in the jury box. "We have, Your Honor."

The judge nodded for the man to continue. He opened a piece of yellow paper from a legal notepad and began reading. "We the jury find Jordan Bradley Heart not liable for the death of Fred Martin." The tall man folded up the paper and sat down.

Mr. Bailey gave Jordan a joyful clap on the back. But Jordan stood still, almost as if he didn't believe the words just spoken.

"You are guilty!" Mrs. Martin yelled at Jordan, the jubilant expression she wore earlier exchanged for rage. "I will find you—you will answer for the death of my husband. We will never forgive you—you butcher, murderer!"

Jordan paled, stepping away from Mrs. Martin.

"Order!" The judge banged on her gavel. "Mrs. Martin, you will restrain yourself."

"Come on now," Mr. Bailey said, taking Jordan by the elbow and leading him out of the courtroom. Once they were in the foyer, Mom brought Jordan to her, cradling him in her arms like a child.

"I'm so relieved. I knew they would do the right thing and find you innocent."

"It's over, son," Dad said, rubbing Jordan's shoulders.

"It's all behind us," Mr. Bailey said. "That's what's important."

"Richard, join us for a celebratory lunch," Dad requested. "I'll make a reservation at the Pearl Blossom."

"I would be delighted," Mr. Bailey said, looking jovial.

Soon the family was headed downtown. Mom called Chelsey from the car, telling her the good news, and asked her to meet them at the restaurant. However, Chelsey wasn't able to join them, as she was currently putting makeup on a bride.

The restaurant looked elegant with gold chandeliers and crystal wineglasses. A young woman trailed her fingers over a baby grand piano, a sweet melody filling the air. Ella felt out of place in her school uniform. Most of the people in the restaurant were wearing a suit or an evening dress.

"I can't decide what to have," Mom said as she looked at the menu. "So many good choices."

"I'm having the prime rib," Dad said, patting his stomach. He turned to Mr. Bailey. "It comes with the creamiest mashed potatoes you have ever tasted."

"Sold," Mr. Bailey replied happily and put down his menu.

A woman in a fancy, cream-colored uniform came over to them. "Are you ready to order?"

"Two prime ribs," Dad began.

"Make that three," Mom added.

"I'll have the chicken breast with mushroom sauce," Ella said. It was her favorite dish at the Pearl Blossom.

They looked at Jordan.

"Nothing," Jordan said.

"Nothing?" Dad's brow crinkled in puzzlement.

"Have something," Mom encouraged. "A house salad, or some soup."

"Nothing. I'm not hungry."

"This is a celebration, Jordan," Mr. Bailey prodded.

"You're right," Jordan said, turning to the waitress. "Bring us your finest champagne. I killed a man and my family wants to celebrate." With that, he threw down his napkin and left the table. A thick silence followed, with the waitress biting her lip, unsure of how to respond.

"Can I see your wine list?" Dad asked. The server looked at him in shock.

"Your wine list," Mr. Bailey said a little more loudly. The server jumped, then scrambled off.

Ella pushed her own chair back and hurried after Jordan. She found him in an alley near the entrance. He was facing a wall, his hands resting on the gray bricks above him.

"I want to be alone," Jordan said as Ella approached him.

"Don't you know you can't get everything you want?" Ella said, trying to lighten the mood. Jordan didn't look up. He was in pain and nothing was going to change that. But it wouldn't stop Ella from trying.

"It's time for you to forgive yourself," Ella said to Jordan. "We have all forgiven you."

"I've told you, some things can't be forgiven," Jordan replied, his knuckles whitening as he clenched his hands. He released his fists, but his voice was dense with grief. "I killed a man, and there is no other way of saying it."

"No, you didn't."

"I wish I could go back and undrink all those beers at Blake's stupid party. But I couldn't let Blake down, not when he could always count on me to win the drinking game or do something asinine. I think that's why he keeps me around. Because I'm the prime example of a screw-up . . . driving a man to kill himself. Makes Blake's failed business ideas seem noble in comparison, right?"

"No," Ella shouted. "You made a mistake. How many times do I have to keep saying it?"

Jordan just shook his head, his shoulders hunched in despair. In that moment, Ella realized he would never forgive himself. His family, friends, the judge and jury could all pronounce him innocent, but he would forever hold himself liable.

"There is something I need to tell you," Ella said. She could not let her brother be burdened with all the guilt. It was time for her to come clean. "I owe you an apology."

Jordan looked at Ella skeptically. "What could you possibly be sorry for?"

"I deliberately sabotaged your first trial," Ella blurted out.

"I know, Ella," Jordan replied.

"What do you mean you know?"

"It was pretty obvious what your intentions were. You went against everything Mr. Bailey told you to say."

"Can you ever forgive me?"

"You don't need my forgiveness. You were reacting to the mess I made of your life. You are human, after all, even if you act like an angel most of the time."

Ella laughed, but Jordan didn't even crack a smile.

"You don't know what it's like," Jordan went on, a teardrop visible on his cheek. His voice was hoarse, straining over his words. "I feel like a bastard every day of my life and there is nothing I can do about it."

Ella had never seen him cry before. She didn't know how to respond. Should she hug him or keep her distance?

"I don't know if my life would be better had the accident never happened," Ella said, her own eyes growing misty. "Maybe I would have injured myself during a recital, or maybe I would become a world-famous dancer and be surrounded by girls just as snobby as Brittany every day of my life." Ella shuddered at the thought. "Who knows? What I do know is the Jordan who caused the accident four years ago is no longer with us."

"You mean that?" Jordan asked, the pain in his eyes slowly disappearing.

"I do," Ella replied, holding his gaze.

Jordan turned his face back towards the wall. He was shutting her out. She had to move fast.

"I would like to eat the chicken I ordered," said Ella. "I'm starving, but I'm not going back inside without you."

"Well, then you will be waiting a while," Jordan replied, his forehead resting on the gray bricks. "I don't plan on joining Mom and Dad for a 'celebratory' lunch."

It was a battle of wills.

"Well, as you intend for us to be here all day, let's play a game," Ella suggested. "Let's list every country in Europe that we know. I'll go first, starting in Eastern Europe. There is Belarus, Czech Republic, that one that starts with an M . . . Moldova."

"Any chance I can get you to shut up?"

"Nope—Slovakia, Ukraine, Poland."

"Alright," Jordan conceded in exasperation. "I'll go back inside."

"Good," Ella said, happy her little plan had worked. "Are you going to have a salad or soup?"

"What am I, a mouse? I want a steak."

They went back into the restaurant. Ella found her chicken by her place, and Jordan found a prime rib by his.

"I took a guess," Dad said, looking hopeful.

"It was a good one," Jordan said as he dug into the thick slab of meat. Ella took a bite out of her chicken. It tasted juicy and delicious.

"There is something I need to say," said Jordan, placing down his cutlery. He waited until all eight eyes were on him, then he took a sip of his water and began, "I'm sorry for behaving like such a jackass." Mom's cheeks pinched. She hated when Jordan swore.

"I'm sorry for driving drunk and causing one of the biggest accidents in Forrest Hill. I don't think I can ever apologize for what I did," Jordan went on. "But I can say thank you for giving me another chance, a chance to prove I'm going to get it right this time. And I will, I swear. The next time I'm in a courthouse, I will be trying a case, not being the one tried." Jordan paused, clearing his throat. "Ella"— Jordan turned to her—"you're a good sister, even when you're acting like a smart—" Jordan stopped when he saw his mother's face, saying instead, "smart bottom."

"Smart bottom." Ella laughed, covering her mouth.

The whole table began to laugh, cutting the tension.

"I'm parched," Jordan said, touching his throat. "I'll get some beer. Can't stand water." He signaled for their server.

"No!" Mom and Dad cried in unison.

"Gotcha." Jordan smiled. "Relax, I'm just getting some soda."

Then Jordan turned to Mr. Bailey, asking him to explain the meaning of the word bifurcation.

"Well," Mr. Bailey said, straightening his shoulders and getting into lawyer mode. "The judge has the right to divide the case . . ."

Ella tuned out the rest of the answer, never much caring about the law. Ella noticed Mom taking Dad's hand into her own, dabbing at her green eyes with the corner of her napkin. It felt like they had been let out of a cage, the accident finally behind them, where Ella hoped it would forever stay.

# CHAPTER 34

"THIS WILL BE your final project in Woodshop," Mr. Geller announced. His hands were covered in lime and beige paint, prompting Ella to wonder what project he had been working on over the weekend.

"You will have two hours in which to complete the assignment," Mr. Geller said. "Setting the timer and . . . begin."

Ella looked at the tools in front of her. She had to build a small storage box to pass the class. She took the Phillips-head and maneuvered a screw into the wooden board. Mr. Geller had given them instructions, a deceptively simple sheet of paper diagramming what went where. The diagram might as well have been instructions on how to build a space shuttle.

She managed to screw together the first two sides of the storage box, remembering the tips Brandon had given her when they built the bookshelf together. She kept the screwdriver straight, careful not to use too much force as she turned the screw in the predrilled hole. Then Ella saw a hammer on Mr. Geller's desk and remembered Brandon's words, "Never hammer a screw." She laughed. Max looked up at her with raised eyebrows. He glanced around for the source of Ella's amusement but quickly gave up and went back to working on his storage box.

Ella bit the inside of her cheek, halting the laughter. She didn't want Max to think she had lost her mind, although it was clear she had lost her concentration. She refocused and worked on attaching the hinge to the top of the box. She peeked at Max. His storage box was coming together like he had twenty years of experience in carpentry. All he had left to do was add the lid and then his storage box would be finished.

Ella noticed his biceps bulge as he worked, no pudge left to pinch. He and Nicole had been nominated as prom king and queen, and Ella had voted for them, wanting to see new rulers; Brittany had reigned long enough.

Ella turned back to her project. She managed the third side. But something went wrong, and the fourth side would not fit. Ella started to cry in frustration. Max lifted his head, giving her a look of pity. With a quick movement he rearranged a couple of pieces in the correct order. All she had to do was connect the lid to the hinges.

Ella dabbed at her eyes, giving a quiet "thanks."

Max nodded before yelling, "Done."

Mr. Geller came over and inspected his work. "Nicely done, Max." Mr. Geller said as he admired the box. "You can go now. Have a good summer, and good luck next year at Indiana University. It's my alma mater."

"Cool, Mr. Geller," Max replied, swinging his backpack over his left shoulder as he made his way to the door.

"Your storage box," Mr. Geller called after him.

Max smiled sheepishly and returned for the box. "Hold the screwdriver the other way," he hissed to Ella. Ella gave a small nod as Max shuffled past.

While Ella wouldn't say she and Max were friends, Max had helped her on more than one occasion, making Woodshop bearable. Thanks to him she might actually pass this exam.

"Done," called Stefan and another boy Ella never could remember the name of. Their boxes matched Max's, sleek and professional. One boy after another called that they were finished, leaving Ella furiously scrambling to complete the project. Soon Ella was the only student left in the classroom. There were just fifteen minutes to go, and Ella still didn't have the top of her storage box attached.

She lined up the hinges of the top with the adjoining wall, screwing in the remaining screw. "Done," Ella yelled, flopping over the storage box, totally exhausted. The box was complete, but the big bad wolf from "The Three Little Pigs" could have easily blown it to smithereens.

Mr. Geller examined Ella's box. He looked like he had never seen anything so awful, turning the box this way and that. "Well, Ella, your storage box is standing," Mr. Geller said kindly. "However, two screws are stripped, and a hinge is jammed. I will pass you, but my advice is never to go into construction. You just don't have the mind for it."

"Thank you," Ella said, not caring that Mr. Geller was not complimenting her. She had passed the class, she would graduate, and that was all that mattered. Ella rushed to her locker, relieved.

Ella wanted to hurry home and tell Brandon the good news, that she had passed Woodshop without stabbing anybody. But then she remembered she was nothing to him now. He wasn't her boyfriend, he wasn't her friend, he wasn't even the farm manager. Ella let out a sigh of regret. She didn't know what to feel; forgetting him was impossible, and loving him was pointless. And no matter how she tried, she just couldn't push Brandon from her mind.

Ella walked to her locker and groaned. Brittany was there putting books away. Ella looked around for Stefan and was relieved to see he was not in sight. She was not in the mood for the lip-smacking session they engaged in whenever they were within two feet of each other.

"You going to the prom tonight?" Brittany asked as she checked out her reflection in the tiny mirror hanging in her locker.

"Wasn't planning on it," Ella answered, taking out her books for next period.

"I guess Barry was taken." Brittany smirked and pursed her cherry-red lips. Ignoring Brittany, Ella unzipped her bag and pulled out a binder, jamming it into the lower locker shelf. Brittany dropped her cell phone by Ella's feet. Ella reached down to get it and noticed a site for guide dogs on the screen.

"I know someone at the hospital who works with guide dogs," Ella offered as she passed Brittany back her phone. Brittany didn't say anything. Instead she put her phone back in her bag and rummaged through it.

"How's your mom doing?" Ella asked.

"Don't," Brittany hissed as she pulled out a Spanish workbook.

"Look, I know what it's like to have your life change suddenly," Ella said. "I can only imagine what you're going through."

"Stop," Brittany cried, slamming her locker shut. "Don't give me this fake sympathy crap. You and the rest of this school are just glad it's not your mom that ran into a tree. Don't pretend that you actually care." With that, Brittany turned on her platform shoes and hurried down the hall.

Ella bit her lip. How could she bury the hatchet when Brittany insisted on using it?

"What are you wearing tonight?"

Ella turned to see Nicole, her blond hair in a side pony.

"My pajamas," said Ella.

"It's original, I'll give you that," Nicole said as she punched in her locker code. "I love my dress. It's puffy and shiny and I'm wearing heels that defy gravity."

"Sounds like you're getting ready to be the next prom queen."

"You think?" Nicole cocked her head to the side, revealing an ear full of little rhinestones all along the outer part of her ear.

"I do." Ella gave Nicole a smile. She touched her own ear, feeling the single piercing she begged her mother for when she was eight. The pain had been too much for Ella to even think about getting a second piercing, let alone a fifth or a sixth.

"Why don't you come tonight?" Nicole asked.

"I don't have a date," Ella replied.

"This is 2018. Dates are not mandatory."

"But they are good for giving rides," Max said, standing beside Nicole. "Ella, how was the exam?"

"I passed." Ella grinned. "But I think I only did because Mr. Geller was terrified I would have to repeat his class if I didn't."

Max chuckled, stretching his hand towards Nicole.

"Good luck tonight," Ella called after them as they headed to their next class. Nicole waved before continuing down the hall.

Ella checked her bag for her cell phone, her heart tugging when she saw she had a text. It sank when she realized it was from her mother, asking her to pick up more milk on the way home. Ella would add it to the popcorn she was planning on buying. Lounging at home was definitely underrated.

Prom night was going exactly as Ella had planned, with a bag of butter popcorn popping in the microwave and the kettle boiling away on the stove for instant cocoa. She decided to have marshmallows with her hot chocolate instead of whipped cream. Change things up a bit.

Ella found she was not as blasé about missing the prom as she had thought. A small part of her wanted to join Maria and Denzel. Yet she couldn't stand the thought of sitting all evening watching them make googly eyes at each other. Ella would have nothing to do but sit in a chair, stuffing her face, watching everyone else enjoying their evening. She could stuff her face just as well at home, thank you very much.

Her cell phone rang; it was Maria. "Els, did you change your mind? Denzel and I have a whole limo to ourselves. We don't mind swinging by."

"I haven't changed my mind, Maria," Ella said. "It seems Johnny Castle will be my date tonight."

"You will regret this," Maria warned. Some part of Ella knew Maria was right, but she brushed the feeling off.

Instead, Ella said, "I bet you look beautiful."

"You can't see me."

"I remember when you tried your dress on for me last Friday. You were born to wear a cocktail dress."

"My mother was acting like your mom, taking a dozen pictures of me. She just couldn't stop. And I still can't believe we have school tomorrow. What high school has prom on a school night?"

"They were hoping that having prom on a Tuesday instead of a Saturday would cut down on drinking and other 'naughty prom behavior,'" Ella mimicked, reciting what the vice principal had told the students when he announced the date of the prom.

"What the school board did was create an unofficial senior skip day. They are crazy if they think anyone is going to show up to school tomorrow."

"That reminds me," Ella said. "You never did tell me what your exact plans were for the prom this evening. Or should I say, after the prom."

"Ella, don't start that again."

"You know you will tell me . . . eventually."

"You sure you don't want to come tonight?"

"I'm sure."

"You know, you were born to do more than study and watch Dirty Dancing."

"I'm beginning to think not."

"Well, have fun with your popcorn and cream-topped cocoa," said Maria.

"I added marshmallows this time," Ella replied. "I'm trying to be more spontaneous."

"Oooo . . . exciting," Maria mocked. "Bye, Ella."

"Bye."

Ella sipped her hot chocolate. Delicious. The marshmallows were a nice touch.

Jordan came into the kitchen in khakis and a denim button-down shirt. He looked a lot nicer than she did in her pajamas. He glanced at the mug she was cradling in her hands.

"Isn't it too hot for cocoa?" he asked. Ella took a defiant sip, sweat forming at her temples. She brushed it away.

"Can I borrow the Volvo?" Jordan asked. "Seeing as you seem to be staying in this evening."

"Where are you going?" Ella asked.

"I'm meeting Brandon and Chris at the shooting range."

"You sure spend a lot of time with them," Ella muttered, taking another sip.

"Is this kindergarten, Ella?" Jordan shot back. "Do I need permission to go out with your friends?"

"We're not . . . oof. It's complicated."

"Figuring out how to manage an escrow account is complicated," said Jordan. "Maybe it would be easier if I told you Brandon and Ranny broke up."

"How do you know that?" Ella asked, her hands and feet suddenly going all tingly.

"Because he asked me how to get his ex-girlfriend to stop calling him," Jordan replied. "I told him to freeze her out, but he said that felt too cold. It seems your badass crush has a big mushy heart—now, where are your car keys?"

"On the hook." Ella motioned with her chin, gripping the hot mug to regain some feeling in her hands. It didn't work. She still felt prickles in her fingers as the news of Brandon's relationship status settled in.

"Got 'em," Jordan said. "Enjoy lounging on the couch."

"Jordan," Ella called.

Jordan swiveled around, giving her an expectant look.

"Tell Brandon I say hi," Ella said. There was so much more she wanted to say, but she didn't trust Jordan to relay it.

"Okay," Jordan called over his shoulder as he headed for the garage door.

"Tell who hi?" Mom asked, entering the kitchen in an evening gown, her red hair twisted into a lovely topknot. Mom looked glamorous—red-carpet glamorous. Chelsey must have had a hand with the makeup, as Mom wouldn't let Chelsey go near her hair even with a hairbrush.

"You look nice," Ella said, brushing off the question. "Where are you guys going?"

"To a charity dinner," Mom replied. She gave herself a once-over in the reflection of the kitchen window.

"Pattie, do you have the checkbook?" Dad asked, looking dashing in his tux.

"Have it right here." Mom waved the checkbook at her husband. "Are you sure you don't want to go to the prom?" she asked Ella. They had been having the same conversation all week. Mom felt Ella was missing out; Ella felt justified in staying home.

"I'm positive," Ella said. "I have a very enjoyable evening planned." She held up the bowl of popcorn.

"Well, enjoy watching Dirty Dancing." Mom kissed Ella on the cheek, leaving behind a smudge of red lipstick.

"Come on, Pattie, or we'll miss the hors d'oeuvres," Dad said. He shared Ella's love of food.

"Have a good night, sweetie," Mom called as Dad escorted her to the garage.

Ella took her bowl of popcorn and her mug of hot chocolate and went to the den. She popped in the Dirty Dancing DVD and snuggled into the couch with her comfort food.

# CHAPTER 35

SHE WAS AT the log dancing scene when Chelsey burst into the den. "Oh good, you're here. I want to practice this new type of hairdo called 'lazy curls.'"

"Alright, after the movie," said Ella, shoving popcorn into her mouth.

"Or you can press pause," Chelsey suggested.

"Fine." Ella gave in, switching off the TV.

"And I need you to shower," Chelsey instructed.

Ella sighed, pushing herself off the couch, and trudged up the stairs. She knew she should tell her sister to stuff it, but then Chelsey would nag her until she listened. It was easier to give in; Chelsey made pit bulls seem like pushovers.

"Thanks," Chelsey called after her.

Ella showered, enjoying feeling cool instead of sticky. Then she got back into her pajamas.

Chelsey came into Ella's room. "Ella, why are you in pajamas?"

"Because I want to be," Ella replied.

"You look awful," Chelsey said. "How about you wear these?" She handed Ella a light-blue T-shirt along with a pair of jeans.

"Alright," Ella groaned, going to the bathroom and changing. "Happy now?" Ella asked after she had done as instructed.

"Very," Chelsey said, patting the bed. While Ella would never admit it, she felt more comfortable in a fresh T-shirt than her sticky pajama shirt, and her hair needed taming from the frizzy mess the humidity had turned it into.

Chelsey blow-dried Ella's hair until it was only slightly damp. She took out a curling iron and made little ringlets in her hair. Then Chelsey ran her hands through the strands, undoing the curls she had just made. The results were perfectly formed auburn waves.

"Gorgeous," Chelsey said, patting Ella's hair. "But I didn't want the waves so defined. I should have only curled the bottom half."

Chelsey brought out a makeup bag and began painting Ella's face with concealers.

"Why are you putting on makeup?" Ella said.

"Because I'm taking pictures," Chelsey replied. "Why do you think I made you put on normal clothing?"

Ten minutes later, Ella was polished and glossy. Her pretty reflection didn't make her happy; instead she thought about how the marshmallows in her cocoa were probably completely dissolved by now. She would have to make the hot chocolate all over again. Chelsey was ruining everything with this spontaneous glamor session.

"Where will the photo shoot be?" Ella asked, wanting this to end as soon as possible.

"On the couch," Chelsey said. "Now follow me." They made their way to the living room with the black leather couches. "Okay, lie down with your shoulder propped up."

"Like this?" Ella asked, getting into a sideways plank on the couch. The leather was cool against her bare arm.

"Perfect," Chelsey said, pushing some hair behind Ella's shoulder. "Now, don't smile; we are going for glamorous, not cute."

Chelsey didn't have to worry about Ella smiling. There was nothing about this photo shoot that made Ella happy.

"That's a wrap," Chelsey said, scrolling through the pictures she had just taken. "You can go back to watching your movie."

"Want to join me?" Ella asked.

"Thanks, but I already promised Tia and Rebecca I'd meet them for coffee," Chelsey replied, reaching for her purse. Chelsey never was one for sitting around in the evening.

Ella returned to the den and settled back into the movie. Just then, the garage door swung open and voices carried down the hall.

"I can't believe I shot the bull's-eye. I'm getting good at this."

Jordan was home—with company, it sounded like.

"You were better than me. I missed so many times the instructor gave me a flyer for a beginner's course."

Ella nearly choked on her stone-cold cocoa. Brandon was here. This night was going nothing like she had dreamed about in class.

"Brandon's here," Chelsey said, taking a seat next to Ella on the couch.

"I know," Ella said. Did Chelsey think she was oblivious to her surroundings?

"Aren't you glad I made you pretty?" Chelsey whispered in her ear, giving Ella a wink. This whole thing had been a setup. How did she not see it?

Jordan and Brandon entered the living room. Brandon paused when he saw Ella.

"Hi, Ella," Brandon said when their eyes met.

"Hi," Ella said back.

"Still watching Dirty Dancing?" Jordan asked, joining them on the couch.

"I am," Ella replied.

"I'm going," Chelsey announced, getting to her feet. "Brandon, how about you take my spot?"

"Alright." Brandon's face flushed as he sat next to Ella.

"Just make sure your date doesn't order wine," Jordan said as Chelsey passed him.

"It isn't a date," Chelsey said, whacking him on the head with her purse.

"Geez, Chelsey." Jordan rubbed his head. It was Christmas morning all over again.

Jordan, Brandon, and Ella sat watching the movie, no one saying anything.

"Well, I'm bored," Jordan said after about ten minutes, hopping up. "Brandon, you coming?"

"I think I'll stay," Brandon said.

"Suit yourself," Jordan replied. He headed upstairs.

"Cindy loves this movie," Brandon said, turning to Ella. "It's not really my thing. Too much dancing, not enough action."

"The movie was a box office success, so I'd say most people don't share your opinion." Ella knew she sounded touchy, but she didn't care. All she wanted was to finish the movie in peace—was that too much to ask?

"I think a movie shouldn't have more than two songs, tops," Brandon continued. "The fact that every other scene has a song makes the movie impossible to watch."

"So does talking," Ella pointed out.

"Fine, I'll be quiet," Brandon said, reaching for the bowl of popcorn on the coffee table. He munched quietly next to her until the movie ended.

"What did you think?" Ella asked, switching off the TV.

"Too much singing and dancing," said Brandon.

"Then why did you sit through it?"

Brandon shrugged. "I guess I hoped it would get better."

Ella fiddled with the remote while Brandon went fishing for the semi-popped kernels at the bottom of the bowl. The quiet stretched on. Ella felt the need to break it. "Brandon, can I ask you something?"

"I never know how to respond to a question like that," Brandon replied. "It always makes me nervous. Well . . . I guess so. Go ahead."

"What do you see when you look at me?" The question fell from Ella's mouth before she felt ready to ask it. Now that it was out, she burned to hear the answer.

Brandon took a breath, letting out the air slowly from his mouth. "You really want to know?"

"Yes." Ella shut her eyes, bracing for the answer.

"I see you giving Dusty too many carrots even when he doesn't deserve them," Brandon began. "You hardly say what you feel—unless you're angry, and then you say too much. Your hair gets frizzy when it's hot and your lips crack when it's too cold. And you care too much what people think."

"Ouch," Ella said, shifting away.

"You asked a question and I gave you an honest answer."

Ella angled her face from him.

"What did you want me to say, Ella?" Brandon asked quietly.

"First off, I was hoping you didn't see all those things," Ella said, pushing hair behind her shoulder. "I was hoping . . ." Ella paused. It's too late to save face; better let it all out. "I was hoping," Ella continued, "that you would say my feelings for you were returned, that even though I'm not perfect . . . I'm still perfect for you." Then Ella shut her eyes once more, waiting for the rejection she feared, waiting to have her heart broken, waiting, waiting, waiting.

"Ella," said Brandon. "I watched Dirty Dancing with you."

"Yeah, so?"

"So?" Brandon cried. "I went to the dance with you. I Googled medical terms before work so you would think I'm smart. I convinced Jordan to drive me here because I told him I wanted to jam—do you see me jamming with Jordan?"

Ella's eyes flew open in disbelief as butterflies took over her stomach.

"I broke up with my girlfriend to give us a chance," Brandon continued, his voice softening. "I mean, what more do you want me to—"

Ella leaned forward, intending to silence him with a kiss. Instead, her hair wacked him in the face, causing him to blink and rub his eyes.

Ella clapped a hand over her face and wished the couch could swallow her up.

"Could we try that again?" Brandon asked. "You kinda caught me off guard."

Ella laughed and moved closer to him. Brandon placed his hands on either side of her face, rubbing his thumb over her cheek. Very slowly, he brought his mouth down to hers. The kiss was as wonderful as in her daydreams, filling every place of her heart. Brandon wrapped his arms around her and pulled her close to him. Ella's hands traveled to his hair, feeling the soft strands between her fingers. They kissed for a while. Ella kept waiting for Brandon to pull back, to get some air. It seemed he didn't need any—neither of them did.

"Hello," called a voice from the kitchen. Shoot. Her parents were home.

Ella and Brandon wrenched apart just as Mom came into the living room.

"Brandon, what a nice surprise," Mom said, her evening gown brushing against the couch. "What are you guys up to?"

"We were . . . talking," Ella replied, meeting Brandon's eyes. He coughed to disguise his laughter.

"I'll get you some water," Mom said, walking to the kitchen.

"That was close," Ella muttered as Brandon cleared his throat.

Mom came back with a glass and handed it to him.

"Thanks," Brandon croaked, drinking the water.

"Did you guys win anything at the auction?" Ella asked.

"Yes," Mom said. "We won a lovely set of knives."

"Sounds like the beginning of a horror movie," Jordan said, leaning against the banister. Ella had not heard him come down.

"They will come in handy when your father begins his cooking course next week," said Mom with a glance at Dad.

"Can't wait," Dad replied, looking anything but thrilled.

"Brandon, ready for me to drive you home?" Jordan asked.

"Sure," Brandon said, getting to his feet.

"I'll come with," Ella offered.

Jordan pinned Ella with his eyes. "I think you guys had enough 'talking' for one evening, don't you?"

Ella squirmed. He had seen them. How embarrassing.

"We'll talk tomorrow," Ella said to Brandon.

"Not if I have any say," Jordan said, clapping Brandon on the back. Brandon paled and walked with Jordan to the back door. He gave Ella a wave, which she returned.

"Did you have a good evening?" Mom asked, joining Ella on the couch.

"Yeah." Ella sighed. It was better than any prom.

"I think you should call it a night," Dad said to Ella. "There is school tomorrow."

"Yes, Daddy." Ella yawned, pushing away from the couch. She gave her parents each a hug before dutifully making her way up the stairs.

Ella didn't have to worry about having sweet dreams that evening—not when she had beautiful memories to replay in her head. And replay them she did until she fell asleep.

# CHAPTER 36

BARRY STOOD BY the podium, giving the valedictorian speech, his sandy hair shaped like a bowl around his face. He never did seem to have a decent haircut. Ella was happy Barry was speaking instead of her, even if it meant she had to settle for being salutatorian. Ella hoped he was nearing the conclusion of his speech. It seemed endless.

Barry's voice rang out from the loudspeaker. "We look towards the future with optimism. For most of our anxiety stems from worries about dreams most of us will never be able to achieve. So today, I give each and every one of you permission to allow your apprehension to desiccate. To let go of your irrational dreams of being efficacious and you will see there is nothing left to worry about."

Mr. Howell began to clap, signaling the end of Barry's speech. Barry seemed pleased with himself, his beady eyes shining brightly behind his large glasses. Ella clapped along with everyone else and noted the looks of relief in the audience. Barry's speech had been painful for everyone, it seemed—except his parents, who clapped as if their son had just received the Nobel Prize. Ella hoped someone had taped Barry's speech. He said many lines that could be turned against him someday.

Ella wiped sweat off her forehead and scouted out the crowd. Of course, there would be a heat wave on the day of her graduation. Her green polyester gown attracted the strong sunrays, making her feel like she was baking inside.

Her parents beamed up at her from the fourth row. Uncle Bruce and Aunt Linda were beside them along with the farm manager, Vicki. Vicki had become more than an employee; Ella often visited her after school to enjoy cornbread and stories about the horses she had worked with over the years.

Ella saw Chelsey's perfectly made-up face, not a drop of sweat to be found. How did she manage that? Then Ella's heart fluttered as she saw Brandon, in a white oxford shirt and navy dress pants, sitting next to Chelsey. Their eyes met, and Brandon winked, filling Ella's heart to the tippy-top. He was really hers at last.

Jordan had admitted that he colluded with Chelsey on prom night by talking about guitars all evening until Brandon suggested they play together. Sadly, Jordan had gone back to law school, unable to stay for Ella's graduation. He made sure to mark her day by sending her a cake that read *Future Doctor* in frosted letters. It really should have read *Future Pre-Med Student*, but Ella decided to let it go.

"Smile, everyone," Mom said as Dad, Chelsey, and Ella huddled together. She snapped a picture, then waved her hand, signaling for Brandon to join in. Brandon stood next to Ella and slipped his arm around her waist.

"Beautiful," Mom said, reviewing the pictures on the camera screen.

The group split up. Dad shifted with her uncle and aunt to the side. Vicki was introduced to Mrs. Salter, and they struck up a lively conversation with lots of hand gestures. Chelsey was speaking with Brandon; Ella distinctly heard the words "jeans" and "out of date" come from her sister's mouth. Brandon didn't look like he was enjoying the conversation; his head kept turning to the refreshments table. Ella was about to rescue her boyfriend from her sister when she saw Maria and Denzel bounding up to her.

"Didn't think Barry's speech would ever end," Maria complained, tossing her raven hair over her shoulder.

"Yeah, he was like an idiot professor filibustering the school for more science classes," Denzel added. "Why couldn't you have been valedictorian, Ella? Your speech would have at least made sense."

"My speech wouldn't have been half as memorable," Ella replied. "I would have encouraged people to go for their dreams."

"Speaking of fulfilling dreams," Maria said with a grin, "rumor has it that you spent prom night with the hottest guy in Greenbrier."

"Guilty," Ella said and returned Maria's smile.

"Hey," Denzel said, nudging Maria's shoulder.

"I said hottest guy from Greenbrier," Maria pointed out. "You're from Nashville, remember?"

"Still, don't like you using the word hot, unless my name or chili peppers comes after it."

Maria rolled her eyes and gave Denzel a playful push.

"Where is the guy?" Denzel asked, craning his neck.

"I have to rescue him," Ella said. "I think my sister is giving him fashion advice."

"Better hurry," Denzel replied. "Brandon looks like he is about to bolt."

"Come on, everyone," Mom called. "Ella, Brandon, stand together. Maria and Denzel, join in the picture." Saved by Mom, Ella thought as Brandon hurried over.

Maria knew all about Mrs. Heart's picture-taking habits and stood patiently, smiling through several shots. Denzel and Brandon didn't seem as forgiving. Their smiles hardened on their faces.

"Mom, enough pictures," Chelsey said, tugging on her mother's elbow.

"One more of just Maria and Ella," Mom begged. Brandon and Denzel leaped out of the shot and headed to the drinks table.

Ella put an arm around her best friend, pressing their cheeks together. Maria playfully stuck her tongue to the side.

"How do you manage to look pretty with your tongue hanging out?" Mom said, shaking her head as she reviewed her pictures. Then Mom went to join Dad, who was talking to some friends on the PTA.

"Are you coming to the graduation party tonight at Stefan's house?" Maria asked Ella.

Ella looked over at Brittany and Samantha making pouty lips at the professional photographer Brittany's parents had hired. Then Ella saw Brittany's mom walk towards her daughter, tapping a long white cane from side to side. Brittany laced an arm through her mother's, clasping her hand.

"Ella," Maria called, waving a hand in front of her face.

"I'm going to Brandon's," Ella replied. "His family is having a BBQ in honor of his graduation and I promised I'd go."

"I told you this would be your best year ever," Maria said, jabbing Ella in the rib.

"I should have known, you are always right." Ella jabbed her back.

"Some things take you a long time to figure out."

"It took me about a second to know how awesome you were."

"You are a genius." Maria put her arm around Ella's shoulders. Then Ella felt sad. She was going to miss seeing her best friend in school every day. New York seemed so far away.

She pushed away the sad thoughts. They still had the summer together. It was too soon to start missing Maria.

"So, are you going to tell me what happened on prom night?" Ella asked.

"Sure," Maria replied. "When you come for a sleepover. That is— after my mom goes to bed." Ella's imagination ran wild.

"Maria," Denzel called, motioning for her to join him.

"See you later," Maria said, as she hurried over to Denzel. Ella saw Colonel Moland in his dark-navy uniform with Dr. Moland, Denzel's mother, by his side. Maria seemed to fit right in like an honorary member of the family.

Strong arms wrapped around Ella's waist.

"Never thought I would be dating the smartest girl in school," Brandon said, resting his chin on her shoulder.

"Well, you do have excellent taste," Ella replied.

"Tell that to your sister."

"Don't take anything she says too seriously. Chelsey thinks it's her calling to make sure everyone looks fashionable."

"Well, I'm a lost cause," Brandon said. His cell phone buzzed, and he looked at the screen. "Gotta go; it seems my own BBQ has started without me."

"I'll be there as soon as I can," said Ella.

"Take all the time you need. It's not every day you graduate from Dellpines bull-baiting Academy."

"Glad I only have to do it once."

"Me too. I don't think I could sit through another speech given by that Barry boy."

There was an audible groan. They both turned to see Barry standing nearby.

"See you at the house," Brandon said. Ella waved goodbye as Barry stepped forward. Ella had the feeling Barry was intimidated by Brandon.

"I never pegged you as the type of girl who likes cowboys," said Barry as soon as Brandon was out of earshot.

"What type of guys should I be into, Barry?"

Barry shrugged. "He doesn't look that bright. That's probably why my speech bored him. I bet he thought when I was talking about 'deep time,' it was time to think about how many duster jackets he had in his closet."

"I doubt he was listening that closely to your speech," Ella replied. "You lost me after you brought up quantum entanglement."

Barry crossed his arms. "That was the best part of the speech."

"There was no best part of your speech."

Barry sighed. "You're all too doltish to understand. I bet no one at Harvard would have any trouble understanding the scientific concepts I spoke about."

"Lucky for us, you're Harvard's problem now. They must not know about your navel fluff collection."

"How did you know about that?" Barry said, anxiously looking around to make sure no one had overheard.

Ella gave a sly smile.

"You're just jealous because I took home the final victory." Barry indicated his valedictorian medal.

Ella rolled her eyes. "The only difference between your medal and mine is that your medal hangs on a blue ribbon instead of red."

Barry looked down at his medal and saw that she was right.

"You were always a worthy opponent," Barry said, a turn of tenderness in his voice. "Johns Hopkins is lucky to have you."

Ella was touched. It was the first nice thing Barry had ever said to her.

"You're not so bad yourself," Ella said, adding, "in small doses."

Barry smiled and stuck out his hand to her. Ella ignored his hand and gave him a hug. It seemed to surprise Barry, but he didn't pull away.

"Barry, don't be afraid to be yourself," Ella said against his shoulder.

"I'm never afraid to be myself," Barry answered.

Ella looked over to Stanley and his family. Barry followed her gaze.

"I think I'm going to miss you," Ella said, wondering where all this sentimentality was coming from.

"Yeah, well, maybe when I'm very lonely and run out material to memorize, I just might miss you too."

Ella nudged Barry's shoulder. Barry was the only other person in school who was just as unsure of himself as she was. She guessed, in a strange sort of way, they had been friends all along.

Ella drove to Brandon's house with the windows open, the Dirty Dancing soundtrack blaring. How many times had she shown up at his home with palms of sweat and nerves in knots? Today she showed up in a peach popover shirt, white jeans, and a heart full of confidence. She knew Brandon was expecting her and would be disappointed if his girlfriend didn't show up.

She drove to Landcork Drive and hauled to a stop. Cars lined either side of the street. This is going to be some party, Ella thought as she got out of her car. She heard little feet pounding the pavement. "Ella," Graham cried. He threw his small arms around her legs.

"Hi, Graham," Ella said, patting his back.

"We are having a BBQ," Graham said, his eyes wide with excitement.

"You don't say?" Ella mocked. She shuffled his blond hair.

"Graham." Cindy rushed to his side and knelt in front of him, her tangerine-colored sundress skimming the ground. "What did Momma say about you and cars?"

"That I can only drive them when Daddy holds the steering wheel," Graham answered dutifully.

Ella and Cindy both laughed as Cindy took his hand.

"He's been waiting for you," Cindy explained. "You're kind of a celebrity around here. Your name is mentioned at least once at every meal."

"Ella!" Holley ran to her, throwing her arms around Ella's neck, almost knocking her to the ground. Holley took a step back. "How do you always look so nice?"

"I have my own personal stylist," Ella replied.

"You do?" Holley gasped.

"It's my sister," Ella admitted. "She's a beautician."

"Can she come over and give us all makeovers?" Holley asked excitedly.

"She would love to," Ella replied. Holley squealed with delight.

"I think you just made Holley's year," Cindy whispered, pushing open the back gate.

The backyard was filled with people Ella didn't recognize, chattering and munching on BBQ fare. A long table was decked out with burgers, chicken wings, red coleslaw and French fries. Ella could hardly wait to dig in.

"Hey, Els," Brandon said, flashing Ella a bright smile. He examined her face more closely. "There's something on your mouth."

"What?" Ella asked, her hands flying up to inspect. Why didn't Cindy or Holley mention anything?

"Me." Brandon grinned, giving her a kiss.

Ella rolled her eyes. "I think you need to fire the person who writes your pick-up lines."

"No need. I already got the girl," Brandon said. His eyes twinkled.

"Yeah you did," Ella said as she gave Brandon another kiss.

"Want something to drink?"

"Sure."

Brandon led Ella to the drinks table.

"I'd love some iced tea," said Ella. "Did Cindy make any?"

"She sure did," Brandon said, pouring the tea into a red plastic cup.

"Thanks," Ella said. She looked around at the many faces she didn't recognize.

"Come, there are some people I want you to meet," Brandon said, taking her hand. Ella was introduced to cousins, neighbors, and Paulina's father, Bob. Bob looked like a male version of Paulina, with blue eyes and a tall, lean frame and wistful smile. The only difference was the gray hair and goatee. Ella discovered that Paulina was an only child whose mother died from ovarian cancer when Paulina was only eighteen. Bob had never remarried; Paulina's mother had been the love of his life.

"Does your mother ever talk about your grandmother?" Ella asked Brandon when they were out of earshot.

"Occasionally," Brandon replied. "I know she was a smart woman, the first in her family to go to college. She also loved animals, had my grandfather buy a ranch—that's how Mom learned to ride horses."

"Your grandfather seems to still miss your grandmother."

"My mother never knew her mother's name till she was older," said Brandon. "Her father was always saying 'Yes dear, no dear.' You know, he used to wake up at five every day to cook my grandmother breakfast. Nothing says love like waking up early for someone. I hate waking before my alarm forces me to."

"Boot camp will change that."

"I know, which is why I'm taking these next few weeks to sleep in while I still can."

"Sleep is wasted on the childless," Chris said, rolling over to them. "Hey, Ella, come to brave the family circus? First embarrassing scene about to happen. Some idiot invited Cousin Jeff and his ex-wife."

"Oh no," Brandon groaned. "Has Mary Ann drunk anything yet?"

"Two beers and a shot of whiskey," Chris replied.

"Then I'd say the show is about to start," Brandon said, looking worried.

"Hello, Ella," Paulina said, elegant in a printed sundress and rhinestone sandals. "Congratulations on your graduation today."

"Thank you," Ella replied.

"We need some more mustard," Paulina said, turning to Brandon.

"But I was just in the kitchen," Brandon moaned.

"I'll go," Ella offered.

"Thanks," Paulina said. "I think there's one left in the refrigerator."

The kitchen looked like a bomb had exploded, with paper wrappings and chip bags scattered everywhere. The sink was filled sky high with dishes. Ella found the mustard in the fridge next to an open bottle of soda. She grabbed it and headed for the deck when she bumped into someone and the bottle dropped from her hands.

There, in a black scoop-neck dress and thong sandals, was the last person Ella hoped to see: Ranny.

# CHAPTER 37

"SORRY," RANNY SAID, picking up the mustard. "I didn't know anyone else was in the house. I just came in to get Graham some juice."

"It's okay," Ella replied. She reached for the bottle.

"I'll take it," Ranny offered. "Save you the trouble."

"It's an eleven-ounce bottle; I think I can manage," Ella said, extending her hand once more.

"I didn't mean . . . oh, just take it." Ranny jammed the bottle into Ella's hand.

The two girls stood in silence. The tension seemed to grow like the dishes piling in the sink.

"Do you hate me?" Ella asked, fearing the answer.

Ranny bit at her nails, which were nibbled to the quick. "I guess I just don't understand it," she finally replied. "I thought Brandon and I were forever, or at least that's what he promised me. I guess I was stupid to believe it, right?" Ranny asked, glancing up at Ella, pain swirling around her gray eyes.

Ella's heart contracted. She would have believed Brandon if he said they were forever. Were they forever? Now that she had him, she couldn't bear the thought of him breaking up with her and choosing someone else.

The silence was becoming painful. "I should take the mustard outside," muttered Ella.

"I'll give Graham his juice," Ranny said.

Ranny headed in one direction, Ella in another. Ella's heart was still racing when she entered the backyard. Ranny's words crawled up like ivy, twisting around her heart.

Ella placed the mustard down, taking a seat next to Brandon at the table.

"I know you're bad at directions, but I had faith you would find your way to the table eventually," Brandon remarked when he saw her.

Ella gave a half smile, not in the mood to be teased. She saw Ranny join the table next to a boy she didn't recognize. The boy was wiry, his T-shirt hanging loose on his lean frame, his dark hair in a crew cut.

"Seth Harris." The boy stuck out a hand to Ella.

Ella returned the greeting. "Ella Heart."

"I saved you a burger," Brandon said, handing Ella a plate.

"Thanks," Ella replied, searching the table for the ketchup. It was by Seth.

Brandon and Seth struck up a conversation about their upcoming enlistment as they dressed their burgers. Seth talked about how wimpy West Point's boot camp would be compared to his Marine training. Brandon countered the remark by replying, "Well, all you need is muscles to be in the Marines."

"I can't believe I'm serving with you people," Ranny huffed, taking a bite out of her burger. Apparently, she was also enlisted.

Ella listened to the banter, not knowing how to add to the conversation, feeling more like an observer than part of the gang.

"Can I have the ketchup?" Ella asked quietly.

"You gotta ask louder than that," said Brandon. "Like this. Pass me the ketchup, Private Harris!" Brandon said to Seth in a loud, commanding tone.

"Sir," Seth said, aiming the ketchup at Brandon's shirt. Brandon jumped out of the way, and the ketchup splattered Ella instead.

"Seth, you are dead meat," Brandon said, leaping up. He looked like he meant it.

Ella put a hand on his shoulder. "It's okay. I'll just add it to my burger." She wiped the ketchup from her shirt onto her bun, making everyone laugh.

"Did you give Ella the present yet?" Seth asked Brandon.

"Thanks for reminding me." Brandon reached under the table and handed Ella a book covered in brown paper. Ella tore open the wrappings to reveal a thick, aging textbook. It was about practicing medicine in the military.

"Saw a similar textbook in your room and I thought you might like to have it," Brandon explained. "Seth's uncle was a medical officer in the army. I asked him if he had any leftover textbooks from the time he served. This is the one he found."

"I told him to get you a gift card," Seth defended himself. "But Brandon insisted you would want the book."

"It is the perfect gift," Ella said as she flipped through the pages. She saw several chapters that interested her. "I'll read it cover to cover."

"As long as you don't read it out loud," Brandon replied.

"I promise I won't read it out loud," Ella assured him. "Thanks, Brandon, and Seth. Oh, and, Seth, please thank your uncle for me."

"You did him a favor," Seth replied. "He needed to get rid of the old thing. I can see if he has more. Save Brandon having to buy you anything for Christmas."

They all laughed. Ella no longer felt like an outsider.

"Hey, how about we go rock climbing after dinner?" Ranny suggested, changing the subject. "I bet Ella has never been to Boulder Climb."

"Great idea. Want to go, Ella?" Brandon asked.

Ella's heart beat faster. She had been to Boulder Climb. It was a rock-climbing park where one could practice rock climbing on almost any type of mountain without fear of falling. She had tried it out once with Maria but was not able to bend her leg enough to climb most of the rock walls.

"I don't know," Ella stammered. She had to think of an excuse. What happened to their original idea of watching Braveheart? While the movie was not Ella's first choice, any movie was better than showing off her ability to fall. Was Ranny doing this on purpose? Suggesting an activity Ella couldn't easily do?

"Oh, come on, Ella," Seth insisted. "I bet you can tell us all about the science of rock climbing, and the best way to reach the top without dying and all that good stuff."

"I don't know anything about geology," Ella said. "And as far as I know, the best way to stay alive is not to fall off the cliff."

Seth laughed. Ella wasn't sure if Seth was laughing with her or at her. One thing was certain: Ella would be sitting by herself watching everyone else have fun if they went to Boulder Climb.

Brandon's eyes met hers. He nodded to her as if she had spoken. "Ella and I are going to stay here and watch a movie," Brandon announced.

"But Seth and I really want to go rock climbing," Ranny insisted.

"Yeah, Brandon," Seth said. "It will be great training when we have to rope climb in the obstacle courses, assuming they do obstacle courses at West Point."

"No one is stopping you from going," Brandon replied as he dipped a French fry into a pile of ketchup on his plate. "But Ella and I are going to stay here. Can you believe Ella has never seen Braveheart?"

"What?" Seth cried, his brown eyes popping out of their sockets. "It's a classic. You have to see it."

"Don't you guys want to do something else besides sit on your butts?" Ranny asked. "We can go rollerblading or paintballing."

"I'm watching Braveheart with Ella," Brandon said, as he placed a hand over hers under the table. Ella's spine tingled at the simple touch. He was choosing her, and Ella couldn't be happier. Then Seth and Brandon began reciting lines from the movie using Scottish accents.

Ranny rolled her eyes. "Boys," she muttered, looking annoyed.

"No one is asking you to join," Seth pointed out.

"No one asked you to join either," Ranny shot back.

"Ey, stop your bickering; there's room enough for both your rutty bottoms," Brandon replied in his best Scottish accent.

"My ancestors would cringe hearing their accent butchered like that," Ella said to Brandon.

"You're Scottish?" Brandon replied in surprise, returning to his normal Southern tone.

"I'm sure some part of me is," said Ella.

"I thought red hair usually means you're Irish."

"Red hair is also indigenous to Scotland."

"How about instead of a history lesson in hair we go watch the movie?" Seth suggested, leaping up from his seat. "I call the armchair."

"No, I call the armchair," Ranny said, hurrying after him.

Brandon waited for Ella as she climbed off of the bench. She was grateful that he didn't offer to help her. She was still struggling with Ranny and Brandon being friends. A part of her worried that the spark would reignite.

"How long is this movie again?" Ella asked, trying to move her mind away from Ranny. She grabbed the textbook, which was heavy in her arms.

"Oh, come on, Ella. You'll love it," Brandon said as he led her to the top of the basement steps. Then he paused.

"There was one more thing I wanted to give you," he said. Ella waited for Brandon to produce a gift, but instead he leaned down and kissed her. She wrapped her arms around him to steady herself, bliss taking over her senses.

"Brandon, Ella—where are you?" Seth called from the basement.

"Coming," Brandon called, taking Ella's hand.

Ranny was in the armchair and Seth was on the far end of the couch, looking defeated. The movie started and so did the commentary. Ranny tried to get the guys to be quiet but had no luck; they just kept on talking in their hideous Scottish accents.

Ella didn't mind the constant comments and accent imitations. The movie wasn't something she was particularly interested in. Instead, she snuggled closer to Brandon, laying her head on his shoulder. She joined in the fun by asking questions, which Brandon and Seth were all too eager to answer.

Ella glanced at Ranny sitting in the armchair, her legs drawn under her. Ella couldn't do that with her legs; she would never be able to bend her right leg that far. Ella thought about the fact that Ranny was enlisting. Will Brandon and Ranny be in the same unit? Will Ranny try to win Brandon back? Ranny's eyes met Ella's. Ranny gave Ella a small smile before her gaze fluttered back to the TV. Ella pushed the thoughts aside; she was being silly. Of course Brandon and Ranny would not be in the same unit; he was going to West Point.

But what if he didn't get in? a voice whispered inside her. Of course he got in, a more assertive voice countered. Brandon would have told you if he hadn't. She turned her attention back to the movie, telling her fears to take a hike. This was a moment to enjoy. She would not let worry ruin it.

If anyone had told Ella a year ago that she would be sitting in her boyfriend's basement, watching a movie with his friends, she wouldn't have believed them. But now, at eighteen, every dream Ella had seemed to be coming true. She was going to her dream college, and the boy she loved asked nothing more from her than to see herself as she was. Ella no longer had to worry about being flawless, something she never could be anyway. She was finally able to let go and enjoy herself—sitting here, watching a movie, hanging out. Life was just about perfect. All that was missing was the popcorn.

THE END

# ACKNOWLEDGEMENTS

As every writer knows, books don't write themselves. They are the creative production of many hands and eyes. I'd like to thank the following people who have brought my lifelong dream to reality. I hope the finished product is everything you hoped it would be.

To my writing group: Melanie, Suzanne, Kibi, Sarah, Aryeh and Deena; thank you for giving me a safe place to read my work and help my writing grow.

To my friend Orna Alexander, thank you for the French tutorial. Je vous Remercie.

To Daniel Sinasohn, thank you for taking time away from your studies and work to answer the legal questions I threw your way.

To Dr. Shimon Brooks, thank you for guiding me through theories of physics and helping me translate the meaning of those theories into understandable phrases.

To my friend Dr. Sophie Silverstein, thank you for answering all my medical questions and guiding me through medical phraseology.

To my cousin, Dr. Mark Shaffer, thank you for staying up late nights answering my questions about medical school and giving me your unending support. Love you, Cuz!

To Steve Diamond, LCDR, US Navy retired, thank you for giving me a deeper perspective of the struggles and sacrifices that every man and woman in the services makes on behalf of their country.

This book would not have been the same without you!

Thank you to Julie Gray, my story editor who guided me through the writing process, Robyn Hunter, my copy editor, who caught countless spelling and grammar mistakes, even in French, and Keri Karandrakis, my developmental editor, who help me tie up loose plot ends and character holes.

To my mentor, Sheryl Kessler Pruitt , M Ed, ET/P, for teaching me to read and never giving up on me when my dyslexia made me doubt what I was capable of.

To Vickie Rinehart, thank you for always believing I would write a book. You are the reason I began this manuscript.

To my sister Dr. Sarah Wolfberg, thank you for always holding me to a higher standard and bringing out my best.

To my parents, Drs. Bernard Wolfberg and Laura Robinson, thank you for your unending love and support; it has been my greatest source of strength!

To my three girls, Shoshana, Aviva and Yael, thank you for cheering on your mama and believing in me. The moment you opened your eyes, I was changed for the better.

And last, to Michael, my love and best friend, thank you for every moment you have spent shaping, reading and editing this book. You brought my dream to life. I don't know what I did to deserve you, but I hope I keep doing it for the rest of my life.